SHIPWRECKED

More books by Siobhan Curham

Dear Dylan

Finding Cherokee Brown

SHIPWRECKED

Siobhan Curham

Shipwrecked
Published in Great Britain 2013
by Electric Monkey, an imprint of Egmont UK Limited
The Yellow Building
1 Nicholas Road
London W11 4AN

ISBN 978 1 4052 6457 0

1 3 5 7 9 10 8 6 4 2

www.egmont.co.uk

A CIP catalogue record for this title is available from the British Library

Typeset by Avon DataSet Ltd, Bidford on Avon, Warwickshire
Printed and bound in Great Britain by the CPI Group

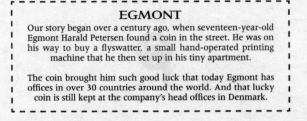

53080/1

For Bea, Luke and Alice.

Best. Siblings. Ever.

Prologue

In the pale light of a half moon she dances around the fire, her body swaying and pulsing in time with the drums. With every jerk of her head her hair whips at the night air and sweat trickles, salty, into her mouth. *Let this be the night*, she thinks to herself, *please, let this be the night*. Then the rhythm takes over and all thoughts are gone. The pounding of the drums merges with the pounding of her heart until she no longer knows where she ends and the music begins. Just when she feels as if she might spiral up into the sky, all movement is sucked from her limbs like an ebbing tide. She collapses to the ground and stares into the flames, waiting for the vision to take form.

She smells the smoke first, and hears the shouting of the men, their voices coarse and sour with hate.

'*Burn! Burn! Burn!*'

Then the image of the crib appears, rocking back and forth, its silhouette black as coal against the flames. But this time, when she looks inside, he waves his chubby hand and gurgles.

This time, for the first time, he's alive.

Tears spill from her eyes, mingling with the sweat on her skin. Tearing her gaze from the fire, she leans back on her heels and looks up into the sky. A swollen cloud scuds across the moon, swallowing it whole.

It is beginning, she thinks to herself, and her lips curve into a knowing smile.

Chapter One

The night before I'm due to go away for the summer I write two lists. I write them while I'm making dinner because I always think best when I'm cooking. The first list is for my mom, reminding her when to water the plants and feed the cat and go to the grocery store, and the second is for myself and entitled 'COSMIC WISH LIST'. Earlier today I read an interview with the winner of *From Trailer Trash to Teen Queen* and she claimed she owed her 'like, super-amazing journey' to writing a cosmic wish list. So I figured I'd give it a go. I mean, if it can help a girl named Happymeal Johnson to fame and fortune then anything's possible. Right?

The first thing I write on my cosmic wish list is: *Please don't let Mom have a total nervous breakdown while I'm gone. Please let her remember how to do stuff – like live a normal life – and not endanger the lives of my plants and cat!* Then I put down my pen and go out on the balcony, which also doubles as our herb garden, and pick a handful of basil. I'm making Mom's favourite tonight, noodles and Bolognese sauce, to try and compensate for the fact that I'll soon be deserting her. I'll only be gone for four weeks, but I know she's viewing it as desertion. Ever since Dad walked out, nearly a year ago, she's had this major phobia about people leaving. Even when our cleaning lady, Constance, goes on holiday, she gets all anxious, like Constance is going to phone us from the beach and tell us she's eloped with a lifeguard or something. But I'm nearly seventeen. I need to get Mom used to the fact that I won't be around forever.

I'm about to go back inside when I hear the sound of laughter from below. I move to the edge of the balcony and crouch down next to a huge pot of rosemary. Having a herb garden is a great cover for spying on your neighbours. Not that I'm advocating spying on your neighbours, but it's good to have a healthy interest in the people who live around you. It shows that you care. That's what I tell myself anyways. This is the first time in my life I've had neighbours. When we lived with Dad we had nothing but the ocean and hills to look at. Living in this apartment block is like living on the set of a soap opera. There are so many different stories going on, it's really hard not to get hooked.

As I pull an Oscar-worthy performance of looking for a

sprig of rosemary, I sneak a glance down into the courtyard. The guy who lives in the ground-floor apartment opposite is standing by his kitchen window. He doesn't have a top on and he's talking to someone, although I can't see who. This is a major development. In the three months he's lived here he's never brought anyone home – let alone brought anyone home when he's half naked. I crouch closer to the pot and peer through the rosemary. In the heat of the evening sun it smells awesome. The man laughs again and a woman appears behind him. She rests her head on his shoulder and they stand there for a moment staring out into the twilight. Then they start to full-on smooch.

I immediately turn away. I wish I could say this is because I do have some principles when it comes to stalking my neighbours. But it's not. It's because seeing anyone getting it on right now makes me feel a weird hollow ache inside. And it's not because I'm single – for the first time in my life I actually have a flesh-and-blood boyfriend who doesn't exist solely in my daydreams. Which is what makes this hollow feeling all the more scary.

I skulk back into the kitchen and head straight for my cosmic wish list. *Please let Todd and I make it through the cruise without killing each other*, I write. Then I put down my pen and sigh. I'm not so sure being cooped up on a cruise ship for four weeks, performing night after night, is exactly what Dr Phil would recommend a couple in our position do. I chop up the basil and take it over to the stove. The Bolognese sauce is bubbling away, turning a rich golden red as the tomato blends with the juices of the meat. I add the basil and give it a stir. What else would I like to happen this summer? I close my eyes and picture myself dancing. In the four weeks since passing the audition for the cruise show we've done nothing but rehearse, but I still can't help stressing that I'm going to mess up. Most of us students at the LA Dance Academy have performed in shows before, but it's different on a cruise ship. If you mess up you can't exactly escape your audience, they'll be there haunting you for days to come at breakfast and dinner and by the pool.

I go back to my cosmic wish list and write: *Please let me remember all of my routines. Especially the Flamenco–Funk Fusion.* Our teacher, Rainbow, thought it would be 'totally rad' for us to showcase dances from around the world. Then she got the crazy notion that it would be even more totally rad to mix these dances up – 'to, like, showcase the diversity of today's world through the medium of dance'. Hmm. I'm not so sure the kind of folk who spend their life savings cruising ocean after ocean, stuck on a ship for weeks on end, are really all that bothered about the diversity of today's world. But I guess I'll soon find out.

'Well, something's smelling mighty fine.'

I quickly stuff my list into my pocket at the sound of Mom's southern drawl. I turn and see her standing in the doorway.

She's wearing one of her home-made, tie-dyed sundresses and she's pulled her hair back into a long, loose braid. She's smiling. This is good. She's also holding Tigger. Tigger is my DGP – Divorce-Guilt Pet – bought for me by Dad when he ran off with his allergist. He started seeing her when he thought he might be allergic to wheat. It turns out he was allergic to Mom and me. Who knew? Anyway, I ended up with Tigger, who is officially the world's zaniest cat, so it wasn't all bad. Mom puts Tigger down and he immediately makes his way over to me and winds in-between my legs. I feel his body purring against my skin. I make a mental note to add, *Please don't let Tigger fall out of love with me while I'm away*, to my wish list.

'I've made a whole pot load,' I say to Mom, nodding at the saucepan. 'We can freeze what we don't eat tonight, for you to have when I'm, you know – away?'

Mom smiles again and sits down at the table. The kitchen table is one of the few pieces of furniture we took from our old house when we moved here. Mom found it years ago in a flea market out in Venice. It's made from random pieces of wood all slotted together like a giant jigsaw. When I was little she would tell me stories about each piece and the imaginary places they'd come from. I still like to sit at the end made from teak that Mom said came from a pirate ship. When I was little, and she and Dad wouldn't let me leave the table until I'd eaten all my vegetables, I'd close my eyes and run my fingers along the grooves in the wood and imagine I was a swashbuckling pirate who never had to do dumb things like eat carrots because I was always way too busy finding treasure.

'I was thinking, Grace,' Mom says. 'Maybe while y'all are away I'll take a drive up to Lake Tahoe. Do some painting.'

'Really?' I nearly drop my spoon in shock.

'Uh-huh.'

I come over to the table and sit down next to her. 'That's a great idea.' It isn't just a great idea; it's a totally awesome, best-thing-I've-heard-in-years idea. Mom is an amazing artist, but she hasn't painted a single stroke since Dad left. I think of my cosmic wish list scrunched in my pocket. Surely it isn't working already? I haven't even done the whole 'releasing my wishes to the stars' bit yet.

'I figure it's time I started getting on with things again, you know?'

Mom's eyes are glassy with tears. I take hold of her hand and notice that for the first time since Dad left she isn't wearing her wedding ring. Relief fizzes through me like soda.

'Now, don't forget to pack your sunscreen,' she whispers. And although she's crying as she says it, I know that this is her way of letting me know it's okay for me to go.

After dinner I go to my room to finish packing. The first thing I see is the light on my cell phone blinking. I have two new messages – one from my best friend, Jenna, and one from Todd. I open Jenna's first.

So, do u think u will sleep with Todd while we're away? ;-) j xoxo

I sigh. Jenna's been asking me this question pretty much every day lately. She's obsessed with my sex life. Not that I have a sex life. It's more like a grope-in-Todd's-car-till-I-tell-him-to-get-off-me life. Jenna lost her virginity when she was fourteen. But what she doesn't understand is that not everyone is as eager as her to have sex. To me, sex is the biggest thing you can do with another person. It's like giving them the most intimate part of yourself; a part you'll never be able to take back, and I don't want to do that until I'm totally ready. Todd and I have only been together for four weeks – and right now I'm totally *un*ready.

I press reply.

Hey! Still not sure I'm ready yet. I know u think he's perfect but I'm not so sure he's perfect for ME.

But once I start typing, it's like unleashing some kind of inner text maniac and I can't seem to stop.

To be honest, I think I might need 2 be with a guy who's a bit quirkier – a guy who actually likes watching movies with subtitles and thinks it's fun 2 lie on the beach at night and count the stars and talk about who wrote the best guitar riff of all time – which of course would be Nirvana, Smells Like Teen Spirit – altho if he said anything by Tom Morello I wouldn't hold it against him!!! ;-) Sometimes when

I talk to Todd it's like we're hollering at each other from opposite ends of the grand canyon. I try and try but he just doesn't seem to HEAR me. Does that make sense?

I stop typing and look at my epic text. It's so long it takes up two screens. I sigh. If I send that to Jenna she'll think I'm nuts. As far as she's concerned, Todd's a total catch. He's cute, an awesome dancer and comes from a 'great' family – which in Jenna-speak means his family own half of Brentwood. But to me that stuff is just the gift-wrap, it's what's underneath that really counts. And that's what I'm not so sure about.

I press delete and type a new text:

Not sure. Don't forget 2 pack ur straighteners! G xoxo

Anyone who knows Jenna knows there is more chance of turkeys wearing *We Heart Thanksgiving* T-shirts than her going anywhere without her hair straighteners. I used to wish I had sheet-smooth blonde hair like hers, but now I know how much work it takes – she has to get up at 6.30 every morning to get it like that in time for school – I'm kind of glad I decided to embrace my auburn curls.

Mom thinks Jenna's way too uptight or, as she puts it, 'that girl needs to take a goddam chill pill!' But Mom doesn't understand. Jenna's immaculate appearance is her suit of armour against the world. We've been best friends since we were seven so I know why she is the way she is. I sometimes wish she hadn't sworn me to secrecy about what happened to her. If Mom knew she'd realize that beneath the sheen of perfection Jenna's just as insecure as the rest of us. She just hides it better is all.

My phone bleeps. Another text from Jenna. I take a deep breath, preparing myself for a lecture about how it really is time I did the deed with Todd. But surprisingly there's no lecture – in fact she doesn't even acknowledge my 'not sure'.

FYI I've packed TWO sets of straighteners!! ;-) c u tomo xoxo

Jenna doesn't have a boyfriend right now; she's actually been single for two whole weeks – which for Jenna is forever. Her single weeks are like dog years. But she's hoping to end her man drought on the cruise and bag herself a member of the English aristocracy. Actually, she just said she wanted to find herself a rich guy – I added the English bit after a Jane Austen-athon the other night.

I click on Todd's text.

hey, babe – looking forward 2 spending next 4 wks with u ;-)

Why did he sign off with a ;-) ? Suddenly, that winking face becomes loaded with a more sinister meaning:

hey, babe – looking forward 2 spending next 4 wks with u
HAVING SEX

I put my phone on the bed and go take down the poster of Jimi Hendrix covering my full-length mirror. I look at my curly hair and sigh. Then I pull up my top and sigh twice – once for each of my non-existent breasts. I used to love being flat-chested. And actually I still do, when I'm going for a run along the beach, or if it's too hot to wear a bra. But ever since I got a boyfriend it feels as if I have a flashing neon sign on my front advertising my uncanny resemblance to a pancake. *But you don't even know if you want to be with Todd any more,* the voice inside my head reminds me. *I know, but sometimes it would be nice to feel like a woman rather than a stick figure,* I answer back.

I pull my top down and go over to the window. My bedroom is next door to the kitchen so it also looks out on to the courtyard. I climb on to my window ledge and look outside. All the lights are off in the guy's apartment below. I try not to think of what he and his new lady friend might be doing in the dark. I see the old man in the apartment directly opposite ours shuffle across his kitchen, preparing his last cup of coffee of the day. I don't need to watch to know that he'll then take this coffee through to his bedroom and drink it in his armchair by the window, with the moonlight glimmering in his silvery hair. I tilt my head back. Up above me the sky is a dark velvety blue and the first of the stars are starting to appear. It reminds me of my cosmic wish list. I pull the crumpled piece of paper from my pocket and re-read it. The winner of *From Trailer Trash to Teen Queen* said that the most important part of making a cosmic wish list – the cosmic part – was releasing your wishes to the stars. Basically this involves setting fire to them. I get down from the window ledge and go fetch the book of matches I use to light my candles and incense. Then I look around my room for something safe to set fire to my list in. I settle upon the ceramic dish my dad brought me back from a recent holiday with The Allergist. I tip the contents of the bowl on to my bed and place the crumpled list inside. Then I take the bowl over to the window and set it down on the ledge. I wonder if I ought to say something while I'm releasing my wishes to the stars. Like a chant or something. The bowl is old and worn – an 'antique' according to my dad, kind of gross in my opinion – but I can just make out an inscription in dark red letters around the rim, above some sort of hieroglyphs.

Vivre éternellement dans l'obscurité de la lune.

I guess it's French but I have no idea what it means. It sounds cool though so I light a match and hold it to the edge of the list and recite the inscription in my most melodramatic French accent. 'Vivre éternellement dans l'obscurité de la lune!' The corner of the paper starts to glow red and curl and then a flame shoots up. I hold the bowl outside the window and pray that none of my neighbours are watching me from behind a herb pot. Gradually, bits of burning paper start peeling off and drifting up into the sky, glinting like fireflies. I feel a sudden rush of excitement as I watch them go. Everything's going to be fine. Mom will start painting again, Todd and I will sort things out, I'll remember all of my routines and Tigger will still love me when I get back. Finally the flame goes out and the last of my wishes flies away. I bring the bowl back into my bedroom and go get a tissue to clean all the black from the inside. But as I wipe the tissue around the bowl I notice a charred scrap of paper in the center. I pick it up and hold it to the light. What I see makes me almost drop the bowl in shock. There, in the middle of the paper, in my handwriting, is the word *danger*.

Chapter Two

It's five in the morning and I'm wide awake. This is not good *at all.* I finally got to sleep at about two o'clock. but it was one of those sleeps that ends up making you feel a whole lot more tired than when you began. It didn't help that I had the most stressful dream ever. Surprisingly, it wasn't about messing up my routines or trying to fend off Todd's advances – my nightmares of choice these past few weeks – it was that I was trapped in a house that was on fire. It was a real old house, with uneven floorboards and shabby furniture, and there was a baby screaming in one of the other rooms. In my dream I was trying desperately to get to the baby, but I couldn't. The smoke in the hallway was so thick it was like the air itself had turned to ash, and the heat from the flames was unbearable.

I turn on my bedside lamp, my heart still racing. The

bowl is on the floor next to the bed where I left it, with the charred scrap of paper still inside. I guess it doesn't take a dream-analysing genius to work out why I might have dreamt of a house-fire. I mean, what was I thinking, setting fire to something in my bedroom? The whole apartment could've burnt down.

It had taken me a long time to figure out where the word danger had come from. And when I did finally work it out I couldn't help feeling spooked. Why did only the 'en' from 'endanger' get burnt? I know that right now I'm chronically over-tired, but that is the first and very last time I write a cosmic wish list.

When I realize there's no way I'm going to get back to sleep I switch on my laptop and log into Facebook. I have seven new wall posts, all from students at the Academy who aren't going on the cruise wishing me luck. Which is really sweet because they all tried out for the job too. Out of habit I click on to Todd's page. His meat-head friend JP has posted a picture of some wrestling chick in a bikini on his wall. Underneath the picture he's written 'dude, I *so* would!' What a meat-head. Then I notice that Todd is now friends with someone called Marley-May McKenzie. I stare at my laptop. What kind of a name is that? Is she sponsored by the letter M or something? I click on Marley-May's profile pic to enlarge it. She looks like a cartoon cheerleader. All perfect, glow-in-the-dark teeth and shiny, princess hair. And breasts rounded like cupcakes. The downside of not sleeping with your boyfriend is that you start to suspect that every other girl he knows would hop into bed with him in an instant. *But why do you even care if you're so unsure about him?* the voice in my head says snarkily. I sigh. Why *do* I care? Maybe somewhere deep down I'm still hoping I'm wrong and that actually Todd and I are meant to be together. Whatever, now is not the time to embark on a session of torture-by-Facebook. I click back on to my own page and decide to update my status instead. I put the cursor in the box and start typing.

Grace Delaney can't wait to go cruising the South Pacific.

I frown and delete. I have this thing about not lying on my status updates. I don't know why – I know everybody lies on their updates, all the time. I guess I just worry that it'll bring bad karma or something. I try again.

Grace Delaney can't sleep.

Geez. I also have this thing about writing chronically boring updates. I delete again and think about the other people going on the cruise. I wonder if any of them are having trouble sleeping. I click on to Jenna's page. She made her last update at just gone midnight.

Jenna Wade is going dancing on a cruise ship!! Super excited!☺

From Jenna's page I click through to Ron's. Ron and Jenna have been friends since kindergarten. Their moms play golf together and go to the same cosmetic surgeon. Jenna calls Ron her surrogate brother. I'm not so sure Ron feels quite the same. I've seen the way he looks at her. It's not the kind of look you give your sister – surrogate or no. But then again, most boys look at Jenna like that, so maybe it's like a biological impulse over which they have no control. I read Ron's status.

Ron Little cannot wait to dance with Jenna Wade and the rest of the guys in the Dance of the Worlds show. Setting sail tomorrow!

Cariss Swayne has left a comment beneath Ron's status: Me too! I click on her profile. Cariss is the daughter of Isaac Swayne – one of Hollywood's top African–American actors who specializes in playing cops with dark secrets and sports stars with drug addictions. Jenna likes Cariss, but I'm not so sure. Cariss is the kind of girl who sashays through life as if the spotlight is always on her and sometimes that can be a real pain. Especially when you're trying to dance together as a team. I read her status:

Cariss Swayne cannot believe her daddy bought her a brand-new iPhone with a diamond heart motif – super-cute!!!

I look at Cariss's profile pic. She's wearing a hot-pink bikini and draped over the bonnet of her Mercedes sports car. Also a present from her daddy. I look at Cariss's perfect body. It's as smooth and shiny as a cocoa bean. I bet she would have sex with her boyfriend all the time. If she had a boyfriend. Cariss prefers to have a collection of male admirers following her about like a pack of puppy dogs. The only boy who doesn't fetch and beg at her every command is Dan Charles. Dan is from downtown LA and is probably the best street-dancer in the Academy. He's there on a scholarship and rumour has it his older brother was in the Bloods gang and was shot in a drive-by – although none of us really know Dan well enough to know if that's true. He pretty much keeps himself to himself. He isn't even on Facebook. I guess we'll get to know him better on the ship. I scroll absently through Cariss's friends list. The other two dancers going on the cruise are Belle Sanchez and Jimmy Patterson, also known as the Flea. Not because he has fleas or anything but because he's real small and has the ability to jump higher and faster than any dancer I've ever seen. Belle and Jimmy aren't really part of our social circle so I'm not able to check out their Facebook pages. Which is probably just as well, as I'm starting to go a little out of my mind with exhaustion. Thankfully, at the precise moment I'm thinking of scrolling through all of Todd's female friends to see which ones look as if they'd like to have sex with him, Tigger pads into my room and leaps soundlessly on to my bed. I curl up beside him and finally the gentle hum of his purr soothes me back to sleep.

Needless to say, when my dad arrives two hours later to take me to the airport I'm not exactly feeling the greatest. And to make matters worse, Dad insists on coming up to the apartment rather than calling me from the lobby like he normally does.

'I thought you might need help with your luggage,' he says lamely as I let him into the hallway. As I stand between Dad in his midlife-crisis Converse sneakers and Mom in her Hello Kitty pyjamas and yesterday's make-up, I feel like the poster child for the nuclear family. That's nuclear as in complete and total disaster on a global scale.

'Okay, well, let's go then,' I mutter, grabbing my purse from the hall table. I give Mom a hug and breathe in the scent of her patchouli oil, as if I'm trying to inhale a part of her to take with me.

'The traffic's pretty backed up already,' Dad says.

'All right, Peter, I'm just saying goodbye to my daughter,' Mom snaps.

I sigh and gently untangle myself from her arms. 'Happy painting,' I whisper.

She smiles at me, but I can see it's taking everything she's got not to cry. 'Happy dancing, sweet pea,' she whispers back. 'Call me as soon as you get there.'

I manage to get Dad and my luggage out of the apartment without any further sniping and pretty soon we're heading down the highway with 50 Cent blasting from the stereo. Yes, 50 Cent, rapping about having sex 'in da club', on my dad's stereo.

'Since when did you like rap music?' I ask, checking to make sure all the windows are closed.

'Ah. Well, Kimberley likes it, so . . .'

Kimberley is the other name for The Allergist. Dad coughs and turns the volume down. I sigh and look out the window. The sky is cornflower blue with the occasional chalky-white wisp of cloud. As we speed along it feels as if the palm trees lining the road are standing to attention, giving me some kind of ceremonial send-off. And then it hits me. This really is happening. I really am going away. And for the first time since I passed the audition I actually feel relieved. For a whole year I've been living in the fallout of my parents' break-up. And for years before that I'd been living in their war zone, having to be the grown-up while they acted like kids. This will be the longest time I've ever had away from them. The longest time I'll have only had to worry about myself. I feel my cell phone vibrate in my purse. I take it out and see that I have a text from Todd.

At the terminal. C u soon x

'It's Todd,' I tell Dad. 'He's there already.'

Dad just clears his throat. He met Todd for the first time a week ago. We went to a Red Lobster for dinner. Basically it was three courses of cringe, with a side order of deep-fried humiliation. I could tell Dad didn't like Todd pretty much straight away. He wasn't rude to him or anything. In fact, he was very polite. Way *too* polite. When I asked him what he thought of Todd afterwards he just said, 'Hmm, okay, I guess.'

But after what he'd done to Mom and me he couldn't exactly be too critical of my relationship choices, could he? I feel a sudden, hot flash of anger.

'Don't worry about parking,' I say as Dad takes the exit for the airport. 'You can just drop me by the terminal.'

Dad looks at me and frowns. 'Oh, I don't know, Grace. I think I ought to come in with you.'

I shake my head. The only good thing about having a parent who's eaten up with guilt is that they pretty much do whatever you tell them. 'There's no need. My teacher will be there. And all of my friends. We'll be cool.'

It turns out all of my friends are anything but cool when I finally locate them in the crowded terminal. I spot Jenna first. She's wearing a super-white tracksuit that's making her tanned skin gleam like syrup. She's also wearing a fearsome scowl.

'Some total douche bag just trod on my vanity case and wrecked it,' she says all in one breath as soon as she sees me.

I examine the immaculate white leather case. It takes me a moment to notice the slightest trace of what I guess could be described as a footprint – or a footprint's really pale ghost. But when Jenna gets in one of her moods it's safest just to play along. I shake my head sympathetically and sigh.

'And my mom had a major hissy fit when I told her we wouldn't be doing any ballet routines in the show,' Jenna adds.

'You told her?' I am genuinely shocked. Jenna's mom used to be a professional ballerina and she spends her entire time trying to control Jenna's every move – and making sure that every move is ballet-related. She's a pretty scary lady and Jenna doesn't normally do anything to deliberately annoy her.

'Yeah, well, I've had just about enough of her ordering me about.' Jenna dumps her vanity case on top of the rest of her luggage and flicks her platinum hair over her shoulder. I can practically see the tension crackling like static in the air around her. 'I wanted her to know that for the next four weeks I'll be doing whatever the hell I want, and there is absolutely nothing she can do about it.'

I wonder if this is a good time to tell her that my dad has started listening to rap. I decide it's probably not.

Just across from Jenna I see Cariss standing supermodel-straight in the centre of a family of Louis Vuitton cases. She's wearing a pair of pale-pink jeans so tight they might have been sprayed on and she's having an argument with someone on her new, matching pink iPhone . . . whilst still looking totally serene. This is quite an achievement.

'I can't believe you'll be away filming over Christmas,' she yells into the phone. 'I don't care if he's directing it – I'm your daughter!'

Hmm, clearly quite a few of us are suffering from parent-induced tension. I look around the terminal and see Todd and Ron over by the Air Hawaii desk talking to our teacher Rainbow. Rainbow isn't coming with us; she's just here to make sure we all board the plane safely. Todd's wearing a new pair of baggy cut jeans and an Abercrombie tee. His floppy brown hair is golden at the ends from the sun. He looks like a *Seventeen* centrefold. So shouldn't my heart be, like, palpitating or something? This sun-kissed Adonis is my boyfriend and all I feel is numb inside. I send him a mental instant message. *Turn around now, if you're the one for me.* Todd keeps chatting away to Ron. Then he lets out one of his really loud laughs and it cuts across the noise of the airport like a trumpet blast.

'Oh my God!'

'What?' I look back at Jenna. She's staring toward the terminal entrance, her pale blue eyes icy with disdain. I turn and follow her gaze. Belle Sanchez is standing in the doorway. She's wearing a bright orange tracksuit and her black hair is scraped up into a high ponytail. As usual her ears are loaded with gold hoops. But I don't think it's her look that's gotten Jenna so pissed. Belle is also clinging to her mom and weeping loudly.

'We're only going for, like, four weeks,' Jenna hisses in my ear. 'What's her problem?'

I shrug. I guess Belle must be the only one of us who isn't about ready to divorce her parents.

A family with four small kids comes spilling into the terminal, but Belle and her mom don't move from the doorway. They're holding on to each other as if the world is about to end.

'Yo, Grace!' I hear Todd yell from behind me.

'Hey.' I turn round and smile at him.

'How long you been here?' he says, bounding over with Ron. 'You should have texted me.'

'I just got here,' I say. 'Hi, Ron.'

Ron smiles, but he's looking at Jenna. 'Hey, Grace. What's up, Jen?'

Jenna is still scowling at Belle. 'What's up with that girl?' she says. 'If she didn't want to come why'd she bother auditioning?'

We all look at Belle and her mom, their entwined bodies convulsing with sobs. Todd hooks his arm around my waist from behind. I lean into him and try to relax.

'It's Latinos,' Ron says. 'Always so dramatic about the slightest thing.'

'Yeah, well, I think it's pathetic,' Jenna says. Ron nods in agreement. His round face and thick black hair always remind me of a Lego-man. It kind of creeps me out.

'So, what's happening, guys? Are we all set?' Rainbow says, striding over with her clipboard. 'Any sign of Dan and Jimmy?'

We all shake our heads.

'Okay, well you go get in the queue for check-in and I'll try and round up the others.'

'You may need a crowbar to prise Belle away from her

mom,' Jenna says. 'Ron, be a sweetie and get my case for me.'

Ron nods his Lego-man head eagerly, despite the fact that he's already laden down with an enormous rucksack.

Rainbow looks over at Belle and her mom. 'Ah. I see. Well, you guys get going and I'll get Belle.'

But before she can move, the door slides open and Jimmy the Flea bounds in. He's wearing a Hawaiian shirt and garland – with pinstripe trousers and a pork-pie hat. Somehow he's actually managed to make this look pretty cool.

'Oh my God. What is he wearing?' Jenna says. 'That guy is a total dork.'

I look at Jenna and wonder why she's acting so mean. Her fight with her mom must have really gotten to her.

Dan Charles slouches in behind the Flea. As usual he's got on a vest top and track pants and has a huge sports bag slung over his muscular brown shoulder.

'Belle, darling girl!' the Flea cries in a mock British accent. He's actually from New York but speaks like a member of the royal family most of the time. He's kind of like a really wired Prince William.

Belle disentangles herself from her mom and promptly throws her arms around the Flea. Dan comes over to us.

'What up, bro,' Todd says.

I can't help cringing. Todd has this habit of lapsing into gangsta speak whenever Dan's around.

'What up,' Dan replies, nodding coolly at all of us.

'Okay, guys, go get in line and I'll fetch Belle and the Flea,' Rainbow says. 'Cariss, can you go with the others please.'

Cariss looks at Rainbow blankly, then looks down at her luggage. 'Who's gonna get my cases?' she asks.

'I'm afraid you'll have to carry your own cases,' Rainbow replies as she heads over to Belle. Cariss looks outraged, like Rainbow just told her she'd have to walk all the way to Honolulu. I notice Dan smirking as he walks right past her.

'The Flea and Belle are a total embarrassment,' Jenna says as she gestures at Ron to pick up her case. 'There's no way I'm sitting anywhere near them on the plane.'

Todd and Ron nod in agreement, but I sigh. I thought I'd be escaping a war zone for the next four weeks, not flying straight into another one.

Chapter Three

In my life BT (Before Todd) I used to have this imaginary boyfriend called Ashton. Ashton was everything I wanted in a boy – funny, smart, liked watching French movies (and therefore the height of sophistication) and, of course, cute. But cute in a wild-haired, piercing-eyed, pirate kind of a way. Every night I'd lie in bed with one arm wrapped around my waist pretending that it belonged to Ashton. 'Don't worry,' Ashton would whisper over the rumble of my parents fighting downstairs, 'I love you.' And then I'd close my eyes and dream of being whisked off on dates to super-romantic places like a Parisian cafe or a second-hand bookstore in Brooklyn, and smooch Ashton's pillow-face until I fell into a blissed-out sleep.

As I sit on the plane to Hawaii, watching across the aisle as Todd tries to put a sick-bag on Ron's head, I wonder if maybe my imaginary boyfriend could be to blame for my doubts about my real boyfriend. Maybe Ashton was too perfect? Maybe he's impossible to live up to? But then if you're going to imagine up a boyfriend why would you choose to give him any character flaws?

Beside me, Jenna and Cariss are hunched over Cariss's new cell phone. In front of us, through the gap between their seats, I can see Belle and the Flea, heads together, deep in conversation. And although I can't actually see Dan in his seat on the other side of the Flea, I figure he'll be plugged into his iPod as usual, head nodding in time to the beat.

A stewardess starts walking down the aisle toward us pushing a refreshments trolley. I love air stewardesses. They are so glamorous and poised despite the fact that their jobs are actually one of the lousiest in the world. I read an article in *The Chronicle* one time that said stewardesses are often infertile because flying between all the different time zones causes their menstrual cycles to go into total meltdown. They also suffer from really dry skin, brittle nails and short-term memory loss due to sleep deprivation. Basically, beneath all the make-up, they're like the living dead. You would never think it looking at this stewardess. Her hair is buttercup blonde and her lips are as glossy and red as Snow White's apple. 'Can I get you any refreshments? Coffee, water, soda?' she says time and time again as she makes her way down the plane, but each time with the enthusiasm as if it's the very first. As she stops at the row in front of us I hear Belle asking for a pack of M&Ms. Next to me, Jenna sighs. Jenna's mom has her on this mega-strict diet. It involves eating tons of raw vegetables and drinking grass-based drinks that look like green paint. Personally I'm glad to see Belle has an appetite. Hopefully it means she's over her sorrow at having to leave her mom.

'This is the first and last time I fly economy,' Cariss hisses. 'There's more leg room in a school locker! It's gotta be, like, breaking the Geneva Convention or something.'

I don't have the heart to tell her that the Geneva Convention was actually created to protect the rights of prisoners of war and therefore it seems highly unlikely that it will also include a clause protecting the leg room of dance students. I shoot a sideways glance at Jenna, ready to exchange a knowing grin, but she's looking at Cariss and giving her arm a squeeze.

'I know, hun,' Jenna murmurs. 'It sucks.'

I get a slightly sinking feeling in my stomach. At school Cariss normally hangs out with Liberty Johnson, daughter of the rock singer Kyle Johnson. Liberty didn't try out for the cruise job because she and her mom are spending the summer on the European leg of her dad's tour. Jenna's always been a little star-struck around Cariss. With Liberty out of the picture she might see a chance to get close to her and I'm not exactly sure where that would leave me. I sigh. Why am I being such a stress-head about everything? Jenna and I have been friends forever. The bond we have doesn't just disappear overnight.

Cariss and Jenna start laughing. Jenna nudges me and passes me Cariss's iPhone. Cariss has uploaded a photo of Belle crying in the airport to her Facebook page. The title under the photo reads: Cry-Baby-Belle. Even though I know Jenna and Cariss are waiting for me to start laughing along with them, I can't do it. I pass the phone back and see the diamond-encrusted love-heart on the back. Seems kind of ironic given that Cariss can be so hateful.

'Can I get you anything, sir?' the stewardess asks Todd. Now she's up close I can smell her perfume, fresh and citrusy. It makes me think of the terracotta pot of lemon grass in my herb garden and I feel a pang of something dangerously close to homesickness.

'Well, that all depends on what's on offer,' Todd says. I cringe and Ron starts to snigger.

'Coffee, water, soda. *Milk?*' The flight attendant deadpans.

Todd's face flushes. 'Coke, please,' he mutters.

Jenna and Cariss order diet sodas. I order a coffee and give the flight attendant an extra-big smile to try and compensate for my idiot boyfriend. As I sip on my drink I think of the summer I was twelve, when my parents and I went on holiday to France. One evening we were eating dinner in a restaurant in Paris and my dad started majorly flirting with our waitress.

Mom and I couldn't understand what he was saying because he was talking in French, but you could tell by the way he was talking all soft and low and the way the waitress kept giggling and playing with her hair that he was most definitely coming on to her. I remember Mom pretending to be all engrossed in the menu, but I could see the tears in her eyes. Guys who flirt with other women while their girlfriends are there are total losers. In all of our imaginary dates Ashton only ever had eyes for me. I close my eyes and fight the panic that's starting to build inside my stomach. I'm about to be trapped on a cruise ship for four weeks with a boyfriend I'm beginning to think is a loser. This is *so* not good.

After the longest five hours, forty minutes on record we get to Honolulu. There's an epic drama in luggage reclaim, when Cariss can't find one of her hundred cases, but finally we make it out into the arrivals hall. We're met by a representative from Oceana Ventura, the company that owns the cruise ship we'll be performing on. His name is Andreas Moon, which sounds calm and zen-like but he's actually all red-faced and super-stressed – apparently Cariss's luggage crisis has put us way behind schedule. Andreas rushes us out to the car park where we have to board a minibus to take us down to the waterfront. After the icy air-conditioning of the airport, the air outside is as hot and thick as soup.

'Come sit with me, Grace,' Todd says as we get on the bus.

I sit down next to him and pull my seat belt on. As I slot it into place Todd puts his hand over mine and smiles. I smile back. And I mean it. This is when I like Todd best, when he isn't performing for his friends or an audience. When I feel like I'm getting the real him. As the bus pulls out of the airport car park Todd leans forward and kisses me on the end of my nose. I feel a tingle of relief. Maybe going away together is exactly what we need to bring us closer.

'Can I ask you something?' I whisper.

'Sure.' He looks at me and smiles.

'Do you ever wish there wasn't so much pressure on us to be a certain way?'

Todd frowns. 'What do you mean?'

I feel my face start to flush. 'I mean, as young people. There's so much pressure to talk and act in a certain way; to be cool.' *Geez, way to talk like a sex ed counsellor,* my inner voice taunts.

Todd laughs and shakes his head. 'You're so kooky, Grace.'

'But don't you ever –'

Just then a Jay Z track comes on the radio and Todd starts rapping along real loud, all the time glancing around the minibus to see who's watching. I turn away and lean my head against the window. When I was on my imaginary dates with Ashton I could always tell him what was on my mind and he never laughed at me or called me 'kooky'. *That's because he was created by you, you doofus*, the voice in my head pipes up. *He was a figment of your messed-up imagination!* I sigh and watch as Hawaii streaks by outside – all green palm trees, white buildings and blue sky. Then I see a sign outside a construction site. DANGER it says in big red letters. That word again. I hug my bag to me and close my eyes.

The minibus takes us to a small harbour on the waterfront. Andreas, still looking really stressed, explains that we're going to be taken by boat to meet the cruise ship, which is currently about an hour away in the Pacific. The cruise, which started in Australia, has been going for several weeks already. We'll be replacing a theatre company as the evening entertainment. The feeling of panic that started on the plane twitches back into life. What if the theatre company was really amazing? What if their play had the passengers whooping in delight night after night? How are they going to feel about watching a bunch of dancing teenagers instead?

We all clamber out of the bus and immediately sweat begins to bead on my skin. I knew Hawaii was going to be hot, but not *this* hot. It feels as if we're standing on a giant grill. I can actually see the heat rising from the sidewalk, causing the air to shimmer like it's melting. I gaze at the turquoise sea longingly.

'Okay, let's get going,' Andreas says as he starts marching over to a jetty where a speedboat is moored.

'Awesome!' Todd exclaims, looking at the boat.

'Could somebody please help me with my bags?' Cariss snaps. Even she is starting to sweat. One of her perfect cheekbones is streaked with mascara.

Ron makes like he's going to help her then glances at Jenna. Jenna gives him one of her smiles that looks all sweet on the surface but her eyes are actually saying 'don't you dare'. She may want to be friends with Cariss but she sure as hell doesn't want to lose Ron as a lapdog. Ron drops his Lego-man head and goes to retrieve Jenna's case.

'Seriously!' Cariss exclaims. 'There's no way I'll be able to carry them all.'

'Well, maybe you should've thought of that before you brought half your mansion,' Dan mutters before collecting his own bag from the trunk of the bus.

Cariss flushes and glowers at him. She looks like a really angry Amazonian queen – whose war-paint has smudged.

'I'll take one,' Belle says, smiling shyly at Cariss.

'Yes, allow me,' the Flea says in his British accent, grabbing another case.

Cariss doesn't even acknowledge them. Then Todd fetches one from the trunk, the biggest one.

'Thanks, Todd, you're a total star,' Cariss says, in a voice so syrupy sweet I wonder how the words didn't stick in her throat. Then, for some random reason, the image of Cariss in her bikini draped over her car pops into my head. 'Make love to me, Todd, you total star,' she says, while beckoning at him provocatively. I blink my eyes hard and look away. The heat must be turning me crazy.

Slowly, we make our way to the end of the jetty, Jenna and Cariss at the front, like two princesses leading a procession of pack animals. Andreas Moon shouts something in a foreign language to the boat and a dark, curly-haired head appears from below deck. It's attached to a tanned, muscular body.

I go statue-still. I want to look away but I can't. It's as if Ashton has clambered straight out of one of my dreams, wearing a faded T-shirt and frayed denim cut-offs.

'This is Cruz,' Andreas says. 'He'll be taking you to the ship.'

'What, his name is Cruise as in cruise ship?' Jenna says with a smirk.

'No, Cruz, as in C-R-U-Z. It's Spanish, he's from Costa Rica,' Andreas explains, as if he's talking to a five-year-old. Jenna gives him one of her death stares but Andreas isn't looking any more, he's saying something else to Cruz in what I guess must be Spanish.

Cruz leaps on to the jetty and starts replying in the same language. His voice is soft and low but he seems real tense and keeps gesturing at the sky. I hear the word *tormenta* a few times and wonder what it means. Belle obviously understands because she also starts looking pretty anxious. But whatever is bugging Cruz, Andreas clearly isn't interested. He just keeps on shaking his head and saying no. In the end Cruz gives a massive sigh and starts hauling our bags on to the boat. Up close he doesn't look much older than us. I figure he's about eighteen, max.

'Oh my God. Isn't there, like, a bridge or something to help us get onboard?' Cariss says, looking horrified at the gap between the boat and the jetty. It's about four inches wide.

Andreas looks at her but doesn't say anything. I can tell what he's thinking though and it isn't pretty.

'What's up? Lost the use of your legs as well as your arms?' Dan says before jostling past Cariss and striding on to the boat. He carries his own bag. Todd and Ron follow him. They leave their bags on the jetty for Cruz. After much shrieking and drama, Cariss and Jenna make it on board. In front of me, Belle whispers something to the Flea and for an awful moment I think she's going to cry again, but the Flea gives her elbow a squeeze and helps her on to the boat. Then I realize that I'm the only one still standing on the jetty and for a split second I get the weirdest feeling. It's like some kind of force is sucking me toward the boat.

'Good luck, guys,' Andreas calls out, clearly a whole lot happier now he's getting shot of us. 'See you in four weeks' time.'

He starts making his way back along the jetty and I pick up my bag. I'm about to hoist it onboard when Cruz reaches out to take it from me. As he grabs hold of the handle his tanned hand touches mine. For a moment we stay motionless, eyes locked. Then Cruz holds out his other hand to help me on to the boat. As I step onboard I feel weightless and giddy, like I'm stepping off a cliff into thin air. And then I'm struck by a truly scary fact – in all the time I've known Todd, he has never, ever made me feel like this.

Chapter Four

For someone who didn't seem to want to take us anywhere at first, Cruz sure is in a hurry once we set off. The boat is going so fast it bounces off the waves like a cork. I go sit at the back and watch Hawaii fade into the distance. Jenna and Cariss have disappeared below deck to protect their hair from the sea spray. They wanted me to come with them but I need to be out in the open to try and clear my head. And it's working – the wind whipping at my face is making me feel a lot saner after the whole touching-hands-with-Cruz-and-turning-into-a-love-struck-statue incident. I turn back and look at Todd and Ron clowning around at the front of the boat, trying to reenact the famous scene from *Titanic*. Then I glance at Cruz steering the boat in the cabin just behind them. The backs of his shoulders are broad and rigid. I look away before I get a

Victorian-heroine-style attack of the vapours. To my left, Belle and the Flea are standing gazing down into the water, deep in conversation once again. To my right, Dan sits hunched over, eyes closed, listening to his iPod. From the frown on his face I'd say he really isn't enjoying the whole sailing experience.

Todd starts making his way down the boat toward me, and I arrange my face into a smile.

'Hey, hun,' he says as he reaches me.

'Hey.'

'Awesome, huh?' Todd says, nodding at the boat as he sits down beside me.

'Uh-huh.'

'One day I'm gonna get me one of these babies.'

I want to say, *why do you have to talk like you're in a really bad movie? Why can't you talk to me like you did the night of the Infamous Root-Beer Floats?* The night of the Infamous Root-Beer Floats was the night Todd and I got together. We'd been in school late, at a street-dance workshop, and afterward Todd had found me crying by my locker. I'd been crying because I was missing my dad, which I thought sounded kind of pathetic, but Todd didn't seem to think so at all. He handed me a sweatband to wipe my tears – he didn't have any tissues – and then he said he was taking me to Denny's Diner for one of his Infamous Root-Beer Floats, as this was the only thing *guaranteed* to bring a smile back to a person's face. Once we got to Denny's we ate hotdogs and drank floats, and I told him all about my messed-up home life and how worried I was about my mom. Then Todd told me all about his sister Ingrid who has anorexia and the strain that puts on his family because everything has to revolve around her the whole time. I know this sounds harsh, but I actually felt relieved that his family was messed up too. It made him seem vulnerable, but in a really good way. And that's why, when he asked me to go out with him, I said yes. I'd thought that, like Jenna, beneath his perfect exterior he wasn't so different to me after all.

'What do you reckon, Gracie? Can you see me at the wheel of one of these?'

I snap back to life and nod at him. 'Sure.'

Jenna appears at the entrance to the deck. 'Hey, Todd, Ron, can you guys come help Cariss open the lock on her case? The key's got jammed.'

'No problem.' Todd gets to his feet and looks down at me. 'Back in a minute.'

I nod and watch as he and Ron disappear below. Then I close my eyes and tilt my head back, opening my mouth slightly so I can catch the salty breeze on my tongue. In my life BT I always thought that having a boyfriend would make things easier and I'd feel less alone. Well, it turns out the novels and the romcoms lied. To me, anyways.

'I'm telling you, he sounded like he knew what he was talking about.' I open my eyes at the sound of Belle's raised voice.

'Chillax, honey-pie,' the Flea says, in his native New York twang. 'The adorable Andreas wouldn't have let us go if he thought we'd get caught in it.'

'What's up?' I call over to them, shading my eyes from the sun.

Belle gestures at Cruz, causing the row of gold bangles on her arm to jangle into life. Her dark eyes are wide with worry. 'He said there's gonna be a real bad storm.'

'But look at the sky, Beau-Belle,' the Flea says. 'My mom always says that if there's enough blue sky to make a pair of cat's pyjamas then it ain't gonna rain. There's enough blue sky up there to make a cat's entire wardrobe – for four seasons!'

We all look up. The sky is a bright, brilliant blue. If it wasn't so humid it would be the perfect day.

'Hey, Cruise-Ship?' Jenna emerges from the hold and shouts at Cruz. She's tied her hair back and is wearing a baseball cap pulled down tightly on her head; ready to do battle with any pesky hair-frizzing spray. 'Got any refreshments on this thing?'

Oblivious, Cruz carries on driving the boat.

Cariss appears at the stop of the steps next to Jenna. Her anti hair-frizzing armour is double-plated – a silk scarf tightly knotted around her head, underneath a hoodie.

'Excuse me,' Jenna yells at Cruz. He still doesn't turn round.

Then Todd appears next to them and yells, 'Yo!' at the top of his voice.

Dan, who'd still been hunched over with his eyes closed, jolts upright and rips his iPod from his ears. 'Wassup?' he says in a weird groaning voice as if he's in some kind of pain.

Keeping one hand on the wheel, Cruz glances over his shoulder at us.

'You got any drinks, dude?' Todd asks.

Cruz looks at him blankly.

Cariss stares at Cruz as if he's just been beamed down from another planet. 'What's wrong with him?'

'I don't think he speaks any English,' Belle says.

'You are kidding?' Cariss replies, without bothering to look at Belle.

'No, he was speaking Spanish earlier.'

Jenna looks around at us in shock. 'Well, that's just great! What if we had an emergency? How would we communicate with him?'

'We do have an emergency,' Todd says. 'It's about one hundred degrees and we've got nothing to drink!'

'I could ask him if you like,' Belle says, fiddling nervously with her necklace. 'I speak Spanish.'

Cariss just shrugs her shoulders.

'Go ahead,' says Jenna.

As Belle goes over to the cabin and starts talking to Cruz in

Spanish we all sit and wait. I see Cariss look at Jenna and raise her eyebrows. Then Jenna starts to smirk. 'So if he doesn't understand any English we could say anything to him, right?'

Ron nods. 'Uh-oh, what have you got planned?'

'What kind of moron doesn't know how to speak English. I mean, hello, twenty-first century!' Jenna says loudly, going over to stand right by the cabin and well within earshot of Cruz.

Ron starts to smirk and Todd laughs.

I stare at Jenna, not sure what has gotten into her. It's like she's showing off. But who's she showing off *to*? Cariss, I guess.

'Not quite as moronic as being a total bitch though,' the Flea mutters.

'What did you say?' Ron snaps.

The Flea just stares at him.

Jenna turns to Ron. 'What did he say?'

'He said not qui–' Ron begins.

'He didn't say anything,' I interrupt.

Belle emerges from the cabin and starts to open a door under one of the seats. 'Apparently there are some drinks in this cupboard.'

Cariss pushes her out of the way and yanks it open.

'Oh great. No diet soda!' she exclaims.

'You're kidding?' Jenna shakes her head in disbelief.

'No, just a load of bottles of water. And they're hot,' Cariss says.

Belle comes and sits down next to me. She's biting her lip and looking a bit teary again. I wish I knew her well enough to be able to give her a hug.

'Geez, I will be so glad when we get to the cruise liner,' Jenna says.

'And I will be so glad when you guys quit moaning,' Dan mutters and the Flea laughs.

'What the hell are you laughing at?' Cariss snaps.

The Flea starts playing with the garland around his neck. 'Chill, Cariss. Stop being so uptight.'

Cariss clenches her hands into tight little fists. 'Don't you dare talk to me like that, you – you – nobody.'

The Flea turns away and although he's still grinning his trademark grin I can see from his eyes that he's hurt.

'Come on guys, let's go to the front,' Jenna says, linking arms with Cariss and looking pointedly at Todd and Ron and me.

Todd holds out his hand to me. I take it but I feel really uncomfortable. 'Sorry,' I whisper to the Flea as I stand up.

For the next hour or so we stay in our separate groups. Belle, Dan and the Flea at the back of the boat and Jenna, Cariss, Ron, Todd and me at the front. The Pacific Ocean stretches all around us for as far as I can see. It's no longer the beautiful pale turquoise of Honolulu but a dark, inky blue. It seems to be getting a whole lot rougher too. Every time the boat leaps off the surface my stomach lurches. I dream of the moment we finally get to the cruise ship and I can go lie down in a darkened cabin.

The only good thing about the rougher water is that it's made Cariss shut up. She's slumped across a seat with her hood pulled way down over her head. All that's visible of her face is her pouting, glossy mouth.

Next to her, Jenna is leaning against Ron, her eyes closed. Ron is just staring blankly into space, looking more like a Lego-man than ever. Even Todd has calmed down, sitting next to me playing Angry Birds on his cell phone.

'I think I'm gonna go back downstairs,' Cariss mutters, lurching to her feet. 'I'm feeling kind of nauseous.'

But before she can move we hear the Flea yell, 'Holy shit!' from the back of the boat.

We all turn to see what's up.

'OH. MY. GOD!' Jenna says, speaking all our thoughts out loud.

There on the horizon behind us is a huge, black cloud, spiralling down toward the sea like a giant corkscrew.

'What the hell is it?' Cariss screams.

When Cruz sees us panicking he turns round too. When I see the look of shock on his face as he turns back I get real scared.

'What is it?' Cariss screams again.

Cruz does something that makes the boat go even faster; then he gets on his radio and starts shouting in Spanish.

'What's he saying?' Cariss screams at Belle.

'He's telling them there's a storm heading our way.' Belle replies.

'What kind of storm?' Jenna yells. 'Why is the cloud shaped like that?'

'It looks kind of like a tornado,' the Flea replies, remarkably calmly given that we seem to be sat right in its path. Right in the middle of the ocean. In a tiny boat.

I try to swallow, but it feels as if my throat has closed up.

'I think it's a waterspout,' the Flea continues. 'I saw this show about them on the Discovery Channel once. It was called *Great Ocean Disasters*.'

'Shut up!' Jenna and Cariss scream at him.

The sea has now gone from being bumpy to swelling in great peaks and troughs. Froth-tipped waves rise and explode over the boat, covering us in spray.

I look at Todd. His tan seems to have paled several shades.

'Oh my God! Oh my God!' Belle cries.

Cruz starts shouting something at us.

'He's telling us to get below deck,' Belle explains.

'Wow! Look at the size of that wave,' the Flea yells. We all turn and see a giant wall of water rising in the distance. It's heading our way.

'Quick!' Todd yells. 'Get down below.'

There's a mad scramble. I go to stand up, but the deck is so slippery I lose my footing and fall flat on my face. The boat tilts sharply to the right and I go crashing into the side. Where's Todd? Why isn't he helping me? I hear the others screaming and yelling as they head for the stairs.

I manage to slither on to my side and look around. They've all gone. I'm on my own. A wave crashes on to the deck and catches me full in the face. I gasp for air as the salt water burns the back of my throat and stings my eyes. I start crawling toward the back of the boat with my eyes shut tight. I think of Mom and Dad and Tigger and I wonder if I'll ever see them again. I want to cry. But I can't cry, because if I cry I'll give up and if I give up I *know* I'll never see them again. And I have to see them. Because I love them. Even my dad in his stupid Converse sneakers.

Then something strange happens – I start feeling really mad. Mad with the ocean and with the storm and with Todd and the others for leaving me here. I'm not ready to die. I haven't even really started to live.

I hear a voice shouting at me in Spanish and I feel a pair of strong arms around my waist pulling me to my feet. Cruz. Together we stagger and slide our way toward the hatch, like we're doing a really bad, drunken dance. I blink and see the wall of water looming over us. Then I close my eyes, grip on to Cruz's hand and we leap down the stairs. There's a horrendous roar as the wave engulfs the boat. We're thrown forward. And everything goes dark.

Chapter Five

For a split second everything seems to freeze and then the whole world tilts on its axis. My stomach lurches upwards – like we're heading for the very highest point on a roller coaster – and then we plummet back down. I go crashing into the corner of the hold, landing on someone.

'Grace?' Jenna gasps in my ear.

'Yes,' I say, trying to wriggle off her. She grips hold of my arm. 'Grace, what's happening? Are we going to die?' Her voice is soft and trembling – and it reminds me of the real Jenna, and why we're best friends.

I take hold of her hand and squeeze it tightly. 'No, of course not. We're going to be fine.' But inside my head all I can think is, *this is it, this is your last living moment on earth.*

There is a roaring sound. The boat tilts again. I feel myself sliding away but Jenna clings on to me. I wonder what it's like to drown. I once read somewhere that it's supposed to be the most peaceful way to die. Clearly whoever wrote it had never been trapped on a tiny boat in the middle of a freakin' tsunami.

'Help!' Cariss screams.

Then I hear someone crying. A boy. 'Oh God. Oh God,' he's saying over and over in between snorting gasps. Ron.

Water starts gushing down the stairs. In the darkness I can just make out figures slipping and sliding, trying to stand up, but then the boat lurches the other way and they're sent flying.

'Jimmy!' Belle cries. 'Jimmy, where are you?'

'I'm here,' the Flea calls out from somewhere on the floor to my left.

'We've gotta get out of here,' Todd shouts. I see his silhouette by the stairwell. Another wave of water rushes down and straight into him. 'Shit!' he cries and stumbles back.

An almighty crash comes from above deck.

Cruz shouts something in Spanish to Belle and yanks open a cupboard door.

'He's saying don't try and go upstairs,' Belle says. 'We have to stay down here.'

'Why? So we can all drown?' Todd shouts.

'Oh my God, I don't wanna drown,' Cariss shrieks. 'Somebody do something!'

'Just shut up and do what you're told,' Dan barks from the other side of the hold.

'Don't speak to me like that,' Cariss replies, but the usual Miss-High-and-Mighty tone has gone from her voice and she sounds like a frightened little kid.

Cruz starts pulling something out of the cupboard. Whatever it is falls to the floor with a loud clatter. Cruz shouts something to Belle again.

'He wants us to put on life jackets,' Belle explains. There's a mad scramble in the dark as we all reach for the jackets. I get two and pass one to Jenna. As I pull my jacket over my head I feel a pinprick of relief; maybe we won't drown after all. But then a much worse thought enters my mind. If Cruz is giving us the jackets because he thinks the boat is going to sink then maybe we'll meet an even worse fate – sharks! I feel Jenna pulling on my hand. I move so that I'm sat right next to her, pressed against the wall. I can feel her body shivering – or is it mine?

'Grace, I'm so sorry, I need to tell you –' she begins, but then the Flea says, 'Listen.'

We all fall silent and listen.

'What?' says Cariss. 'I don't hear a thing.'

'Exactly,' says the Flea.

The roaring noise has stopped. The boat is still rocking violently, but it's upright.

Cruz says something and starts making his way up the stairs.

'He's telling us to stay here while he checks on deck,' Belle explains.

We all sit in stunned silence.

'Grace, are you okay?' Todd asks.

'Yes,' I say, but my voice comes out wobbly and strange. Todd makes his way over to me and grabs hold of my free hand. I know I should be relieved, but all I can think of is how he left me before to get below deck.

'I'm sorry,' he whispers in my ear. 'I should've waited for you. I panicked.'

'It's okay,' I whisper back, but I feel sick. I would never have left him to drown.

'I think I'm bleeding,' Belle says and then she starts to cry.

The Flea scrambles over to her. 'What happened?'

'I hit my head.'

'Hey, don't worry, you're gonna be okay.' The Flea's voice is so gentle and caring it makes me want to sob.

'Are you all right?' I whisper to Jenna.

I feel her nodding. Todd puts his arm around me and Jenna lets go of my hand.

'Ron, where are you?' she asks.

'Here,' Ron says from the other side of the hold.

'Could you come here please?'

Just as Ron scrambles over, Cruz reappears at the top of the stairs. 'Okay,' he calls down to us.

'What does he mean – okay?' Cariss demands.

Belle asks something in Spanish and we all wait while Cruz replies.

'He says the storm has passed. The boat's damaged but it's okay to come upstairs,' Belle says.

We stumble to our feet and cautiously make our way over to the stairs, water sloshing around our ankles. I feel dizzy with shock.

Todd is the first up on deck. 'Oh, man!' I hear him exclaim.

'What is it? What's happened?' Belle asks anxiously from right behind me.

I emerge into the fresh air and can't stop myself from gasping.

It's as if a giant has reached down his hand and crushed the boat between his huge fingers. The metal railings have been bent out of shape and Cruz's cabin is completely destroyed, with the boat's radio and controls ripped out and scattered across the deck. I see Cruz trying to call someone on his cell phone, but he clearly can't get any reception. One by one the others emerge, blinking and gasping on to the deck. The sky is a strange purple-grey colour, but the air feels a whole lot fresher and the wind has dropped.

'All right!' Dan exclaims as he climbs up, his face breaking into a grin.

Todd reaches out to high-five him. 'Looks like we made it, bro.'

'Yeah, man,' Dan replies.

'Is it okay? Has the storm passed?' Cariss asks as she emerges. Her clothes are soaked and clinging to her skin and her headscarf has slipped down around her neck, leaving her normally super-sleek hair sprouting from her head in frizzy clumps.

'Yep, sure has,' the Flea says, taking a good look at the sky. He turns to Belle. 'See! I told you we'd be okay.'

Belle gives him a watery smile. Blood is trickling down her face from the cut on her head.

'Hey, let me take a look at that.' The Flea gently brushes Belle's hair from her forehead. Once again his tenderness gives me a pang of longing. I look at Todd. He's copying Dan's macho, wide-footed stance.

Cruz sees the cut on Belle's head and fetches a first aid box from under one of the seats. We all watch as he sets about bandaging the cut and talking to Belle in Spanish. For a split second I wish that I was the one he was bandaging – his tanned hands are big and weather-beaten but they are so gentle. I sigh and turn away . . . and wonder if I might be suffering from some kind of post-traumatic stress. What else would explain the fact that I'm swooning over a guy like a love-struck middle-grader when we just very nearly died?

'God, that girl is such an attention-seeker,' Jenna whispers in my ear while scowling at Belle. 'I mean, I got battered black and blue down there but I'm not making a big song and dance out of it.'

My heart sinks. 'I don't think she's –'

'What's he saying? What's going on?' Ron blurts out, staring at Cruz.

'He says that the boat has no power and the radio's damaged,' Belle tells us.

'So what does that mean?' Cariss snaps.

'It means we're screwed,' Ron says flatly and he starts biting on his bottom lip.

'No, we're not,' I say. 'The cruise company know we're on our way. They'll be sure to tell the coastguard.'

Todd starts to nod. 'That's right. All we have to do is sit tight.'

'But what if there's another storm?' Cariss says, her voice shrill with panic.

'There won't be,' says the Flea. 'Look over there.'

We all turn and look behind us and sure enough the sky is fading from grey to blue. It's quite possibly one of the greatest sights I have ever seen.

Cruz says something to Belle and puts the finishing touches to her bandage.

'He says we just have to stay calm and wait,' Belle explains. 'He's going to go below and have a look at the damage.'

Cruz nods at her and goes off downstairs.

'Well, this is just great!' Cariss says, kicking at the side of the boat like a two-year-old. 'The first thing I'm gonna do when we get off this shitty boat is get my daddy to sue the ass off Oceana Ventura.'

'What for?' the Flea asks with a baffled grin. 'You can't exactly blame them for the storm.'

'No? Well, I can sure as hell blame them for putting us on this crappy boat, and with someone who can't even speak English.'

'Absolutely,' says Jenna. 'Those guys won't have a leg to stand on.'

I stare at them, incredulous. I can't believe that after everything we've just been through they're starting to bitch already.

'Look at the state of it,' Cariss says, looking scornfully at the damaged boat. 'We're lucky to be alive.'

'Yes. We are,' I say. 'So why don't we all just shut up and show a bit of gratitude for that fact.'

Everyone falls silent. I hear someone cough and see Cruz standing at the top of the stairs staring at me. His dark brown eyes are impossible to read.

I wait for Jenna or Cariss to take a snipe at me, but thankfully they must be too tired or too shocked as they both just look away.

Feeing dangerously close to tears, I go to the front of the boat and start picking up bits of debris from Cruz's cabin and piling it on one side of the deck. I don't know why, I just need a bit of time to get my head together and try and make sense of what's happened. But straight away Jenna comes to join me.

'You okay, Grace?' she says, picking up a small piece of wood and turning it over in her hand. Her white tracksuit is now covered with dirty black streaks, making her immaculate French manicure look kind of out of place.

'Yes,' I say, although I feel anything but okay.

She bends in close to me, so close I can smell the faint remnants of her perfume. 'I don't think it's very constructive to pick on Cariss in front of the others,' she whispers.

'What do you mean, pick on Cariss?' I stare at her. 'I wasn't picking on Cariss, I was just trying to get everyone to stop fighting.'

Jenna smiles at me. 'Just remember that Cariss is one of us, is all I'm saying.' Then she puts down the piece of wood and walks off.

I watch her go back to Cariss. Then I carry on piling up the debris. Jenna has this thing about loyalty. Her therapist says it's down to what happened to her when she was a kid – it's left her with 'chronic control issues'. Most of the time I can deal with it, but there are times, like right now, when it makes me want to throttle her. I look at the pile of wood I've assembled on the deck – and wonder why I bothered. I mean, it's not as if having a super-tidy deck is going to make us more likely to be rescued. I think of Mom in our apartment, the phone ringing and some stranger's voice telling her that our boat has gone missing in a storm. Panic starts chattering away inside my head. How will Mom cope? What will she do? Who will she turn to? Just as I think I'm going to burst into tears someone places their hand on my shoulder. I turn and see Cruz.

'Gracias,' he says, nodding at my pile. And then he smiles. And a pair of dimples appear like quote marks either side of his mouth.

'Yo, Grace!' I jump at the sound of Todd's voice.

'You're – uh – welcome,' I say to Cruz before turning round. Todd is sat on the back seat of the boat. He gestures at me to join him. I go sit with him, and close my eyes. And wish that when I open them this could all have just been a dream.

Chapter Six

'Aha. Rock! I do believe that beats your scissors, my good lady.' The Flea, having reverted to his British accent, waves his fist in Belle's face.

Belle giggles and snips her scissor fingers at him. 'I sure wish there were other versions of this game,' she says wistfully. 'It gets kinda tedious doing the same three things the whole time.'

'Tell me about it,' Jenna mutters next to me.

I ignore her and look around the boat. We've been drifting for hours now with no sign of rescue. Todd, Ron, Jenna and I are slumped across the back seat. Dan and Cariss are sat on what's left of the side seats – on *opposite* sides. Cruz is sat cross-legged at the front of the boat, trying to fix the radio, and Belle and the Flea are engaged in an epic rock, paper, scissors battle on the deck in front of us.

'Well then, let's invent our own, by God,' says the Flea. 'How about a musical version? How about rock, reggae, hip-hop?'

Belle laughs. 'So what beats what?'

The Flea takes off his storm-battered pork pie hat and scratches his head. 'Well, rock would definitely beat hip-hop . . .'

Dan lets out a snort. 'Says who?'

The Flea looks at him, indignant. 'Well, Jimi Hendrix, Kurt Cobain and Freddie Mercury, for starters.'

I smile at him and nod.

'Hmm, but ain't those dudes all dead?' Dan says with a grin. 'Hip-hop has to beat rock. At least all the top hip-hop artists are still alive.'

'Tell that to Tupac,' the Flea mutters.

'Or you could have a military version,' Todd says, stretching out his arms in front of him. 'How about rocket launcher, nuke, shotgun?'

'Yeah, but wouldn't the nuke win every time?' Belle asks.

Todd frowns. 'I guess.'

'It should be nuke, shotgun, radiation suit,' the Flea says. 'That way the radiation suit would beat the nuke, but the shotgun would beat the radiation suit because you could shoot a hole in it.'

Belle shakes her head and laughs. 'But how would you do a hand sign for a radiation suit?'

Jenna and Cariss sigh in stereo.

Todd grins. 'You could cross your fingers, you know, like a skull and cross-bones – but without the skull.'

'Okay.' Belle nods. 'But how about the sign for a nuke?'

'That's easy,' the Flea says, before throwing his arms up in panic.

Everyone starts laughing – apart from Jenna and Cariss.

'Do you guys really think it's appropriate to be joking around right now?' Jenna says, giving Ron a death stare. Ron's smile fades quicker than a New York minute. 'Sorry,' he mutters.

I look down at the dark-blue sea. It's pretty calm right now, but I can't get any satisfaction from that fact. Not now I know what it's capable of. It's like watching a slumbering monster, knowing it could wake up at any second and devour you.

'Did you know that the Pacific Ocean covers one-third of the world's entire surface?' the Flea says, breaking the silence.

'No shit?' Dan stretches his legs out in front of him. The tips of his snowy-white trainers are now scuffed and stained.

'Uh-huh. And it's seven miles deep in some places.'

'Would you please just shut up!' Cariss yells from beneath her hood. Her words echo around the deck and out across the seemingly endless ocean. One-third of the world's surface is pretty hard to comprehend, and for once I don't want to leap to the Flea's defence. Seven miles deep? I look at our battered boat. It seems as tiny and helpless as a tin can. What if we drift for days? What if no one finds us? What's going to happen to us? Clearly Belle is having similar thoughts. She goes to sit in a corner and starts playing with the crucifix around her neck.

Suddenly there's a faint crackling sound from the front of the boat and Cruz leaps to his feet, holding the radio.

'He's fixed it!' Jenna cries.

Todd and Dan let out whoops. But then the crackling sound goes dead. I see a look of despair flicker across Cruz's face.

Cariss pulls back her hood. Her eyes look puffy, like she's been crying. 'Is it working?' she says.

Belle jumps to her feet and goes to ask Cruz. We all sit motionless, watching.

Cruz shakes his head and puts the broken radio down on the deck.

'What are we going to do?' Ron says, starting to pace up and down the deck. 'We've got no radio, no power and no phone signal. How are they going to find us?'

Todd gets up and puts his arm around Ron's shoulders. 'Take it easy, bro. They'll find us.'

Ron turns and stares at him. 'How?'

Todd shrugs. 'Search and rescue helicopter, I guess.'

'That's right,' the Flea pipes up. 'I saw a show on Discovery one time about a plane that came down in the sea. They were all rescued by helicopter. Well, the ones that didn't get eaten.'

Cariss stares at him in horror. 'What do you mean, the

ones that didn't get eaten? What were they eaten by?'

'Sharks?' Dan says.

The Flea shakes his head gravely. 'No, sir. They started eating each other.'

'Oh my God!' Jenna exclaims. 'Will you please shut up!'

Ron and Todd sit back down. Belle comes and slumps down next to the Flea and Cruz goes back to fiddling about with the radio. We all sit in silence. I don't have to be a mind-reader to know that we're all imagining a nightmare scenario in which we end up chowing down on each other.

'So, how much food do we have on board this thing?' Jenna asks.

We all immediately look at Belle. Belle calls out something in Spanish to Cruz. Cruz shrugs and shakes his head.

'Well, that's just great!' Ron exclaims. 'No radio, no power, no phone signal and no food.'

I make a silent vow that if it comes to it, Ron will be the very first person who gets eaten.

'I have some candy in my bag,' Belle says, going over to her rucksack.

'Figures,' Cariss mutters and Jenna gives a tight little laugh.

Belle roots around and pulls out a couple of misshapen Hershey bars.

'I say we leave them till later,' the Flea says. 'When we really start to get hungry.'

'And who made you the boss?' Jenna snips.

The Flea visibly winces and looks away.

'It makes sense,' I say. 'We don't know how long we're going to be out here for.'

'Thanks for the reminder,' Ron mutters.

I sigh and look out across the sea. The sun is starting to sink; a ball of red slowly being swallowed by the horizon. Dread swoops down on me like an icy fog. What's it going to be like out here when it gets dark? Up above us a circling seagull lets out a piercing screech. It feels kind of like that nightmare where you're running and running up a hill, but never getting any closer to the top.

We all jump as Cruz suddenly leaps to his feet and starts shouting and pointing.

'What's up?' Dan says, taking off his baseball cap and blinking.

Todd gets to his feet. 'Land,' he whispers. Then he turns and pulls me up. 'Look, it's land!' he yells.

Everyone else gets to their feet and rushes to the front of the boat. Sure enough, there's a definite bump on the smooth line of the horizon.

'I don't believe it,' Belle whispers next to me.

I turn and see tears sliding down her face. I put my arm around her shoulders and hug her to me. She looks so shocked I immediately let go.

Slowly, the bump on the horizon grows.

'Where do you think it is?' Ron asks.

'Who cares?' says Cariss, pulling her hood back up. 'It's land, that's all that matters.'

Belle takes hold of the Flea's hand.

'I just want to see my mom,' she whispers to him.

The Flea nods. 'I know, sweet-cheeks. And you will. Just think, as soon as we get to land you can call her and tell her you're safe.'

I think of my own mom and feel a warm rush of relief. How cool will it be to hear her voice, and to let her know I'm okay? As the boat drifts in closer to the land I picture us sailing into a harbour and people waving to us from a jetty. And friendly local officials throwing garlands round our necks and welcoming us to their island. Maybe we've just been drifting in one enormous circle and we're actually back at Hawaii? But as we draw closer I see that, wherever we are, it definitely isn't where we set off from. A mountainous peak juts out of the centre of the island like a craggy pyramid, the sunset behind us making it glow a deep red. A band of dense rainforest circles the base of the mountain like a thick green scarf. And, below that there's a large, sandy bay.

'Wow! Check out that beach, man!' Todd calls out.

'Yeah, baby!' Dan whispers.

As we drift into the bay, pure joy rushes through me. We're

going to be okay. We aren't going to drown. We aren't going to be shark food. And we aren't going to have to eat each other.

The boat shudders as it runs aground on the beach and Todd and Ron and Dan start leaping around high-fiving and back-slapping. Then Todd jumps down into the shallow water and starts splashing about like crazy.

'We made it!' he yells. 'We freakin' well made it!'

The Flea helps Belle off. And Ron and Dan help Jenna and Cariss. I scramble down after them, then turn and look back at Cruz. He's staring at the island. And for the first time since we've been on the boat I see a look of absolute terror upon his face.

Chapter Seven

The moment I make it on to the powdery white sand my legs buckle. I hear Todd and Dan's whoops mingled in with seagull cries and it sounds more beautiful than anything even Mozart could've come up with.

We're safe.

As I fall to my knees, hot tears spill from my eyes. I love everyone and everything and I –

'*At last . . .*'

I jump at the sound of a whispered voice over my shoulder. But when I turn round all I see is sand, and the towering, green wall of the rainforest. I guess it must have been the breeze, but I can't help shivering. I have the weirdest feeling that we're being watched. But if there is anyone watching us wouldn't they have shown themselves by now? I peer into the darkness of the forest and hear a rustling sound. Directly ahead of me some branches begin to thrash about, like one of the palm trees is waving its arms in distress. Then a bird shoots out, squawking loudly. The relief I'd been feeling at reaching dry land starts turning to apprehension. Something doesn't feel right.

I look back toward the sea, shielding my eyes from the setting sun. Jenna and Cariss are hugging each other and crying a little ways down the beach. Belle is sat on the sand sobbing, the Flea crouched behind her with his arms wrapped around her like a human cloak. And Cruz? For a moment I don't see him; then he appears on the deck of the boat with some of our bags. I stumble to my feet.

'We're gonna be okay, Gracie!' Todd yells, running over and swooping me into a bear hug.

We're gonna be okay. I repeat his words in my head like a mantra to try and reassure myself. *We* are *going to be okay*. Never again will I moan about Todd. Never again will I moan about *anything*. This is going to be one of those life-changing moments that tearful guests talk about on chat shows. We're alive and that's all that matters.

'Pretty crazy, huh?' Todd murmurs in my ear before letting me go.

I nod and gesture toward the boat. 'Shall we go get our stuff?'

'Nah, let him do it,' Todd says, nodding dismissively at Cruz. 'I wanna explore.'

He looks up the beach to the rainforest.

I can't help frowning. 'Are you sure? I mean, we don't know if it's safe in there.'

Todd sighs and shakes his head, like I'm some dumb-ass two-year-old. 'Geez, Grace, we've just survived a shipwreck. I don't think a few trees are gonna hurt us!'

I frown. Why is it every time I try to like Todd he does something to make me *not* like him even more?

'Well, I'm going to get my bag,' I say.

'Sure.' Todd bounds over to Ron. 'Yo, Ron. You up for a little reconnaissance mission? See if we can find any signs of life?'

I turn and walk back down the beach toward the boat.

'We made it, huh,' Dan says, falling into step with me. He's taken off his baseball cap and for once I can see his eyes. They're as dark as molasses and framed with long black lashes. If the eyes really are the window to the soul then Dan has a real soft and twinkly soul. Totally at odds with his hard-man swagger.

I nod and smile. 'Now we've just gotta figure out where we've made it to.'

'Well, I know one thing,' Dan says, grinning at me. 'It sure beats South Central.'

I follow his gaze to a cluster of palm trees swaying in the wind like hula dancers. 'I guess.' I've never ventured into South Central, but I've seen enough crime reports on the news to know what he's talking about. I wonder what it must be like for him to have to live there. 'You don't . . .' I look back at the rainforest. There's no sign of Todd and Ron.

'What?' Dan looks at me.

I want to ask him if he senses anything weird about the place, but I can't. Not after Todd's reaction. So I shake my head and force myself to smile instead. 'Nothing.'

When we reach the boat Dan shouts up at Cruz. Then he points at the luggage and holds his arms out. Cruz gives a look of understanding and passes him a bag. Dan then passes the bag along to me. We carry on working in a chain-gang formation like this until pretty soon all of the bags are piled up on the beach. Jenna and Cariss sashay over. Jenna links her arm in mine and smiles.

'You are funny, Grace,' she says.

'What do you mean?'

'Helping out the guys like this. You're such a tomboy.'

It's better than being a pampered princess like Cariss, I think, but then I see that Jenna's smile is genuine rather than mocking and I let it go.

'So, how cool is this?' she says, casting her free arm out across the beach.

'Very cool,' I reply, wishing I could truly mean it.

'Oh my God, my luggage is ruined!' Cariss shrieks, picking up one of her designer cases. There's a thin white tide mark running around the middle of it, like a very faint line in chalk.

'It's only water,' Dan mutters.

'It's Louis Vuitton!' Cariss exclaims.

'Don't worry, hun, it can be replaced,' Jenna says.

Cariss gives her a weak smile. Then she opens the case and starts rummaging about inside. 'Oh no!' she wails.

'What now?' Dan says.

'Everything's soaked.'

'That's okay. We can lay it out on the beach,' Jenna says, 'the sun'll soon dry it.'

'What sun?' Cariss sniffs. 'The sun has set.'

I glance up at Cruz and see a look of complete contempt on his face. I guess he doesn't need to understand what Cariss is saying to realize that she's a total brat.

'It'll be back up again in the morning,' Jenna says calmly. 'They'll be dry in no time.'

I glance back up at the rainforest – still no sign of Todd and Ron. I try to ignore the sick feeling growing in my stomach.

Belle and the Flea join us and fetch their bags from the pile. Belle pulls her phone from her purse and starts frantically pushing buttons. 'There's no signal!' She drops to the floor and puts her head in her hands.

Cariss instantly gets her phone out, as if the fact that it's got a diamond-encrusted heart on the back is going to give it better reception. She scowls. 'Nothing on mine either.'

One by one, we all check our phones. When I turn mine

on and see the screensaver of Mom and Tigger I feel a pang of longing so strong it nearly floors me.

The Flea starts to laugh as he pulls a top from his bag and starts wringing water from it. 'Guess I won't be wearing my PJs tonight then.'

'Where do you think we are?' Belle asks no one in particular. Then she says something to Cruz.

Cruz jumps down from the boat, shaking his head and answering her in Spanish.

'He doesn't know exactly where we are, but it's not one of the Hawaiian islands,' Belle says despondently.

'Oh great!' Cariss raises her perfectly plucked eyebrows and lets out a weary sigh. 'Does he actually know anything useful?'

I glance at Cruz, wondering why he looked so afraid when we first got here if he has no idea where we are. He catches my gaze and I quickly look away.

'Where have Todd and Ron gone?' Jenna asks.

'To see if they can find anyone,' I say. 'Maybe we should go see if they're okay?'

We all turn and look toward the rainforest. On cue, Todd and Ron come sauntering out. My entire body sighs with relief.

'Any sign of life?' I call out to them.

Todd shakes his head. 'Not unless you mean wildlife,' he shouts back. 'I've never seen so many darn parrots!'

Cariss lets out another melodramatic sigh. 'So what are we supposed to do now?'

'I say we set up camp for the night and then go look for help in the morning,' Jenna replies.

The Flea nods and rubs his hands together like he's ready for business. 'Cool. How about we build a fire? That way any rescue helicopter will be able to see us in the dark.'

'Good thinking, Batman,' Todd says, as he and Ron reach us. 'Come on, guys, let's get some wood.'

All the boys, including the Flea, bound off in the direction of the forest. Belle looks bereft.

'Are you okay?' I ask her cautiously.

Her eyes immediately fill with tears. 'I just wish there was a way I could contact my mom. I thought –' she breaks off.

I want to hug her, but after the way she reacted before I make myself hold back.

'Well, you know, we'd all like to be able to contact our folks, but there's no point making a big deal out of it,' Jenna says breezily. 'So why don't we do something useful and go find a good place to set up camp. Ask Cruise-Ship if he'll bring our luggage up the beach. Come on, Grace.'

Jenna and Cariss start walking up the beach. I look at Belle. 'I'm sorry,' I say. 'We've all had a really tough day. I guess the pressure's getting to everyone.'

Belle just looks at me coldly. Then she says something to

Cruz and points at the luggage. He smiles at her and nods. I go fetch my own case and start dragging it up the sand. It's okay, I tell myself, we're going to be okay. Tomorrow will be a new day and we'll all feel miles better.

I follow Jenna and Cariss to the top of the beach. They head over to one side, where a crescent of palm trees has formed a natural alcove between the beach and the forest. It's the perfect spot to set up camp. I dump my case down and hear someone coming up behind me. It's Cruz. He's carrying one of Cariss's huge suitcases in one hand and a pack of water bottles in the other. My eyes are drawn to the taut muscles in his arms. He puts the case and the water down next to me. Our eyes meet and a weird kind of jolt runs through my body. He takes a step back, looking shocked, as if he felt it too.

'Thanks, Cruise-Ship,' Jenna calls out and Cariss laughs.

Cruz drops his gaze and starts walking back down the beach. I stand there motionless for a moment, not sure what just happened. Did Cruz feel it too? Whatever *it* was? Don't be stupid, I tell myself. He probably thinks you're a pampered brat like Cariss, there's no way he'd be interested in you. And why would you want him to be interested in you anyways when a) you already have a boyfriend and b) you've just been real-life shipwrecked and should be thinking about way more important things, like *how the hell we are going to get back home?* I sigh and look up at the forest and, looming above that, the mountainous peak at the centre of the island. Now the sun has set it's no longer red, but a jagged black silhouette against the darkening sky.

Just at that moment Todd and Ron come out of the forest clutching armfuls of wood.

'Hey, guys,' Jenna calls out to them. 'I've found us a spot for our camp.'

Seconds later the Flea and Dan arrive. They all dump their assorted sticks and driftwood into a pile.

Todd starts arranging the wood into something vaguely fire-shaped. 'Alrighty, let's get this baby going.'

'Haven't you forgotten something?' Cariss says, sitting cross-legged and bolt upright on the sand, like a haughty, ultra-thin Buddha.

Everyone looks at her blankly.

'Matches. To light it with?'

'Ah,' says the Flea. 'Excellent point, madam.'

'No sweat,' Dan says, producing a lighter from his bag.

Todd grins and claps his hands. 'All right!'

After a few false starts the fire finally catches. We all huddle round, watching as the flames start licking greedily at the wood.

'I need a drink,' Cariss says, ripping the box of water bottles open and pulling one out.

'I guess we ought to go easy on the water,' the Flea says. 'You know – just in case.'

Cariss glowers at him before taking a huge swig from the bottle. 'Just in case what?'

The Flea looks away. 'Nothing.'

Todd starts handing out the bottles. I take one eagerly, but the Flea's words play on my mind and I stop myself from downing it in one go.

'I'm starving,' the Flea says. 'Where'd you put that candy, Beau-Belle?'

Belle gets the Hershey bars from her bag.

Cariss looks around at the rest of us. 'Is that all we've got to go round?'

Dan looks in his bag again. 'I've got some beef jerky.'

'Gross,' Cariss mutters.

We all root around in our bags. All I have to offer is a pack of key lime pie flavoured chewing gum. 'Dessert?' I say, raising an eyebrow.

Dan chuckles. 'Man, I love key lime pie.'

My stomach grumbles. 'Me too.' Suddenly I'm ferociously hungry.

Just then Cruz appears out of the shadows. He drops something down on the ground by the fire.

'Coconuts!' Jenna exclaims. 'My, my, Cruise-Ship, you do have some uses after all.'

Cariss, Ron and Todd start sniggering.

Cruz pulls a small machete type knife from the back of his

belt. He chops one of the ends off, then pierces a hole in the coconut flesh and hands it to Belle, showing her to drink the juice from the centre.

'Gracias,' Belle whispers to him with a grateful smile.

Jenna gets up and moves around the fire till she's right next to Cruz. 'That was awesome,' she says in the slightly breathless voice she always uses when she wants something from a guy. She looks longingly at the other coconuts. 'Could I have one?' She looks from Cruz to Belle. Belle is about to start to translate when Cruz slices the top off another coconut and hands it to me. I feel my face start to burn and keep my eyes fixed on the coconut.

'Gracias,' I whisper, trying to ignore the tremors shooting up my arm from where his hand touches mine. I'm starting to feel like one of the heroines in the crazy Pioneer Romance novels Mom got addicted to after Dad left.

'Here, let me have a go,' Todd says, reaching for the knife. But Cruz has already swiped it up. He slices and pierces the remaining coconuts, wipes the sweat from his forehead with the back of his hand, then heads back off to the boat.

'What a freak,' Jenna hisses, taking a coconut.

'You're telling me,' Cariss mutters.

'I don't know why he couldn't have let me have a go,' Todd says sulkily.

Next to me, Belle sighs.

I put my coconut to my lips, close my eyes and tip my head back. The liquid trickles into my mouth, refreshing and sweet. The only time I've drunk from a coconut shell before was one summer when I was about six or seven. I'd gone with my dad and Grandpa to the state fair and Grandpa won a load of coconuts on a game. Later that night Dad and I had sat out on Grandpa's porch swing, snuggled under a blanket, drinking coconut milk and counting stars. I open my eyes and look at everyone around the fire. They suddenly seem like complete strangers. Why didn't I hug Dad goodbye at the airport? Why was I such a bitch to him in the car?

I don't know if the others are having similar pangs of homesickness, but we all fall silent. Behind us, in the forest, the creaking call of the cicadas seems to go up a notch. Fear shimmies up my spine.

'Maybe we should try going to sleep,' Belle eventually says.

'Sleep?' Cariss snips. 'And what exactly are we supposed to sleep *on*?'

Dan pushes his cap back and looks at her. 'The sand? Or maybe you'd prefer to hang by your claws from a branch.'

The Flea chokes back a giggle.

'Yeah, well, some of us aren't used to sleeping rough,' Cariss shoots back.

Dan jumps to his feet and glares at her across the fire. He's about to say something, then obviously thinks better of it and stalks off to one of the trees.

'We can sleep on our towels and use our clothes for blankets,' Jenna says, smiling at Cariss.

'But my clothes are soaked,' Cariss whines.

Jenna turns to Ron. 'Don't worry, Ron'll lend you some, won't you, Ron?'

'Sure,' Ron says, leaping to his feet and fetching his bag.

Jenna also stands up and takes a look around the alcove. Then she looks straight back at me. 'So, how about us girls sleep over on the left and the boys on the right?'

'Okay,' I say.

'No way,' Todd says. 'I want to sleep next to Grace.'

'I bet you do,' Ron says with a snigger that makes me want to bury him headfirst in the sand.

'And I want to sleep with the Flea,' Belle says.

'Darling, I've told you, you're just not my type,' the Flea says with a cheeky grin. 'You got a few too many X chromosomes going on.' He chuckles and pulls Belle toward him for a hug. 'But if you would like to sleep *next* to me I would be honoured.'

'Fine then,' Jenna says, and I can tell she's really pissed. 'You guys do what you like, I was only trying to be appropriate.' Then, completely ignoring me, she gets up and takes hold of Cariss's hand. 'Come on, Cariss, let's go find a spot.'

As I watch them stalk off I feel hurt and confused. Jenna's been pressuring me to sleep with someone for years. Why is she so concerned with being 'appropriate' all of a sudden? Not that I want to sleep with Todd. Right now I can't think of anything worse than losing my virginity to a boyfriend I'm not even sure I like, surrounded by half my class, and right after the trauma of being shipwrecked. I watch Jenna help Cariss make a bed out of Ron's clothes and I have that sick feeling you get when you realize that, no matter how hard you try to be all feisty and empowered, your happiness is always dependent on other people.

I look down toward the boat. It's so dark now I can only see its outline against the rippling water. I think of Cruz all alone in there and I wonder how he's feeling. To be stuck on an island with a bunch of people you don't know and can't understand can hardly be a picnic.

'Come on, Grace,' Todd says, standing up and holding out his hand. My heart pounds, but not in a good way. I take a hold of his hand and let him pull me up. As I imagine him making a move on me in the night I think of the jujitsu classes I took back in middle grade. I could always get Todd in a choke hold if he tried anything on. *Gee, that's romantic*, the voice in my head says sarcastically. I sigh. Tiredness rolls through me in numbing waves. I trudge after Todd toward the trees. This time, the voice in my head morphs into a Facebook status. Grace Delaney is about to lose her virginity in the worst way imaginable, it announces. I frown and mentally hit delete.

Chapter Eight

When I wake the next morning my whole body feels as if it's turned to stone. The sand, which had felt velvet-soft when we first lay down, now feels hard as rock. My eyes are dry and stinging and my bones ache.

Todd and I ended up making our beds at the end of the palm tree alcove furthest away from Jenna and Cariss. Thankfully, he didn't try anything – in fact, he was asleep and snoring gently within minutes of lying down. Unfortunately, sleep didn't come nearly as easy to me. All night long the forest had gotten noisier and noisier, and every time I felt myself drifting off there would be another strange shriek or croak and I'd be wide awake again, picturing a freakish army of lizards and birds descending upon us. When I did finally fall asleep I plunged right back into the nightmare I'd had the night before about being trapped in the house fire. This time I managed to make it to the room with the crying baby. But when I looked inside its crib, the baby was dead, its face all charred like an ebony doll. I woke up shaking, tears streaming down my face.

I roll on to my side away from Todd and prop myself on to my elbow. The sea is sparkling like a sequinned blanket in the early morning sun. I take a deep breath, hoping to get rid of the tension in my body. But the air smells sticky and sweet. Too sweet. Unable to bear the pain of lying on the sand any longer, I quietly get to my feet. Over to my right, Dan stirs and murmurs something, but he and the others remain fast asleep. The sunlight is such a pale, buttery yellow I figure it must still be very early. I start tiptoeing down toward the water. The battered boat is tilted to one side on the sand. It reminds me of the vagrants you see downtown, stooped from liquor. As I get close enough to see the wreckage that used to be Cruz's cabin I can't help shivering. It's a miracle we survived at all.

Just as I reach the water's edge I hear a splash. I see a head bob up in the water a few yards out, then vanish again. I watch, waiting for it to reappear. When it doesn't I start to panic. Was it Cruz? Is he in trouble? I wade into the water. It's so cool on my hot skin it makes me catch my breath. I carry on walking until I'm waist deep and my shorts are soaked, my eyes scanning the water for any sign of movement. I'm just trying to figure out whether I should dive under and take a look when Cruz resurfaces a few feet in front of me. We both gasp in shock.

'I thought you were in trouble,' I say, before remembering that he can't speak English. I point to myself, then to him, then I do a really bad impression of someone drowning. Cruz looks baffled for a moment, then he starts mimicking me.

'No!' I say, laughing. 'I don't want you to copy me. I thought you were drowning.'

Cruz grins at me and his brown eyes twinkle. His curly, pirate hair is gleaming wet. I try to ignore his tanned torso and the way the water is trickling through the hairs on his chest. Cruz points at himself, then to me, then he leaps up like a dolphin and dives back into the sea.

'You want me to do that?' I say to the empty space where he'd been standing.

I turn and look back up the beach. There's still no sign of life from the camp.

'Alrighty then.' I take a deep breath, and launch myself at a wave. As the water hits my face it takes my breath away. I open my eyes and see Cruz up ahead of me, swimming through the clear water like a fish. He turns to see if I'm following him and gives me a thumbs-up sign. Then he shoots below the surface again. I follow him and come up about a foot away from him. He looks at me and laughs. I laugh back and start wondering if it's possible to get high from looking at impossibly cute dimples. Then I tell myself off for acting like one of the heroines in Mom's gush-fest novels again. Cruz points to himself, then me, then does a forward roll in the water.

'Oh yeah?' I say, feeling a stab of gratitude for my childhood spent living on the coast. I wait for him to resurface then I do a flawless forward roll, followed by another. I turn to look back at him and bow my head. He laughs again and it doesn't seem to matter at all that we don't speak the same language. I guess laughter is the same the world over.

Cruz is just pointing to me again when I hear a yell from the beach. I look back and see Todd standing by the water's edge. He seems tiny. I had no idea we'd swum so far out. I shrug my shoulders at Cruz and whisper 'gotta go' before swimming back to shore. When I get to the shallow water I stand up and take a good look at the island. I'm shocked to see that it wasn't the sunset last night making the mountain appear red – it really is red. Blood red – unlike anything I've ever seen. Just like before when I looked at the forest, unease starts creeping its way inside of me.

'What are you doing?' Todd asks as soon as I get within earshot. He's standing with his hands on his hips, looking like a sulky kid who's just been told he can't have any candy.

'I woke up early so I decided to go for a swim.' As I walk toward him water streams from my T-shirt and shorts.

Todd brushes his hair back from his face. He's still frowning. 'Why didn't you tell me? I was really worried when I woke up and you weren't there.'

At first I feel touched that he cares, but then I see him glaring at Cruz, who's just emerging from the sea behind me, and I can't help wondering if the real reason Todd's so mad is more to do with who I was swimming with.

'It's lovely in there, you should go in,' I say, trying to appeal to Todd's inner surfer dude.

'I can't, we're having a meeting. And Jenna wants him to come too.' He nods at Cruz, then looks at me as if he wants me to ask him.

'I don't speak Spanish.'

Todd continues to pout. 'Well, you seemed to be getting on just fine out there in the water, I'm sure you can make him understand you.'

I sigh and turn to Cruz. I point to him, then I point to Todd and I and gesture up toward the camp. He nods, then mimes putting some clothes on. I smile and nod back.

'He's going to get dressed first,' I say to Todd.

'Yeah, I got that. Come on.' Todd grabs my hand and starts marching back up the beach. I glance over my shoulder at Cruz. He's watching us, but his expression is unreadable again.

Back at the camp the others are all at different stages of getting ready. Jenna and Cariss are dressed and doing their make-up. I see that Cariss is wearing one of Jenna's sundresses, and again I can't help feeling stupidly hurt. Belle and the Flea are packing away their makeshift bedding, Ron's staring into the forest and Dan's just waking up and rubbing his eyes.

'What happened to you?' Jenna asks as soon as she sees me.

'I went for a swim,' I say, going over to get my towel.

Jenna stares at me like I just told her I'd been drowning puppies. 'In your clothes?'

'Yeah, well it was kind of spontaneous.' I pick my towel up off the floor and a cloud of white sand shimmers from it like glitter.

'Didn't you get enough of the sea yesterday?' Cariss says, plucking at one of her perfect arched eyebrows with a pair of gold tweezers.

'The water's really calm now. It's beautiful down there.' I grab a change of clothes from my bag and duck behind a tree to get changed.

'Uh-huh,' the Flea says theatrically. 'I'll say, girlfriend!'

I peer around the tree and see Cruz striding up the beach toward us. He's wearing his faded denim shorts and a T-shirt with a picture of Bob Marley on the front.

I hurriedly get changed then go join the others by the remains of last night's fire.

'We need to ask Cruise-Ship if he has any idea at all where

we might be,' Jenna says, looking straight at Belle. Belle, who had been fiddling with her cell phone again, goes over to greet Cruz.

'Man, I wish I spoke Spanish,' the Flea sighs.

I have to try real hard not to nod in agreement. I watch Cruz's face intently as Belle asks him the question. He shakes his head and shrugs his shoulders, but then I see him look up at the mountain and I see that same look of fear he had last night when we first arrived.

'I say we head into the forest.' Todd helps himself to a bottle of water and looks around the group. 'Sooner or later we're bound to come across someone.'

'Oh, I don't know.' The words burst from my mouth in some kind of weird reflex action. Everyone turns to look at me. I try to figure out a way of explaining the bad vibes I've been getting from the forest that doesn't make me sound like a fruit-loop. My mind draws a blank.

Cariss puts her tweezers and compact down on the sand. 'But what if we don't come across anyone? What if we get lost in there? Then no one will find us.'

The Flea picks up a handful of sand and lets it trickle through his fingers. 'Good point. At least if we stay on the beach we'll be visible to any rescue helicopters.'

I nod in agreement, as if this was exactly what I'd been thinking too.

Belle turns to the Flea, her eyes wide with worry. 'Yes, but how are they going to know that it's us and we need rescuing? They might think we're a bunch of holiday-makers.'

'We need some kind of a sign,' Jenna says, looking around the camp.

The Flea grins and picks up a charred stick from the remains of the fire. 'How about smoke signals?'

Jenna flicks her hair over her shoulder and ignores him.

'We could write something in the sand,' I suggest.

'Good plan,' Dan says, finally getting out of his bed of towels and crawling over to join us.

Ron frowns. 'But how will they be able to read it from up there?'

Belle sits bolt upright. 'I know, we could make the letters out of something.'

'How about bits of wood?' I say, looking at the firewood.

Dan nods. 'Uh-huh. But what do we write?'

The Flea gets up and starts pacing around the circle. 'Help! We've been tragically shipwrecked and we don't know how to get back home.'

I grin up at him. 'Maybe we should just stick with "help".'

'Yeah man, we don't want to have to go chopping down the whole damn forest,' Dan says.

'Whatever!' The Flea pulls his hat down over his face, pretending to be upset, but I can see his mouth is smiling.

'Let's do it then!' Belle leaps to her feet, causing her earrings and bangles to jingle like crazy.

'Okay, you guys go get the wood and I'll make the sign,' Jenna says.

'Why should you be the one to make it?' Cariss asks indignantly. 'There's no way I'm setting foot in that forest. Did you hear the noises coming from there last night? There could be, like, real live alligators in there.'

Dan snorts with laughter. 'You know, I'm pretty sure I saw a real live T-rex stampeding by just now. Chasing a real live lion.'

'Don't mock me!' Cariss's voice rises an octave. 'I'm telling you, I'm not moving from this beach.'

'Okay, okay, we'll both make the sign,' Jenna says, smiling sweetly.

I glance over at Cruz. He's hovering by the edge of the camp watching us intently.

'Belle, tell Cruise-Ship he needs to help us fetch some wood,' Jenna says.

'Geez, what did your last slave die of?' the Flea mutters under his breath.

'Being a dork,' Jenna hisses back at him.

Belle and the Flea exchange glances, then Belle stomps over to talk to Cruz.

'Come on,' Todd says to me, nodding toward the forest.

I take a deep breath and get to my feet. Time to confront this stupid fear for once and for all.

Stepping into the forest is like stepping into the gaping mouth of a giant Venus flytrap. Everywhere is a whirlpool of green. From the moss-covered floor, to the fern leaves as big as fans, to the canopy of branches high above us.

'Pretty awesome, huh?' Todd says.

I force myself to nod, but the forest is so humid and crammed full of vegetation I'm finding it hard to breathe. It's as if the plants are sucking all the air from the place.

A loud squawk from right above my head makes me jump out of my skin. I look up and see a bright-red parrot with a huge hooked beak perched on a branch. His beady black eyes are watching me intently, as if he's getting ready to swoop in for the kill.

'Watch out for snakes,' the Flea calls out from somewhere behind us.

'And alligators,' Dan adds with a chuckle.

'I'm being serious,' the Flea says. 'You get all kinds of critters living in these places. Did you know that more than half of the world's animal species originate from the rainforest?'

Hmm, including psycho parrots, I think to myself, moving away from the branch.

Dan looks back at him with a bemused grin. 'No way?'

The Flea nods proudly, as if he'd discovered that very fact all by himself. 'Yes way. They also say that rainforests are the lungs of the earth.'

'Is that so?' Dan says, struggling to break a small branch off a tree.

'Uh-huh. They're actually responsible for twenty-eight per cent of the world's oxygen turnover – not to be confused with oxygen production, which is a quite another thing entirely.'

I take a deep breath in hope, but it's like breathing in steam.

'Man, does that guy ever shut up?' Todd whispers as we both bend down to pick up some sticks from the ground.

'I think he's funny,' I say.

'Yeah, well, you're not exactly known for being a great judge of character,' Todd mutters.

I stop what I'm doing and look at him. 'What's that supposed to mean?'

'The company you like to keep.' Todd glances over at Cruz, who's hacking away at a branch with his machete.

'Maybe you have a point there,' I snap back at him. 'I am going out with you, after all.'

We carry on working in icy silence. But inside my head is noisy with outrage. How dare he talk to me like that? What's his problem? I'm so angry I almost don't notice the glint of silver beneath a pile of leaves by my feet. I brush the leaves aside and see a pendant half buried in the earth. I pick it up and brush the dirt off. The pendant is oval, about the size of a quarter, and it's engraved with something. It's hard to make out what it is in the gloom of the forest. I hold the pendant up to a thin shaft of sunlight filtering through the leaves and see that the engraving is of a snake stretching upwards, its tongue extended, above the letter H. There's something weirdly familiar about it but I can't think what. For some reason it makes the hair on the back of my neck stand on end.

'What's that?' Todd says when he sees me looking at it.

'I'm not sure. Some kind of pendant.'

Dan, Ron and the Flea gather round to take a look.

'Awesome,' the Flea whispers. Then he winks at me. 'See, I told you there were snakes in here.'

'Buddy, it means that there are *people* in here,' Ron says and he and Todd laugh and high-five.

'All right!' says Dan, joining in the high-fives. 'Now we've just gotta find them.'

Cruz comes over and looks at me questioningly. I hand him the pendant, expecting it to make him happy too. But instead of smiling and looking relieved he stares at it for a few seconds, then starts shaking his head and muttering something under his breath. He thrusts the pendant back at me and starts striding back out to the beach. High above us a sudden breeze rustles through the leaves, causing shadows to flit through the forest like ghosts. Then I hear a sound behind me, like a female voice whispering.

'*This way*,' it seems to say. '*This way*.'

I turn around, half-expecting to see Jenna or Cariss standing there.

'*This way*,' the whisper comes again from behind a tree.

I hesitate, then walk over to the tree. My palms feel suddenly cold and clammy. A prickly vine is coiled all around the trunk, like barbed wire.

'What are you doing, Grace?' Todd asks.

I pause, unsure of what to say. 'I – I thought I heard something.' I peer round the tree into the gloom. But all I see are more trees and thick strands of vine strung between them like tripwires. As I lean forward I catch a waft of the same sickly-sweet scent I smelled first thing this morning.

'Can you see anything?' the Flea asks.

I turn back to the others, thankful that the gloom will hide my blushes. 'No. It must have been the wind in the trees.'

'*Good. They mustn't know – they wouldn't understand.*' This time I'm certain it's not the breeze. The voice came from right behind me, so close I could feel breath on my ear; light as a feather, but clear enough to make out the words.

What the hell is going on?

I stare at the others, hoping for some sign that they've heard the whispered voice too. But they're all just standing there, waiting for me to come back.

Slowly, I look over my shoulder, my heart pounding with fear. But there's still no one there.

Chapter Nine

'Come on, let's go show the others the pendant,' Ron says.

I take a deep breath and hurry back over to them.

'You okay?' the Flea says. 'You've gone really pale.'

I nod. Thankfully the whispering has disappeared. I try to reassure myself. It *must* have been a combination of the heat and the breeze. Whatever, I just want to get out of this green maze and back to the wide open space of the beach.

We all pick up our sticks and make our way out of the forest. Jenna and Cariss are halfway down the beach. They've dug out HELP in huge letters in the sand.

'What's his problem?' Todd says as we watch Cruz dump his sticks by Jenna, then head straight down to the boat.

'Don't ask me,' Dan says.

'The guy's a freak,' Ron says with a scowl.

'Maybe he's scared of snakes,' the Flea says.

I look down at the pendant. It had made me feel uneasy too.

'Hey, you guys, come see what Grace found,' the Flea calls out to Jenna and Cariss. Belle runs over from where she's been collecting driftwood down by the water's edge. Everyone gathers round and I hold out my palm with the pendant on it. Jenna immediately grabs it.

'Where did you find it?' she asks.

'On the floor in there,' I nod toward the forest. 'Under a bunch of leaves.'

'Awesome!' Cariss exclaims. 'It must mean there are other people nearby.'

'Not necessarily,' Belle says glumly.

Jenna stares at her. 'What do you mean?'

Belle dumps her driftwood down on the sand. 'Well, if it was under a pile of leaves it could've been there for ages. The person who dropped it could be long gone.'

'Geez, ever thought of trying out for the world's most depressing person award?' Cariss says, glowering at Belle.

'I was just saying,' Belle mutters.

'Yeah, well maybe you should think before you *just say* anything in future,' Jenna snaps. 'We're trying to be positive here.'

'Well, I'm trying to be realistic,' Belle says, blinking hard, before bursting into tears and running back up to the camp.

‘Beau-Belle!’ the Flea calls, running after her.

Dan glares at Jenna and Cariss. ‘Good work. She had a point, you know, the pendant could’ve been there for ages.’

‘All right, all right,’ Jenna says. She turns away from Dan and looks down at the boat. ‘What’s up with Cruise-Ship? He looked like he’d just seen a ghost.’

‘Don’t ask me,’ Todd says. ‘He took one look at the pendant and freaked out.’

‘No he didn’t,’ I say. ‘He just seemed a bit worried.’

Todd gives a dry little laugh.

Jenna shoots him a look, then glances at me. ‘But why would he be worried?’

‘He’s a Latino,’ Ron says. ‘I told you, they’re complete drama queens, I mean, look at madam.’ He nods toward the camp, where Belle is sitting hunched over beneath a tree, her shoulders quivering.

‘Maybe it was something to do with the picture on it,’ Dan says.

Jenna looks back at the pendant. ‘But it’s just a snake.’

‘Yeah, but maybe it’s some kind of spooky Costa Rican symbol.’ Dan lets out one of his throaty chuckles.

Jenna rolls her eyes. ‘All right, already, let’s just quit with the freaking out and carry on making the sign,’ she says, putting the pendant in her shorts pocket.

We set about filling in the letters in the sand with sticks.

It feels good to be doing something constructive – something that might actually get us rescued. As I get to work on the letter E, I glance over to the boat and see Cruz on the deck. He seems to be trying to fix the radio again.

'Man, I'm starving,' Dan says as we put the finishing touches to the sign.

'Me too.' Todd rubs his stomach. 'You got any more of that beef jerky?'

Dan shakes his head.

'I guess we'd better get some more coconuts then,' Ron says. 'Should we ask psycho-boy to come with us?' he asks, nodding toward Cruz.

'No, we don't need him,' Todd says, giving me a pointed look.

Dan, Todd and Ron saunter off to a nearby cluster of coconut trees, leaving me alone with Jenna and Cariss.

'Grace, is everything okay with you and Todd?' Jenna asks as soon as they're out of earshot.

'Yes. Of course. Why shouldn't it be?' I say, a little too defensively.

Jenna flashes me a smile. 'It seemed a bit tense between you guys just now.'

Cariss lets out a bored yawn so wide I can see every one of her porcelain white teeth.

'It's fine,' I say. 'Shall we go see how Belle and the Flea are doing?'

'Oh, do we have to?' Cariss says. 'I'd really rather rub sand in my eyes.'

Jenna shrieks with laughter. 'Cariss, you're too funny!'

I feel as if I'm drowning in syrup.

'Okay, well, I'm going to go see how they are,' I say and I start heading off to the camp. I've only gone a few feet when I hear Jenna mutter something and Cariss start to laugh. As I keep on walking I mentally rewind through the past twenty-four hours, trying to find exactly what I did to make Jenna want to trade me in for Cariss on the best-friend market. But my mind draws a blank. When I reach the camp Belle and the Flea are hunched over on the sand, deep in whispered conversation. As soon as I get close they shut up and look away. I'm starting to know how Jehovah's Witnesses must feel.

'Are you okay?' I ask Belle.

'What do you care?' she snaps back, her dark eyes glinting with anger.

'Of course I care,' I say.

Belle looks away. 'Yeah right, just like your good buddies Jenna and Cariss.'

The Flea takes one of her hands and smiles up at me. 'Grace isn't like them, Beau-Belle.'

I don't know whether to be pleased or ashamed by his remark. All I know is, I suddenly feel dangerously close to tears too. 'Thanks,' I mumble. I go over to my bag and fish out my cell phone. I turn it on and watch the right-hand corner of the screen, praying that by some miracle the island now has reception. But the magical bars don't appear. My screensaver of Mom and Tigger does though and it makes me want to wail. I take a deep breath and try to compose myself. Everything's going to be okay. The pendant proves that there must be other people somewhere on the island. As soon as we find them, or they find us, we'll be able to get back home again. The thought of the pendant makes me think of Cruz and I squint down along the beach toward the boat. There's no sign of him on the deck, but then I see him walking over to where the boys are collecting coconuts. I feel a stab of concern as I think of how hostile Todd and Ron have been toward him. But then I figure Cruz can more than hold his own.

'Hey, Grace,' the Flea calls over to me. 'I was thinking maybe we could start work on some kind of a shelter. Just in case we're here for another night.'

'Don't say that!' Belle exclaims.

The Flea turns back to her and takes hold of her hand. 'We have to be practical, honey, it did get pretty cold last night in that breeze.'

Belle sighs. 'I guess.'

'Sure,' I say, leaping to my feet, stupidly grateful to be included in something.

'Okay, so I saw this documentary on Discovery once about

what to do if you found yourself stranded in the wild,' the Flea says, standing up and rubbing his hands together like he's been waiting for this moment his whole life. I can't help grinning – I'm starting to wonder if he's sponsored by the Discovery Channel.

Belle reluctantly gets to her feet. 'What did it say?'

'Well, there was a whole bunch of stuff about how to avoid being eaten by grizzly bears, but I guess we won't be needing that here.'

'Thank God!' Belle says.

'Uh-huh.' I grin.

She looks at me and I see her gaze soften. 'So what do we need?'

The Flea takes off his hat and ruffles his hair. 'Branches to build the frame, and sticks and moss and leaves for insulation.'

I get a sinking feeling. 'I guess that means we have to go back into the forest?'

The Flea beams at me. 'Yes indeedy! Are you up for it, Beau-Belle?'

Belle nods. 'It beats sitting here doing nothing.'

My stomach starts churning. I try to ignore it and walk over to them. 'But won't we need some kind of knife for chopping down the branches?'

'Good point.' The Flea looks down the beach toward the boat. 'We need to enlist the help of Don Juan and his machete.'

'He's going off somewhere with the boys, look,' Belle says.

We follow her gaze down to the edge of the cove where Cruz, Todd, Ron and Dan are disappearing from view.

'Ah well, heaven can wait,' the Flea says with a sigh. 'How about we get the smaller sticks and stuff and the others can get the larger branches later on?'

'Sounds good to me,' I say, although, as we start walking toward the forest, my entire body seems to be telling me that going back in there is a very, very bad idea indeed.

Chapter Ten

I don't know if it's because I'm more on edge, or because there's just three of us, but the forest feels even more claustrophobic this time. I think the Flea feels it too because straight away he says, 'Let's not go too far,' and I'm not about to argue with him. As we set about gathering piles of leaves and sticks, Belle starts singing a song in Spanish under her breath. It doesn't matter that I don't understand the words, the melody is beautiful; haunting and soothing at the same time. When she gets to the end I turn to her and smile.

'That was lovely.'

She blushes and looks down at the ground. 'Thank you. It was my favourite lullaby when I was a baby. It's about the moon goddess, Luna, and how she watches over you when you sleep. My mom still sings it to me whenever I'm stressed.'

I nod.

'I just wish . . .'

'What?'

'Nothing.' Belle sighs and starts tugging at a small branch on the tree next to her.

'It'll be fine,' the Flea calls over to her. 'We'll be out of here in no time.'

Belle nods. We carry on working in silence. Somewhere from deep within the forest a bird starts to screech. It reminds me of a witch's cackle.

We work all morning collecting sticks and leaves for the shelter. There are no whispers, or strange smells. By the time we stop and return to the camp I feel light-headed from exhaustion and relief. The sun is now high in the sky, beating down on the sand and making it shimmer a blinding white.

'Good to see they're hard at work,' Belle mutters, nodding toward Jenna and Cariss, who are now in their bikinis and sunbathing next to the HELP sign.

'They are working,' the Flea says, taking off his hat and wiping the sweat from his brow.

'On what? Their tans?' Belle says.

'No – they're forming human exclamation points for our sign.'

I look down at Jenna and Cariss, puzzled, and then I realize what the Flea means. They're both lying next to the P, with their heads at the foot of the sign. From the air their long thin bodies and round heads would make them look like a couple of exclamation points. Belle and I start to giggle.

The Flea takes a look inside the case of water bottles. 'Hmm, we're running pretty low on water.'

'Seems kind of ironic given that we're surrounded by it,' Belle mutters, looking down at the ocean.

The Flea looks at her and nods. 'You're telling me. Water, water everywhere and not a drop to drink. Well, two bottles left to drink, but still, it's not exactly a lot. I say we just take a couple of sips for now.' He hands her a bottle.

'Great.' Belle takes a sip from the bottle and passes it to me. My heart sinks as I think she might start crying again. The thought of only having a sip of water isn't exactly thrilling to me either. My mouth is as dry as the sand we're standing on, and my body is covered in a sticky film of sweat. I take a sip, then pass the bottle back to the Flea with a longing gaze.

The sound of whooping and hollering rings out across the beach and I look over to see Dan, Todd, Ron and Cruz heading back into the cove.

The Flea jumps to his feet. 'They've got something.'

'What is it?' Belle asks.

I stand up. 'It looks like –'

'– fish!' the Flea cuts in. 'Holy mackerel! They've got fish!'

As we start heading down to meet the boys, even Belle looks excited. Jenna and Cariss also get to their feet and pretty soon we're all congregated in the middle of the beach.

'Look,' Todd says to me. 'Look what I caught!' He's holding a huge silver fish. My stomach gives an appreciative growl. I can't help grinning at him, even though I'm still pissed about what he said to me in the forest. He grins straight back. Clearly I've been forgiven.

'But how did you catch them?' I ask.

'He showed us,' Dan says, nodding at Cruz. 'We found a bit of turtle meat and used it as bait, on pieces of string. It was awesome.'

'Wow, good job!' Jenna exclaims, treating Cruz to one of her best boy-catcher smiles.

I look away, feeling slightly sick, even though Jenna is the one who doesn't actually have a boyfriend and is therefore entitled to flirt with whoever she likes.

'We were looking for a freshwater source and we found an inlet, through those rocks, on the other side of the bay,' Ron says to Jenna, stepping between her and Cruz. 'It wasn't freshwater but it's full of fish so we definitely won't be going hungry.'

'But I'm vegan,' Cariss whines.

'Yeah?' Dan says. 'Well, I'm starving. Let's go cook these monsters.'

'Honey, you have to eat,' Jenna says to Cariss, reaching out and stroking her arm.

Cariss starts to pout. 'But fish makes me bloat.'

'Jesus!' Belle mutters, turning away.

'I wouldn't expect someone like you to understand,' Cariss snaps.

Belle turns back and stares at her. 'What's that supposed to mean?'

'Well, it's obvious you don't give a damn about your figure. I mean, you clearly spend your whole life bloated.' Cariss stares at Belle's slightly rounded stomach and I see Belle clench her fists.

'Hey!' I say.

'What the hell?' The Flea glares at Cariss, then goes to stand by Belle.

Jenna gives me a pointed stare. I give her one right back.

'It's okay, we got a whole load of coconuts earlier,' Todd says to Cariss. 'I can prepare you one if you like.'

'Oh, would you?' Cariss gushes, as if Todd had just offered her a life-saving kidney. 'Thank you. That would be awesome.'

I catch Todd's glance sweeping across Cariss's concave stomach and lingering a little too long on her breasts. I turn away, feeling a weird mixture of anger and confusion, and see Cruz looking at me. It's as if I can read the question in his widened eyes. *Are you okay?* I nod and give a weak smile.

'Come on, y'all, let's get a fire going,' Dan says. 'We'll all feel a whole lot better when we've had something to eat.

We trudge back to the camp, where Dan and Todd set about starting a fire while Cruz guts the fish with a pocket knife.

'This is so cool,' the Flea says. 'It's just like being in an episode of *Survivor*.'

Cruz throws a bunch of fish innards on the floor and Cariss makes a retching sound and goes to cower behind her luggage mountain.

Cruz then shows us how to peel some sticks, which he uses to skewer the fish. He arranges the sticks in a pyramid formation over the fire and we all watch, drooling, as the fish slowly turn from silver to golden brown. I don't know if it's my hunger, or the relief at finally eating something other than a coconut or a key lime pie gum, but that first mouthful of hot salty fish is one of the most delicious things I have ever tasted. The warmth slides down into my empty belly and starts radiating out to every cell in my body. And as it does it's as if the world turns from black and white to colour.

'Oh man!' Jenna exclaims. 'This is awesome!'

'I know,' I say. 'Even better than your mom's wheatgrass soup.'

When she starts to laugh I feel a surge of relief.

'And her tofu meatloaf,' Jenna says. 'Do you remember

when she tried to force-feed you that the year you came for Thanksgiving?'

I grin. 'Uh-huh. Thank God for Diamante.' Diamante is Jenna's mom's show poodle. She also doubles as a curly-haired, four-legged trashcan for all of Jenna's mom's crazy Californian food fads. Again Jenna smiles at me and I feel another wave of relief. Maybe things can start getting back to normal now.

Somewhere in the distance there's a low rumble.

'Well, excuse me!' the Flea exclaims, rubbing his stomach.

'What was that?' Cariss asks from behind her luggage.

'I don't know,' Jenna says.

Belle looks up at the sky. 'I think it was thunder.'

We all follow her gaze. The sky's still bright blue but there's no doubting it's getting incredibly humid. There's another rumble – a little louder this time.

'Hey, you don't think the volcano's about to erupt, do you?' the Flea says.

'The volcano! What volcano?' Cariss shrieks, leaping out from behind her cases with a look of total panic on her face.

The Flea points up at the red mountain. 'That volcano, of course.'

'How do you know it's a volcano?' I say, trying not to sound nervous.

The Flea looks at me, super-serious. 'The Pacific islands

are full of volcanoes. Most of them are dormant now, but you never know when one of them is gonna decide to wake up.'

I stare at him, speechless. Surely we would have to be the unluckiest people on the planet to survive a shipwreck only to be hit the very next day by a volcanic eruption?

Belle asks Cruz something in Spanish. Cruz nods.

'Oh my god! It is a volcano. We're all going to die. It's going to be like that place in Russia all over again!' Cariss shrieks.

'What place in Russia?' the Flea says, looking baffled.

'You know, the one where the whole town was covered in lava and preserved for, like, millions of years.'

'Pompeii?' I say.

Cariss nods and starts backing down the beach toward the sea.

'I think you'll find Pompeii is in Italy, not Russia,' the Flea calls out to her.

'I don't really give a damn,' Cariss hisses, 'I just want to get out of here.' With her hair now fully afro from the humidity and her eyes as wide as saucers, there's no doubting Cariss is looking more than a little nuts right now.

Jenna gets up and goes to stand by her. 'It's okay, honey, I'm sure he's only kidding.'

The Flea looks genuinely outraged. 'I'm not kidding. I saw a whole series on volcanoes on National Geographic. That's why the Pacific rim is also known as the Ring of Fire.'

'Didn't that Johnny Cash dude do a song about that?' Dan asks, his baseball cap pulled right down over his face.

'But if it is a volcano and it's about to erupt wouldn't it be, like, smoking or something?' Ron asks.

We all gaze up at the blood-red peak. I breathe a sigh of relief as I see there isn't even the slightest wisp of smoke.

The Flea starts nodding his head. 'Very good point, Ronald. If she were about to blow she'd be smoking like an outlaw's pistol.'

Jenna squeezes Cariss's arm. Cariss continues to look deranged with fear.

There's another rumble, this time much louder, and Cruz starts running off toward the boat.

Cariss throws her arms up in the air. 'Oh my God, where's he going? What's he doing?'

Dan takes off his cap and frowns. 'How should I know?'

We all watch as Cruz clambers up on to the boat and disappears below deck.

'I think he wants us,' Belle says, pointing to the boat. Cruz is shouting up at us and waving his hands.

We all start running down the beach. When we get close to the boat Cruz picks up a couple of large plastic containers from the deck. He gestures at Dan to come closer, then he throws the containers down to him. Then he picks up another couple of containers and throws them down to Todd.

'What the hell is he doing?' Cariss says. 'What use are they going to be if the volcano erupts?'

'The volcano ain't gonna erupt,' Dan yells. 'There's no freakin' smoke!'

Then the Flea tilts his face up to the sky and he starts to laugh and laugh. 'Belle was right. It's a storm, look.'

We all follow his gaze to where a cluster of dark clouds have gathered on the horizon.

'Oh no! Not again,' Cariss cries. 'My clothes!' She races back up the beach to where her clothes have been drying in the sun, and starts grabbing them up into her arms.

'But why is Cruise-Ship giving us those containers?' Jenna asks.

Ron shrugs. 'God knows. The guy's a total loose cannon.'

'I know! I know!' the Flea cries, like he's just worked out the winning answer on *The Wheel of Fortune*.

'What?' Jenna asks, without looking at him.

'To collect rainwater in!' the Flea says triumphantly. 'He isn't a loose cannon, he's a genius. Once the storm breaks we'll be able to collect some drinking water.'

Cruz passes another couple of containers down to us and we all head back to the camp. We set out the containers well away from the shelter of the trees and then we grab our stuff and head into the entrance to the forest and wait. As the storm clouds roll in, the sounds from the forest all quiet down, like its inhabitants know what's coming and have taken shelter too. And then, finally, the first fat raindrop falls. Followed by another and another. The wind starts whipping at the trees above us and the sky goes dark, but this time I'm not afraid. In fact, I'm so relieved to hear the water dropping into the containers I want to leap around and celebrate.

'*I'm singing in the rain*,' the Flea starts warbling.

'*Just singing in the rain*,' I reply.

He looks at me and raises his eyebrows. I nod and grin and the next thing I know we're both on our feet and dancing out into the rain, Gene Kelly style.

'Grace, you'll get soaked!' Jenna cries.

'Who cares?' I say, picking up a stick to use as a pretend umbrella. The rain is coming down in sheets now but it feels exhilarating to be dancing in it, however dumb we might look. And I can tell the Flea feels the same, from the crazy grin on his face. Before long, Dan has joined us, followed swiftly by Todd. I tilt back my head, open my mouth and let the fat raindrops fall into my parched mouth. It feels awesome.

'Come on, Beau-Belle!' the Flea calls.

Shaking her head and laughing, Belle joins us too and soon we're doing a 'Singing in the Rain' conga across the sand. I'm at the end of the conga and as we snake past the entrance to the forest I see Cruz watching us, grinning and clapping along.

Only Jenna and Cariss stay sheltered beneath the trees. Ron is hovering between them and us, clearly torn between his devotion to Jenna and loyalty to Todd.

Then I break free from the conga and fling my arms open. I start spinning round and round in ever wider circles, making my way down the beach. As I laugh and sing along, the wind seems to be joining in, whipping my hair and howling around me. I feel as light as air. This is why I love to dance. No matter how much crap you have going on in your life; dancing lets you shed it like a butterfly breaking free from a cocoon. I spin faster and faster. The wind wails louder and louder. I throw my head back and smile. We have water. We have food. We're on dry land. Everything is okay.

And then Jenna screams.

Chapter Eleven

'What is it? What's happened?' I hear Todd call out.

I stop dancing and squint through the rain. I can just make out the others racing back up the beach. I start running after them but the rain's so heavy now it's like running into a wall of water. I bend over double as the oxygen is sucked from my lungs. Somewhere above the howl of the wind I hear Cariss shouting, 'Oh my God' over and over again. I am putting one foot in front of the other, but it's like trying to go up a downward escalator. When I finally make it back to the camp, drenched and exhausted, I find the others all clustered in a semi-circle formation, peering into the forest. I stand on tiptoe and look over Todd's shoulder. Jenna is backed against a tree, her face ashen. Cariss is sitting on the floor at her feet, hugging her knees to her chest and rocking from side to side.

'What happened?' Todd asks.

Ron goes over to Jenna and puts his arm around her shoulder. 'What is it, Jen?'

Jenna just points a shaking finger toward a tree a little ways inside the forest.

Ron frowns and starts walking toward the tree. Then he stops in his tracks. 'Oh . . . no!'

'What? What is it?' The Flea goes over to join him. 'Holy skeletons! Okay, people, it would appear that we have company.'

'What company?' Belle follows the Flea, and we all follow her. And then I see what's freaking everyone out. There, hanging from a branch, like a super-sinister dream-catcher, is a lily-white skull.

'Look at its eyes,' Cariss moans.

Stuffed inside the eye sockets are two dark-red flowers. In the half light of the forest they make it look as if the eyes are filled with blood. I instinctively glance across at Cruz. His lips are moving, as if he's whispering something to himself.

'What the hell?' Dan says, taking off his cap so he can get a better look at the skull.

'Why is it there?' Cariss cries.

Dan looks back at her and gives a heavy sigh. 'Well now, let me just check my Beginner's Guide to Spooky Shit That Happens on Desert Islands.'

'Shut up!' Cariss shrieks. 'I've just about had it with you

and your sarcasm. If you haven't got anything polite to say then don't say anything at all!'

Dan takes a step back and glares down at Cariss. 'How about if you haven't got anything *intelligent* to say then don't say anything at all?'

'Okay, guys, let's just cool it for a second,' Todd says, reaching out to touch the skull.

'Don't!' Cariss screams, making us all jump about a foot in the air. 'It could be cursed!'

Todd pulls his hand away like it just got burnt.

'Why would someone do something like that?' Jenna says, her voice trembling. 'Why would they hang a skull in a tree like – like some kind of decoration?'

I go over and put my arm around her. 'I bet it's not real. I bet it's one of those plastic ones, you know, like the kind you get at Halloween for trick or treating. Someone probably put it there as a prank.'

'But why?' Cariss says, getting to her feet.

'I don't know. Maybe they wanted to freak out other people who came to the island.'

'Yeah, well, it certainly worked,' Jenna says, brushing some sand from her T-shirt. 'It scared the crap out of me. Didn't you guys see it when you came in here before to get the wood?'

Todd shakes his head. 'No, we must have walked straight past it.'

I look at the skull, swaying back and forth in the breeze, unsure how we could have missed it.

'This place is creeping me out. Can we please go back to the camp?' Belle says, turning away.

But the Flea is still staring at the skull, transfixed. 'Shouldn't we do something with it?'

'Like what?' Todd says.

'I don't know. Bury it?'

'But why do we need to bury it if it's only made of plastic?' Cariss's voice is getting dangerously high again.

'I say we leave it be.' Dan puts his cap back on and starts walking out.

'Yeah, man, let's just leave it,' Todd says. 'Grace is right, it's probably just a Halloween prank.' He turns to me and smiles, but I notice an uneasiness in his eyes.

A pale shaft of sunlight falls like a spotlight on the floor in front of me. I look up and see tiny specks of blue through the mesh of branches high above us.

'Hey, looks like the storm's past,' I say, gesturing upward.

'All right!' Todd says, clamping his arm around my shoulders. 'Let's get out of here.'

We hurriedly make our way back to the camp. The black clouds are disappearing behind the volcano like a retreating army and the sky over the beach is bright blue again. I glance at the HELP sign. It's still intact. If it weren't for the fact that the sand is now soaking, it's as if the storm never happened.

'They sure have some freaky weather out here,' Dan says, fetching his bag from where he'd sheltered it under a tree.

I watch as Cruz goes over to the row of containers. He looks inside them then turns back with a smile.

'Looks like we've got some drinking water,' I say, grinning back at him.

Todd comes over and takes hold of my hand, all the time staring at Cruz. 'Awesome. Let's go get some.'

We each get an empty water bottle and go over to the containers. The storm has left them almost full to the brim. I fill my bottle, then sit on the damp sand and gulp the water greedily.

'What now?' Ron says, once we've all finished drinking.

'I say we make a start on building a shelter,' the Flea says, using a stick to make a picture of a house in the sand.

Cariss scowls at him. 'What's the point in that? The coast guard is gonna find us anytime now. And if they don't, my daddy will. He has his own helicopter.'

The Flea gives a theatrical gasp. 'Really? Oh my gosh, that's, like, incredible!'

Belle smirks and turns away, but Cariss clearly doesn't possess a sarcasm detector. 'Uh-huh. I just know he'll be up there right now, looking for me.'

We all gaze up at the clear blue sky as if half expecting a

Black Hawk to suddenly appear with Cariss's daddy hanging from it, action-hero style.

'But just supposing your daddy doesn't find us today?' the Flea says, adding a cartoon-style helicopter to his picture in the sand. 'What if it rains again in the night? We'll be soaked.'

'He's got a point,' Jenna says, looking really pissed at actually having to agree with the Flea on something. 'But there's no way I'm going back in the forest to get any wood. Not with that *thing* in there.'

Cariss nods. 'Me neither.'

The Flea throws his stick away and jumps to his feet. 'Belle, can you ask Cruz if he'd be kind enough to go get his knife and help us with the shelter?'

Belle scrambles to her feet and goes over to Cruz, who's sitting by the water containers.

We all watch as Cruz nods, then sets off to the boat to get the knife.

'This is gonna be awesome,' the Flea says, rubbing his hands together. 'Just like being in a an episode of –'

'*Survivor*!' Dan and Todd exclaim in unison and we all start to laugh.

By the time dusk falls we've assembled the basic framework for the shelter, but there's still no roof or walls. Dan, Todd, Ron and Cruz have gone off to catch more fish for dinner and the rest of us are all sat around on the sand.

The Flea looks up from the palm leaves he's weaving together and gives a massive sigh. 'It sure didn't take this long on *Survivor*.'

Jenna continues sorting her clothes into colour-coordinated piles. 'I say we finish it in the morning, when it's light again.'

'We?' Belle mutters under her breath.

Jenna shoots her a piercing stare. 'What?'

Belle stares right back at her. 'Why did you say, *we* finish it in the morning? You haven't done a thing to help.'

Jenna jumps to her feet. A thin film of sand is stuck to her legs, making it look as if she's wearing white nylons. 'Well, somebody had to keep look out for planes or boats.'

'Exactly,' Cariss hisses, from behind her mirror. 'Anyway, Jenna and I aren't built for manual labour. We're not heavy-boned like you.'

Belle's dark eyes immediately glisten with tears. Quick as a flash, the Flea puts his leaves down and takes a hold of Belle's arm. 'Okay, how about we get a fire going ready for when the boys get back?'

Belle gets up and stomps away. The Flea heads off after her. I look at Cariss. She's still looking at herself in her mirror. My whole body tenses with anger.

'Why don't you give her a break?'

Jenna lets out a shocked gasp. 'Grace!'

I carry on looking at Cariss. She puts her mirror down and stares at me. Her mouth is pursed into a tight little pout. Then she looks up at Jenna, as if to say, *are you going to let her speak to me like that?*

Jenna sighs and comes to sit down next to me. 'It's great that you're being so charitable and all, but really, Grace, she isn't worthy of your friendship.'

I stare at her. 'What do you mean?'

Jenna hunches in closer to me. 'She isn't one of us,' she whispers dramatically.

'Yes, she is. We're all from the same school. We're all dancing in the same show – or supposed to be.'

'Yes, but we're not all paying the same fees to go to the same school, are we?'

'Exactly,' Cariss says, taking a tube of lip gloss from her make-up bag.

'She's on a *scholarship*,' Jenna whispers with a shudder.

'But what's wrong with that?'

'Oh my gosh!' Cariss lets out a horrified little laugh and for a split second I want to leap over and make her eat her lipgloss.

Jenna puts her hand on top of mine and opens her mouth to speak. But before she can say anything we hear the sound of the boys' voices as they make their way back up the beach. Jenna removes her hand. 'We'll talk about this later,' she says with a smile, but it sounds dangerously close to a threat.

Dinner is strained to say the least. Belle sits with her head bowed the whole time – probably so she doesn't have to make eye contact with Jenna and Cariss. Cariss risks chronic bloating for a couple of mouthfuls of fish. Jenna keeps smiling at me as if to say, *don't worry, you're one of us*, and the boys talk a bit about fishing, but their earlier excitement seems to have vanished. Even the Flea is subdued and doesn't mention the Discovery Channel a single time. I imagine a huge comic-style thought bubble hanging above all our heads, reading: *We're doomed to stay on this island for another night!*

After the last of the fish has gone we all sit staring into the flames. Well, all of us apart from Cruz, who's sat under a tree at the edge of the camp, carving something from a piece of driftwood with his pocket knife.

'What if they never find us,' Cariss says, fiddling with the beading on her silver sundress. She's slicked her hair back into a ponytail and it gleams like ebony in the firelight.

Jenna leans her head on Ron's shoulder, causing his Lego-man face to instantly light up. 'You'd have thought we'd have seen some sign of life by now,' she says with a sigh.

'We have,' the Flea says. 'We found the pendant – and the skull. Although I guess the skull's more of a sign of death.'

Next to him, Belle shivers and pulls her towel tighter round her shoulders.

I glance into the darkness behind us, where the forest is creaking and hissing, like an ancient monster rousing from sleep. I picture the skull hanging from the branch, its blood-red eyes gaping out into the pitch-black, and my skin starts to crawl. What if I really did hear someone whispering to me? What if they come back again in the night while I'm asleep? Panic pinballs inside my ribcage. I need to do something to distract myself or I'm going to go nuts.

'Let's have a party.' The words spring from my mouth before I have time to censor them.

Todd frowns at me. 'What?'

'Let's have a party,' I mumble. 'To take our mind off things.'

'What kind of party?' Ron asks.

I shrug, already wishing I hadn't said anything. 'I don't know. A dance party?'

Cariss frowns. 'But how can we dance? We don't have any music.'

I'm about to concede defeat when Dan starts to nod. 'We could make our own music,' he says. 'Like we did before when it was raining.'

The Flea claps his hands together in excitement. 'I could sing for you again.'

'Oh, please, no!' Jenna exclaims. Then she starts to smile. 'I guess we could have a dance-off. After all, we really should be keeping in shape for the show.'

'I can give you a beat.' Todd picks up a couple of discarded coconut shells and starts tapping them together. Dan starts beat-boxing along. The Flea whoops and leaps to his feet. We all watch as he starts body-popping around the fire, his thin body as bendy as rubber.

'All right!' Todd cheers as the Flea does a perfect backflip over the flames. Then he throws his hat high into the air, coming down into the splits and somehow catching the hat on his head.

Everyone bursts into applause. Apart from Cariss, who's jumped to her feet and moved into the middle of the circle. 'My turn,' she announces, shoving past the Flea.

'That was so cool,' I say as he collapses down on to the sand next to me.

'It was nothing,' he pants, with a wink.

'Okay, give me a beat,' Cariss says.

Todd starts drumming a beat on the coconut shells, a rapt expression on his face. There's no denying that Cariss is beautiful when she dances. Her body twists and turns like a snake and her skin shimmers gold in the firelight. Even Dan seems impressed. She moves right up to him until, as if hypnotized, he gets to his feet and starts dancing with her. As they shimmy closer and closer the tension between them is sizzling.

'Okay, someone else's turn,' Jenna hollers, breaking us all from our trance. 'Grace, it was your idea, how about you have a go?'

Dan goes and sits down, looking really mad at himself for succumbing to Cariss's charms.

Cariss sashays over to the other side of the circle and slides down into a lotus position with a smug smile on her face.

When I first stand up I feel really self-conscious, and curse myself for ever suggesting this. Dan and Todd start tapping out a beat and I close my eyes and try to find the rhythm, but my body feels stiff and disjointed. Then Belle starts softly singing the lullaby she'd sung in the forest earlier. As Dan and Todd begin to drum in time, her voice grows louder. I sway along and imagine the music entering my body. When Belle hits the high notes I lift my arms high. When her voice comes back down, soft and low, I bend my body down. This is the kind of dancing I like best – freestyle and totally at one with the melody. When the song comes to an end I open my eyes and I find myself looking straight at Cruz. He's staring back at me so intently I have to look away. The others start to clap and cheer and I take a deep breath and go back to the circle. As I walk past Belle I mouth the word 'thank you'. She nods and almost smiles.

'That was great, babe,' Todd says as I go and sit down next to him.

'Okay, my turn,' Jenna says, jumping to her feet. 'But I'm going to need a partner.' She marches straight over to Cruz and grabs a hold of his hand. 'Come on, Cruise-Ship, let's see what you're made of.'

Cruz stands frozen for a second, then he pulls his hand away.

'What's up,' Jenna says. 'I want to dance with you. You know – *dance*.' She starts doing a real exaggerated dance mime.

Cruz shakes his head.

'I'll dance with you, Jen,' Ron says, stepping forward. But Jenna is furious. Even in the dying fire-light I can see her face flushing an angry red.

'This was a dumb idea,' she snaps. 'Let's just go to bed.'

We all watch as she stomps off toward the palm trees.

Cariss gives Cruz a filthy look. 'Who the hell do you think you are?' she spits at him before marching off after Jenna.

'Geez, looks like the ugly sisters won't be going to the ball after all,' Dan says with a chuckle.

For the first time all night Belle smiles.

'Don't speak about Jenna like that,' Ron snaps, before going off to join them.

'Oh yeah? And what you gonna do about it?' Dan yells after him. He gets to his feet and yanks his cap off. He looks real mad. 'I swear, somebody better find us tomorrow before . . .' he breaks off, but we all know what he's thinking. Somebody better find us – before we start killing each other.

Chapter Twelve

I look at the half moon through a gap in the palm trees and wonder if there really is a goddess called Luna watching over us, like in Belle's lullaby. I sure hope so. Right now, I'd take anything.

It's ages since we went to bed. This time Todd started kissing me the second we lay down. His kisses were so fierce and urgent I immediately pulled away. He rolled off in a sulk and now I'm lying here in the sticky heat feeling hollowed out with hunger and loneliness.

'Good night, Mom,' I whisper up at the moon, hoping it will act like some kind of a satellite dish and beam my words down to her at home in LA. I close my eyes and take a deep breath. To try and block out the fearful thoughts that I know are just waiting to race into my mind, I decide to count my blessings. This was a trick my grandpa taught me when I was five years old and afraid of the dark. 'Thank you for the food and water,' I whisper. 'Thank you for letting us get through a day without anyone actually killing each other. Thank you for keeping us safe. Thank you for giving me the opportunity to dance. Thank you for –'

I hear a splashing sound and open my eyes. I'm just starting to think I imagined it when I hear another splash, and another. I try to ignore it, but it's no good, now my mind is full of questions. What if it's the person who left the skull in the tree? What if it's the person who's been whispering to me?

I sit bolt upright and rub my eyes. Then I look around the camp to see if anyone else has heard it, but there's no sign of movement. I get to my feet as quietly as possible. If I don't go check it out I'll never get to sleep.

I start tiptoeing across the sand, ready to race back to the others at the first sign of danger. When I get halfway down the beach I stop and squint at the sea. It takes a few seconds for my eyes to adjust, then I see someone sitting by the water's edge in the shadow of the boat. I can tell from the outline of his long curly hair that it's Cruz and I breathe a sigh of relief. Then I look back toward the camp, not sure what to do. I feel wide awake now, and the thought of going back to lie on the rock-hard sand isn't exactly appealing. So I keep on walking down to the water, not really knowing what I'm going to do when I get there. When I'm a few yards from Cruz I cough softly. He turns and, instead of looking surprised, he smiles, like he's been expecting me. I go sit down next to him. The sea stretches out in front of us, an endless glassy sheet, glimmering silver in the moonlight.

Cruz picks up a stone and throws it into the water. I watch as the ripples spread out like the rings in a tree trunk, then dissolve away again. It's a little cooler down here and I start feeling a bit more human. I tip my head back and look up at the sky and see a strange glowing band of cloud arching over us. 'Wow! What *is* that?'

'The Milky Way,' Cruz says softly.

'You're kidding? The actual Milky Way?' Then I look at Cruz, my eyes wide with shock. 'You spoke! I mean, you spoke English.'

Cruz looks back at me and grins. 'Did I?'

'Yes! And you just did it again!'

'I guess I did.' He looks back up at the sky. 'Did you know that the Milky Way is supposed to be the pathway between the earth and the spirit world?'

I don't know what to be more excited about. The fact that I'm sitting under the Milky Way, or the fact that Cruz can speak English. I decide that it's definitely the fact that Cruz can speak English.

'But why have you only been speaking in Spanish? Why didn't you tell us?'

Cruz carries on staring at the sky but I can see from the dimple by the side of his mouth that he's grinning. 'Maybe I did not want to.'

'But why not?' I fall silent. I'm pretty sure I can guess why not. After the way Jenna and the others have treated him why would he want to talk to us? I start cringing with embarrassment as I think of all the mean things they've said about him, while he's been able to understand every single word.

'I'm so sorry,' I say, doodling like crazy with my finger in the sand. Even though I haven't said anything nasty about Cruz I feel just as guilty as if I had.

'Why?' He turns and looks at me.

'You must've heard all the stuff they've been saying about you.'

'Yes. But they do not think I hear it. So who has the last laugh, huh?'

I grin back at him. 'You, I guess.'

'Right.'

'So how come you spoke to me?'

He looks away again. 'You are the only one I want to know.'

It could've sounded cheesy but he says it in such a matter-of-fact way it takes my breath away.

'I am?'

'Yes.'

'Oh. Well, thanks.'

'No problem.'

It's as if the last couple of days have been one of those movies with a killer twist at the end. Now I have to re-run everything in my head knowing the truth – that Cruz could understand us all along. Then I think of the storm and how Cruz dragged me to safety.

'You saved my life!' I blurt out.

Cruz continues looking straight ahead at the sea. 'Yes.'

'Thank you.'

He turns to me and smiles. 'I am glad.'

I smile back. 'I'm glad too.'

Then I remember how scared Cruz looked when we first arrived on the island, and when we found the pendant. 'Do you know where we are?'

He shakes his head. 'No.'

'But –' I break off, too shy to ask him why he'd looked scared.

He looks at me. 'But?'

I take a deep breath. I don't want to risk upsetting him when we've only just started talking. 'You looked a little – uneasy – when we first got here, as if you knew something about this place.'

Cruz runs a hand through his hair. He suddenly looks nervous. 'I do not know for sure, but I think . . .'

'What?'

'I think I *might* know where we are.' He puts down his handful of stones and turns to face me.

'Where?'

He takes a deep breath. 'Île de Sang.'

'Île de Sang?'

'Yes.'

I shake my head. 'Sorry, I've never heard of it.'

'It is French. For Blood Island.'

'Oh.' My heart sinks. 'Why's it called that?'

Cruz frowns, as if he's trying to figure out whether to tell me or not. He picks up a piece of driftwood and starts turning it over in his hand. 'In the South Pacific they say Île de Sang is haunted by the spirit of a voodoo queen.'

'Really?'

He nods. 'Her name was Hortense Buchet. She was driven out of New Orleans in the nineteenth century for putting a curse on her master.'

I'm confused. 'But we're miles away from New Orleans. Why would her spirit be here?'

Cruz puts down the piece of driftwood and looks at me. 'People say that she went to live on a mystery island.'

'What do you mean, a *mystery* island?'

'Well, no one really knows if the island exists. It isn't on any maps.'

'But if it doesn't exist then it can't be true, can it?' My brain feels as if it's being tied in knots.

Cruz glances over his shoulder at the volcano looming behind us. I'm half expecting him to start laughing and say, 'Just kidding.' But when he looks back at me his face is poker-serious.

'I learnt how to sail boats when I was fourteen years old,' he says, quietly. 'The guy who taught me had a book – a book of seafaring legends. Sometimes, he would read them to me – he liked to, you know, spook me a bit, see if I had what it took for life on the ocean.'

I nod.

'One of the stories was of a boat that ran adrift on Île de Sang about one hundred years ago. Only one of the crew members managed to escape. He said that the others were all killed in some kind of voodoo sacrifice by Hortense.' Cruz lowers his voice till it's just a whisper. 'There was a picture of the island at the start of the story. That moment when we first got here, when I looked uneasy?'

I can feel sweat beading on my back. 'Yes.'

'It was like the picture had come to life. The rainforest, the red volcano. Nowhere else do you get red volcanoes. They are always black, or grey – never red.'

'But that doesn't mean –' I break off.

Cruz nods. 'Maybe it is all bullshit. I don't know. It's just that something doesn't feel right in this place.'

'What do you mean?'

'Something is wrong – the skull in the tree . . .'

'But that could have been here since last Halloween.'

'No. The flowers in the eyes. They were fresh.'

'Oh.' I think of the whispering I heard in the forest. And the strange, sickly smell. Despite the heat I start to shiver.

Cruz moves closer. 'Are you cold?'

'Yes. No. I don't know. A little scared, I guess.'

Cruz places a hand on my back. Its warmth soaks into me. 'You mustn't be scared. We just need to be careful.'

I nod. He's so close it's making me dizzy.

'I loved to watch you dance before.'

Embarrassment jolts me back to reality.

Cruz looks out to sea. 'You dance like the wind dances in the trees.'

'Oh.' I desperately rack my brains for something slightly more interesting to say. But I've never been in this situation before. Todd's idea of sweet-talk is telling me he loves the way my pale skin makes his tan look deeper. The only examples I can draw upon are from Mom's Pioneer Romance novels, where the heroines cry 'Bless your heart' or 'Lord have mercy', when a handsome stranger compliments them.

Cruz turns back to face me and his face is deadly serious again. 'You know, in Navaho culture they say that if you save a person's life you are responsible for them for the rest of your days.'

'Oh.' *Say something else*, the voice inside my head yells.

Cruz nods. 'So you will be okay. I'm looking out for you now.'

I have the sudden and totally inappropriate urge to crawl into his strong arms. Instead I stumble to my feet. 'I ought to be getting back.'

He nods and stands up too. Then he takes something from his pocket and hands it to me. 'I want you to have this.'

I look down and see that it's the piece of driftwood he'd been working on earlier by the fire. He's carved it into a beautiful flower. 'Wow, that's amazing!'

'It is the guaria morada. The Costa Rican national flower. It brings good luck. Take it.'

'Okay.' My hands tremble slightly as I take it from him. 'Thank you.'

'Good night.'

'Good night.'

I walk up the beach, clutching the wooden flower. It feels as if my head is whirring louder than the cicadas as it tries to process the night's events. Up ahead of me, the forest sways and groans in the dark. Could the island be haunted by an evil spirit? Could all the things Cruz told me be true? Is this why

I've felt so uneasy since I've got here? I feel sick with dread. Then I look back over my shoulder. Cruz is standing by the boat, motionless, watching me.

Instinctively I raise my hand. He waves back and his words echo through my head. 'I'm looking out for you now.'

I take a deep breath and keep on walking.

Chapter Thirteen

'Oh my God! It's missing!'

I wake with a start at the sound of Jenna's voice and feel something digging into my leg. I reach down and find the wooden flower that Cruz gave me. Memories from the night before start scrolling through my mind like the headline banner on CNN. Cruz and I sat together by the sea last night. Cruz and I sat *talking* by the sea.

'What's gone missing, hun?' Cariss calls.

'The pendant,' Jenna replies.

I feel a rush of dread as I remember what Cruz told me about Île de Sang and the voodoo queen.

'Hey.'

I jump as I feel Todd's hand on my shoulder. Quickly hiding the flower under my sweatshirt pillow, I turn to face him. His golden hair is tumbling into his face, making him look like a sleepy puppy.

'You sleep okay?'

I nod. Guilt tiptoes into my head and sets up camp.

'Who's taken it?' Jenna yells.

I close my eyes and wish that when I open them again she would still be asleep. And this day wouldn't already be starting badly.

'Yo! What's all the noise about?' Dan calls from beneath his blanket of clothes.

'Someone's taken the pendant,' Jenna yells. 'It was in my shorts pocket and now it's disappeared.'

'Maybe it fell out?' the Flea mutters, his voice thick with tiredness.

'It couldn't have, it was there last night and now it's gone.'

'Man!' Dan sighs. 'Does it really matter? It's not like it belonged to you.'

'It's okay, honey, we'll find it, 'Cariss says. 'How about we do some yoga to take your mind off it?'

Todd puts his arm around my waist and pulls me toward him. 'How about we sneak off for a bit of alone time today?' he whispers in my ear.

I nod, because nodding feels like the easiest thing to do right now, but in my head, things are going crazy. Last night is starting to feel like an insane dream. I wriggle out of Todd's arms and sit up. Belle is curled on her side facing me, clutching the crucifix round her neck and whispering something to herself. I figure she must be praying. Jenna's pacing up and down at the other end of the camp, scouring the sand. Next to her, Cariss is doing some kind of hardcore yoga move in a microscopic bikini.

'I don't suppose you've seen it, have you, Belle?' Jenna asks.

Belle freezes. 'Why would I have seen it?'

'Oh, I don't know. I was just asking.'

Belle rolls over to face Jenna. 'Well, why don't you *just ask* any of the others?'

'So, what's for breakfast?' I say, trying desperately to steer the conversation off collision course.

'Coconuts?' the Flea says with a sigh.

'I'm telling you, if I have one more coconut I'm gonna turn into a freakin' macaroon,' Dan says, sitting up.

'Todd, could you fix me a coconut?' Cariss calls, as she pushes herself up into a headstand.

Todd sits up and looks over at her. 'Sure,' he says, brushing his hair from his face.

But something weird happens. Even though Cariss looks just as perfect upside down, even though her breasts are practically spilling out of her bikini top, and even though Todd's eyes are almost in another zip code to his head, I don't care. 'Today's the day my daddy finds us, I just know it,' Cariss says, coming out of her headstand and going straight into a downward dog.

Dan averts his eyes from her butt and gets out of bed. 'I'm going for a swim,' he mutters.

'He's probably got Navy Seals on the case by now,' Cariss continues.

'Say what?' the Flea mutters from beneath his hat.

'Navy Seals. They're a crack commando unit trained for super-high-level rescue operations.'

'I know who they are,' the Flea replies, taking his hat from his face and sitting up. 'But don't you think they'll be a little preoccupied with other things right now? Like fighting the war on terror? Or ridding the world of the axis of evil?'

Cariss comes down into a cobra pose and glares at the Flea like she's about to sting him with her tongue. 'For your information, my daddy is a very influential man. He was once voted FHM's Guy I'd Most Like to Play Call of Duty With!'

The Flea jumps out of bed. 'Okay. Whatever. Hey, Beau-Belle, fancy going for a swim?'

'Sure.' Belle gets up and they both grab their towels and swimsuits and head off down the beach.

Cariss watches, stunned, like she can't believe the Flea wouldn't be totally spellbound by tales of her daddy's awesomeness.

'Shall we go get some more fish?' Todd asks Ron.

Ron nods. 'Sure. Is that okay, Jenna?'

Jenna nods and comes to sit down. 'As long as you don't ask that creep Cruise-Ship to go with you.'

'We don't need him,' Ron says scornfully. 'Anyways, after what he did to you last night I don't care if I never have anything to do with him again.'

Jenna smiles at Ron and his pale cheeks visibly glow.

I wonder if I ought to offer to go with them.

Todd jumps up and pulls a clean T-shirt from his bag. 'Okay, Ron dude, let's go get us some breakfast!' Then he looks down at me and grins. 'Don't forget what I said about later, Grace.'

I nod and force a smile.

'What's happening later?' Jenna immediately asks.

Todd's face flushes and he turns away. 'Nothing. Come on, Ron.'

I decide against going with them. I'm going to need to mentally prepare for my alone time with Todd.

'What did he mean?' Jenna says, the moment Todd and Ron have gone. 'What's happening later?'

'Nothing.' Now my cheeks start burning with embarrassment.

'He must've meant something.' Jenna glares at me.

'It was just something – private.' I get up and start folding away my bed.

'Oh, I see.' Jenna stands up and marches over to her own bed. 'Well, I never thought you'd be one of those girls, Grace.'

'What girls?'

'The kind who puts her boyfriend before her best friend.'

'What?' I stare at her, unsure I just heard her right. 'But I don't put –'

'Don't worry about it.' Jenna turns to Cariss, who's now sat in a lotus position staring at us intently, like she's watching her favourite soap. 'I'm gonna make sure Oceana Ventura fire Cruise-Ship's ass the second we're out of this place,' Jenna says.

I stare at her in disbelief. 'Why? Because he wouldn't dance with you?' I'm feeling so mad at her right now. How dare she accuse me of being a bad best friend after the way she's been acting these past couple days?

Jenna and Cariss both look at me like I'm deranged.

'But I had asked him to dance with me,' Jenna says.

I start stuffing my towel into my bag. 'What if he didn't feel like dancing? Maybe he's shy. Maybe he can't dance.'

'Grace, what on earth has gotten in to you?'

I stop packing my towel away and look at her. 'What do you mean?'

Jenna sighs and smoothes back her hair. 'Ever since we've been on this island you've been acting super-strange.'

Oh, and you haven't? I want to yell at her. *Sucking up to Cariss like she's a popsicle. Practically freezing me out. Being a super-bitch to Belle and the Flea. And Cruz.* I look at them both staring at me blankly and I realize there's just no point. 'I'm going for a swim,' I mutter and march off to the beach.

I'd hoped that after my swim things would get better. But when I get back to the camp, starving hungry, Todd and Ron are pacing up and down, grim-faced and empty-handed. 'We couldn't find any bait,' Todd mutters when I look at him questioningly.

Ron looks at Jenna. 'What are we going to do?'

Jenna frowns. 'We're going to have to get Cruise-Ship to catch us some fish. But I don't want you guys going with him. We have to stand together and let him know we're unhappy with him. Otherwise how will he ever learn to show us respect?'

'Exactly,' says Cariss.

Jenna looks at me. 'Grace, can you go tell Belle to ask him to get us some breakfast.'

I want to tell her to go herself, but if she goes anywhere near Belle it'll only lead to more conflict, so I head off down the beach. Belle and the Flea are sitting by the water's edge, staring out at the crashing waves.

'Hey, Belle,' I say, trying real hard to sound joyful and carefree, like we're one big happy family on vacation. 'Jenna asked me to ask you if you'd ask Cruz if he could go catch us some fish for breakfast. Wow, there sure was a lot of asking in that sentence.'

No one laughs. Belle looks up at me. 'Why don't you *ask* your boss to do her own dirty work?'

I frown. 'She's not my boss.'

'Oh, no?' Belle gets to her feet and glares at me. 'You guys think you're so special, don't you, just cos your parents have got money. You think it gives you the right to order people about and talk to them like they're pieces of dirt.' She clenches her fists like she's actually about to sock me. 'It's bad enough when we're at school, but I'm not putting up with it here, I have enough to deal with.'

'But I – when have I ever treated you like that?'

'All the time!' Belle cries. 'When have you ever asked me how I am, or talked to me at break time, or sat with me in the lunch hall?'

'But –'

'It's like you're all members of this exclusive little club where everything's perfect and nothing ever goes wrong and anyone who's slightly different doesn't get a look in.'

'But that's not true. My life isn't perfect.'

'Yes it is.'

I'm starting to feel mad now too. 'No it isn't, and you have no right to tell me it is. You don't know the first thing about me.'

Belle smiles triumphantly. 'Exactly! And whose fault is that?'

The Flea gets to his feet and grabs a hold of Belle's arm.

'Sorry, Grace, Belle's under a lot of pressure right now, she doesn't mean it.'

Belle turns on him. 'Yes I do.'

'Well, then you can go to hell,' I yell. My throat tightens and my eyes start to sting with tears. I turn and start running off along the beach, away from them, and away from the camp. I've had it with Belle. What gives her the right to decide that my life is perfect? What gives her the right to decide that she's the only one who has it tough? *Try having to be the adult your entire childhood*, I want to yell back at her. *Try living with parents who only care about their own stupid dramas and don't even notice how much it's hurting you*.

I stop running and bend over to catch my breath. All I want to do is get away but there's nowhere to go. I hate this damn island! I carry on along the beach, blinking back tears. As the waves crash over my feet I think of how much I loved the sea when I was a little kid. How exciting and mysterious it seemed. Now the vast expanse of water feels like an endless prison wall. I'm just about level with the boat when Cruz appears on deck.

'Hey,' he calls down to me.

'Hey,' I say, but it's no good, I can't make myself smile.

Cruz leaps over the railing and splashes his way over to me. 'What's up?'

I turn away and take a deep breath. I have to stay cool. I

can't let him see I'm upset. 'Everyone's falling out and we've got no food and the boys tried to go fishing, but they weren't able to catch anything because they couldn't get any bait and I don't know what to do.'

So much for playing it cool.

Cruz looks puzzled. 'But I have bait from yesterday still. Why they do not come to me?'

I look at him, unsure of what to say.

He starts to laugh. 'Don't tell me, the ice queen told them no.'

I smile and nod. And I know it sounds petty, but right at this moment I'm really glad he doesn't like Jenna. I'm really glad he hasn't been dazzled by her platinum hair and Colgate smile, the way most guys are.

Cruz grins at me. 'So, you have any plans right now?'

I look around the island and shrug. 'Surprisingly, no.'

'You want to learn how to fish?'

I shake my head.

He looks genuinely disappointed. 'You don't?'

'I already know how to fish. But if you want me to come with you I'd like that.'

Cruz looks mortified. 'I am so sorry! I just – what is the word? – assumed.'

I grin at him. 'What? That because I'm a girl I wouldn't know how?'

He shakes his head. 'No, not because you're a girl – because none of your friends know how.'

My face flushes. 'Yeah, well, I'm not like them.'

'Oh, yes, I know that already.' He grins at me. 'Okay then – let's go fishing!'

To get to the inlet you have to clamber over a rocky outcrop at the edge of the beach, then go through what looks like a cave but is actually a really long, dark tunnel. You come out on the other side into a thin cove surrounded by high walls of red rock. A narrow stream of seawater runs through the centre of the cove, splitting it in two. Unlike the bay, with the spooky forest at one end and the ocean on the other, the cove feels safe and secure. For the first time since we arrived on the island I actually feel like I have some privacy.

Cruz leads me to a cluster of rocks forming a natural jetty over the stream. We sit down and he fetches some string and bait from his bag.

'So, how did you learn to fish?'

'My grandpa taught me. He lives on a lake in South Carolina. We go night-fishing together whenever I stay with him.'

Cruz looks suitably impressed. 'I bet you never fished like this before though, huh?' he says, attaching a piece of turtle meat to the end of his string.

I laugh and shake my head. 'No. This is a first for me.'

After we've threaded pieces of turtle meat on to our lines we cast them out and sit in silence for a while. But it doesn't feel awkward like it does when Todd and I fall silent.

'When I buy my farm I'm going to have a lake and go fishing there every day,' Cruz says.

'You're buying a farm?'

'Yes. That's why I work for Oceana Ventura. To earn the money.'

'That's great.'

He looks at me and smiles. 'So, you want to be a world-famous dancer?'

I laugh and shake my head. 'No, not especially.'

'Why do you do it then?'

I cast my string out a bit wider and stare down into the clear water. 'Because it's the only thing that makes me forget all my worries.'

He frowns. 'What worries?'

'Oh, you know, the usual. Parents. Divorce.' I put on a jokey, TV-presenter-style voice. 'Being the product of a broken home.'

Cruz shakes his head. 'No, I do not know. My parents are still happily married.'

'Oh. Well, consider yourself lucky.' Suddenly I spot a fish shimmering through the water and I move my line toward it. 'Yes!' I cry, as it goes for the bait. I pull the string up and the fish streaks silver through the air. I kill it quickly with a sharp slap against the rock and put it down. It's a big one – about two pounds. My grandpa would be proud.

Cruz high-fives me as we laugh and cheer. Then he hands me a fresh piece of bait. 'Fishing is the thing that makes me forget my worries.'

I look at him, curious. 'Really? Doesn't it just give you more time to dwell on them?'

He shakes his head. 'It makes me, you know, switch off.'

I nod and we carry on fishing.

'Do you really believe that the island's haunted?' I say after a while.

Cruz frowns. 'I don't know. After we spoke last night I was worried you'd think I was a crazy person. I didn't mean to scare you, I –'

'You didn't scare me!'

He looks at me with one eyebrow raised, which strangely makes him look even cuter.

'Okay, maybe you did just a bit. But I'd already been feeling spooked.' I instinctively lower my voice. 'You were right – there is something weird about this place.'

Cruz nods and sighs.

'I'm glad I've got you to talk to, though.' I stare at the water, embarrassed at being so forward.

'Me too,' Cruz says.

I look at him and smile. 'So, in that book you were telling

me about, did it say why the voodoo queen was banished from New Orleans?'

'For putting a curse on her master.'

'Yes, but why did she do that?'

Cruz pulls his line out of the water then turns to face me. 'You know it could just be folklore, right?'

I nod.

'Well, the story is that her master, François Buchet, the guy who brought her to New Orleans in the first place, was a very wealthy and powerful man. He owned one of the largest cotton plantations in all of Louisiana. But the moment he set eyes on Hortense he became infatuated with her. She was like a drug to him, you know, like – like – opium?'

I nod.

'They became lovers immediately, and then Hortense fell pregnant with his child. When his wife found out she went crazy and threatened to tell everyone. Buchet could not afford to have his reputation ruined, so he told his wife Hortense had put a spell on him, that he hadn't been in control of what he was doing; and then he cast Hortense out.'

'And that's when she went to live on the island?'

Cruz shakes his head. 'No. At first she went to live in the French quarter of New Orleans. That's where she built her name as a voodoo queen. But then strange things started happening.'

'What strange things?'

'Well, first Buchet's cotton crop failed in mysterious circumstances. Then his daughter – she died.'

'And he thought it was Hor—'

'Hortense. Yes. Buchet's wife became certain she had placed a curse on the whole family. Hortense had become a well-known voodoo queen by this time.'

'What exactly *is* a voodoo queen?'

Cruz yanks his line out of the water. A fish wriggles on the end of it, its skin flashing a rainbow of colours in the sunlight. 'They were supposed to have supernatural powers. People would go to see them if they wanted something done.'

'Like what?'

'Like a cure maybe, if they were sick. Or a curse, if someone had, you know, done wrong to them.'

'Oh.' I stop watching the water for fish and look straight at Cruz. 'So what did Buchet do to her?'

Cruz carefully places his fish alongside mine on the rocks. 'The story says he sent a gang of men to her place in the dead of night and they burnt it to the ground. With Hortense and the baby still inside.' He looks at me, grim-faced. 'The baby died.'

I shiver. 'But Hortense didn't?'

Cruz shakes his head. 'They thought at first that she did, but then rumours started that she had somehow used her powers to escape. Several people saw her around New Orleans after the fire, and one night she was seen boarding a boat with a small group of people.'

I frown. The story is sounding more and more like a fairy tale by the minute. 'But how did they know she'd gone to an island?'

Cruz starts putting some fresh bait on his line. 'About two years after Hortense was last seen, a young woman turned up at a church in New Orleans. You know the word zombie?'

'Sure.'

'Well, that is what she was like. Although her body was still alive it was like she was dead on the inside.'

I frown again. 'But what did she have to do with Hortense?'

Cruz puts his line down. 'She never spoke a word when she was awake, but when she slept she would have terrible nightmares and scream out about Île de Sang and all the terrible things Hortense did there.'

'Oh. I see.' I'm still not convinced. Zombies seem way too Scooby-Doo to me.

'And she had Hortense's symbol branded on her back.'

'Her symbol?'

'Yes. The voodoo snake god Papa Labas, above the letter H.'

The palms of my hands go clammy. 'A snake above the letter H? But that's . . .'

Hc looks at me and nods, his expression now deadly serious. 'I know. The symbol on the pendant you found.'

Chapter Fourteen

I make my way back to camp with eight fish and about a hundred questions. The biggest of which being, where is the pendant? When Jenna said it was missing I'd assumed she'd just lost it, but now I don't know what to think. Cruz has taken a couple of fish and gone back to the boat, and although part of me feels sad he's now effectively an outcast, another part of me is relieved that he won't have to be treated like crap by the others.

When I reach the camp, Todd, Ron and Dan are working on the shelter and Jenna and Cariss are practising dance routines. Belle and the Flea are nowhere in sight.

As soon as Todd sees me he drops the branch he'd been hammering into the ground and comes running over.

'Where've you been?' Then he notices the fish I'm carrying. 'Where did you get those?'

'I caught them – well, five of them anyway.'

'All right!' Dan exclaims. 'Looks like you could teach these boys a thing or two about fishing, Grace.'

Todd just glares at me. 'How did you catch them?'

'With string.'

'But –'

'I have been fishing before, you know.'

'When?'

'At my grandpa's in South Carolina. I always go fishing with him. I've told you that.'

Todd looks blank. 'Oh, I . . . I don't remember.'

'What's going on?' Jenna says, coming over with Cariss. 'Where did you get those fish?'

'I caught them.'

'On your own?' Cariss's eyes widen.

'No.' I take a breath. 'With Cruz.'

I'm not sure who looks the most furious, Todd or Jenna.

'You went fishing with Cruise-Ship?' Jenna says.

I nod.

'But . . .'

I turn away from them to face Dan and Ron. 'So who's going to help me cook them? I'm starving.'

'You got it,' Dan says. 'Come on, Ron, let's get the fire going again.'

Dan and Ron head off, but Todd stays staring stony-faced at me.

'How could you go fishing with him, after what he did?' Jenna says.

I frown at her. 'You were the one who wanted him to go fishing for us.'

'Yes, but I didn't mean for you to go too.'

'Well, I did go. And now we have breakfast, so shall we just move on?' As I march over to Dan and Ron I feel buzzed like I just downed two espressos. I'm so used to doing anything and everything to keep the peace, it feels weird talking back to Jenna like this.

'Grace!' Todd calls after me.

'I'm going to gut the fish,' I yell over my shoulder.

Todd waits a second, then comes and sits down opposite me – so I can be treated to a clear view of his sulky face, I guess. All the time I'm preparing the fish, he just sits there in silence. Jenna and Cariss stay by the beds, huddled over in conversation. I tell myself that I don't care, but I do. My friendship with Jenna has been the one constant thing in my life – now it's unravelling it feels like someone's ripping the safety net out from under me.

Once the fish are cooking, the Flea and Belle reappear.

'Do I smell brunch?' the Flea says with a wink.

I nod and smile, grateful for someone to talk to.

'You okay?' he mouths and I nod again.

Belle studiously avoids my gaze.

'Grace here's been a fishin',' Dan tells him.

The Flea looks genuinely impressed. 'You have? Is there no end to your talents, young lady?'

I grin. 'Why, thank you, kind sir.'

'I think we should have a meeting,' Jenna calls over abruptly.

Dan groans. 'What for?'

'To decide a few things.'

'Like what?'

'Well, like what we're going to do, for starters.'

Belle, who's sitting a little ways from the rest of us, immediately looks up. 'What can we do? We're stuck here until someone finds us.'

Jenna shakes her head. 'Not necessarily.'

'What do you mean?' Belle edges a bit closer.

'We could go looking for help.'

We all look toward the forest. My stomach tightens as I think of the skull – and what else might be lurking in there. As if on cue, a circling gull lets out a scream.

Belle gets to her feet. 'We can't. We have to stay here.' Her voice is shrill and her eyes wide with fear.

Jenna scowls at her. 'But we could end up staying here forever.'

Belle marches over to her. 'Don't say that!'

The Flea reaches up to try to take hold of her hand. 'It's okay, honey, take it easy.'

But Belle is looking totally panic-stricken. 'We can't stay here forever. I have to get off this island. I have to get back home.'

'What the hell is wrong with you?' Jenna is on her feet now, her face inches from Belle's. 'Quit acting like a baby. We're all in the same position, you know.'

'No, we're not!' Belle shoves Jenna, making her stagger backward.

Jenna regains her balance and turns to face the rest of us. 'Oh my God! Did you see that? She physically assaulted me!'

'I wouldn't call it physical assault –' the Flea begins.

'What the hell was it then?' Jenna yells. 'She pushed me. You all saw it. Didn't you?'

Ron immediately leaps to his feet and goes to stand next to her. 'Yes, we saw it.'

Belle looks at Jenna, her fists clenched. 'I'm not leaving this beach and you're not going to make me,' she shouts. Then she stalks off toward the sea.

'Belle!' the Flea calls out after her.

'Leave me alone,' she yells. 'All of you.'

The Flea sits down, looking deflated.

Jenna shakes her head. 'That girl is a psycho!'

Cariss gets up and grabs a hold of Jenna's hand. 'I cannot believe the way she spoke to you, honey. It was so uncalled for – and so ugly.'

'So ugly,' Jenna echoes.

'Yeah, well, we can't go anywhere if Belle doesn't want to,' the Flea says. 'We're not leaving her here by herself.'

'I vote we stay on the beach a couple more days,' Dan says. 'The coastguard's bound to show up soon.'

'Fine by me,' Todd mutters.

Jenna purses her lips, then sits back down. Cariss and Ron immediately sit down either side of her, as if their movements have been choreographed.

'Well, if we're staying on the beach I think we need to establish a few rules,' Jenna says.

Dan looks at her suspiciously. 'What kind of rules?'

'General housekeeping. Assign chores, that kind of thing.'

Dan sighs. 'Great.'

'What would you like me to do, Jen?' Ron looks up at her with puppy dog eyes. He literally seems one step away from rolling over and begging.

'I think you boys should be responsible for keeping the fire going and fetching the food and building the shelter.'

Dan coughs. 'Right. And what do you girls do while we're doing all the hard work?'

'We keep the place clean and tidy and cook the food.'

'How very Stepford,' the Flea mutters.

Jenna immediately trains one of her ice-cool smiles on him. 'I thought you could help us girls, Jimmy, seeing as you're more, you know – one of us.'

Cariss stifles a snigger.

The Flea glares at her and I don't know whether to hug him or kill Jenna. What hope do we have if the Flea gets mad? He's the only one of us who's been resolutely cheerful this whole time. I sigh and look down the beach. Belle is hunched over on the white sand, gazing out to sea. I would've felt sorry for her, but I'm still smarting from what she said to me earlier and I don't like the way she's making out that being here's worse for her than it is for the rest of us.

'Grace, why don't you and I go get some firewood?' Todd says suddenly.

'But she can't!' Jenna exclaims.

Todd frowns. 'Why not?'

Jenna's face starts to flush. 'Because – because she needs to help out here.'

Todd ignores her and holds out his hand to me.

Jenna jumps to her feet. 'I know – why don't we all go

play a game of beach volleyball?'

I stare at her. What the heck has gotten into her?

'Er, cos we don't have a ball?' the Flea says.

'We can improvise,' Jenna snaps.

Dan gets to his feet. 'I have an inflatable beach ball in my bag.'

'You do?' Jenna claps her hands together excitedly. 'So, how about it?'

'Great idea!' Ron gets to his feet. So does Cariss. But Jenna's still looking at Todd.

'You guys do what you want. I want to spend some time with Grace,' Todd says, still holding his hand out to me.

I'm shocked and not just because Todd has pulled a massive U-turn. Him turning down volleyball is like *The National Enquirer* turning down a celebrity scoop. But I figure it would be good to get a chance to clear the air between us, so I take his hand and get to my feet.

'But you love volleyball,' Jenna says.

'Yeah, well, I love a lot of things,' Todd replies.

Ron immediately starts to snigger. 'You guys be careful. Be sure and watch out for *snakes*.'

I give him my deadliest death stare.

'Okay, well, let's go then,' Jenna snaps.

As the others all head off for the beach, Todd and I start walking in the opposite direction – toward the forest.

'Do we have to go in there?' I say.

Todd shrugs. 'Where else can we go? It's not as if we can book a room at the Hilton.'

My heart sinks faster than an anchor. But I have to come clean with Todd about the way I'm feeling. And I can't exactly do that within earshot of the others so I trudge on after him up the beach.

The minute we get into the forest I gasp. The air is so sticky it's as if the trees are sweating. The sickly sweet smell is back again too, stronger than ever. Todd doesn't seem to have noticed it though. I feel for the wooden flower in my pocket and grip it tightly.

'So what's going on?' he says, as soon as we've got a little ways in.

'What do you mean?'

'You know what I *mean*. Why are you being so distant?'

It feels as if someone's pressing a pillow over my face. My heart starts racing with panic. All of the things I wanted to say to Todd become a jumbled mess of words in my head.

'What? I – I don't know . . .'

Todd gives a sarcastic little laugh. High above us a parrot screeches. 'Yeah, right. What about last night when I was trying to kiss you? You couldn't get away from me fast enough.'

I take a breath and almost gag on the humid air. 'That's not true. It's just . . .'

'Just what?' He looks down at the floor. 'You're not the only girl who wants to go out with me, you know.'

'*What?*'

He keeps on looking at the floor. 'I'm just saying.'

'So, what? I should be eternally grateful?'

Todd scuffs the tip of his flip-flop in the dirt and doesn't say anything.

'Are you for real?' I don't know if it's the heat or my anger, or a mixture of both, but I feel really dizzy and sick. I reach out and grab on to a nearby tree. The forest starts spinning around me in a kaleidoscope of green. 'What's that smell?'

'What smell? Look, don't change the subject, Grace. I need to know what's going on. It's not good for my rep to have a girlfriend who isn't into me. It makes me look like a tool in front of my boys.'

Tiny sparks of light dance before my eyes. I retch and bile burns at the back of my throat.

'I can't breathe,' I gasp.

'Grace? What the hell?'

'I have to get out of here!' I start staggering back toward the opening, focusing on the patch of blue sky to guide me there.

'Grace! What's up with you?'

I stumble out on to the beach and collapse on all fours on the sand.

'Grace!' Todd stands in front of me. 'If this is some kind of stunt to get out of answering my question, then it's a pretty low blow and –'

But before he can say any more I try to push myself up – and throw up all over his feet.

Chapter Fifteen

'It must've been the fish. Maybe we didn't cook it right.' The Flea passes me a bottle of water and I take a sip.

After I hurled all over Todd we came straight down to the sea to clean up. The others are now gathered round me in a circle – minus Belle who must still be off somewhere in a huff. And Cruz, who I guess is on the boat.

'I knew I should have stayed vegan,' Cariss wails. 'Now we're all gonna get food poisoning.'

I shake my head. 'I don't think so. I think it was the heat in the forest. And that smell. I could hardly breathe.'

'What smell?' Jenna asks.

'I don't know,' Todd says. 'I couldn't smell anything.'

'It has to be the fish then.' Cariss starts wringing her hands together. 'Oh, God – I look so ugly when I vomit.'

I take another sip of water. 'But I'd only just eaten the fish. Doesn't food poisoning take a few hours to kick in?'

Cariss frowns. 'Well, maybe it's some kind of super-fast food poisoning. You know, like in those movies where psycho terrorists develop a mutant strain of, like, chicken flu, to wipe out the entire planet.'

'Well, I'm feeling fine,' the Flea says.

'Me too,' says Ron.

'I feel sweet,' says Dan, and Todd and Jenna nod.

'I guess it must be heatstroke then,' Jenna says.

I nod. 'I'm feeling way better already.'

Ron smirks and pats Todd on the back. 'Looks like you'll be playing volleyball after all then, bud.'

Todd smiles, but I can tell he's pissed. Then I remember what he said to me in the forest about making him look bad in front of his friends. But I don't feel angry any more. I feel relieved. Now I know for absolute certain that I have to end things with him.

'Okay, Todd, you come on my team,' Jenna says, throwing him the ball.

'Shouldn't someone sit with Grace?' the Flea asks. 'What if she gets sick again? We don't want her choking on her own vomit. Although it would be very rock 'n' roll to get shipwrecked *and* die like Janis Joplin all in one week.'

Jenna glances at Todd. Todd stays where he is and starts

twirling the ball on his fingertips.

'I'll be fine,' I say.

'I don't mind doing it.' The Flea comes over to stand by me.

'Okay, great. You keep Grace company and we'll play ball,' Jenna says quickly.

The Flea and I make our way over to a small cluster of palm trees.

'Thank you,' he says, as soon as we've sat down in the shade.

'What for?'

'For being sick.' He smiles apologetically. 'Not that I want you to feel lousy or anything, but the glamorous world of beach volleyball isn't exactly my scene.'

I look at him and laugh. 'Me neither.'

'Really?' He looks genuinely surprised and I think back to my fight with Belle. I guess he must have the same low opinion of me.

'So you're more into fishing then?'

I nod. 'Fishing's great.'

The Flea grins. 'Awesome. You remind me of my mom.'

'I do?' I don't quite know what to make of this news.

The Flea nods, then looks worried. 'That's a very good thing by the way.'

'Oh. Well, thank you.'

'She's what the Women's Institute of America might term, a very spunky gal.'

'*Oh.* Well, thank you again.'

'You're welcome.' The Flea looks down at the others, then back at me. 'Can I ask you something – and if it's too personal please feel free to slap me and call me a darned cad.'

I giggle. 'Okay.'

'Why do you hang out with those guys?'

I immediately look away. 'Jenna and I have been friends for years.'

'And?'

'She's not always how she is in school. She's been through a lot. I guess I'm friends with her because I get to see the real Jenna, although . . .'

'Although she's been a Class A bitch ever since we got here,' the Flea finishes for me.

I don't say anything, but I do smile at him. 'You know what Belle said earlier, about us all acting like we're special because our parents have money?'

The Flea nods.

'I'm honestly not like that. My life isn't perfect at all.'

The Flea reaches out and squeezes my arm. 'Honey, I know that. And Belle wasn't thinking straight, she was just lashing out.' He looks away. 'You know, the first day we started at the Academy I really wanted to be your friend.'

'You did?'

'Uh-huh. I saw you with your nose buried in a copy of *The*

Great Gatsby and I thought to myself, that's my kind of woman. Not that I have a kind of woman, you understand, but in terms of reading material . . .' His face starts to flush.

I laugh and nod. 'I understand. Why didn't you say something?'

He frowns. 'Your buddy Jenna has a great way of erecting an exclusion zone around you guys.'

'Oh. Right. Well, I hope we can be friends now.'

The Flea takes off his hat and grins at me. 'Are you kidding? We've been shipwrecked together! That kind of shit makes us practically family.' Then he looks over his shoulder at the forest. 'This place is a little on the creepy side, isn't it?'

I nod, and for a second I wonder if I should tell him what Cruz told me. But then I'd have to tell him that Cruz can actually speak English and I'm not entirely sure the Flea would be able to keep news that big to himself.

'So, what was the smell you were talking about?' he asks, looking concerned.

The minute I think of the smell I feel sick all over again. 'I don't know. It was real sickly and sweet. Kind of like really strong incense. I felt like I was suffocating.'

The Flea nods. 'There's something very weird about that forest.' He leans closer to me. 'I want to tell you something, but you have to promise not to mention it to the others. I haven't even told Belle . . . I don't want to make her more stressed.'

'What is it?'

'You know the skull, that you thought was left over from Halloween?' he whispers.

'Uh-huh.'

'I don't think it could have been.'

'Why not?'

The Flea glances around before looking back at me. 'It wasn't made of plastic. I've watched enough episodes of CSI to know that that was a *bona* fide skull – excuse the pun.'

I hug my arms round myself. Further down the beach Jenna shrieks with laughter as Todd wrestles the ball off her.

The Flea looks at me, worried. 'Sorry. I didn't mean to rattle you.'

I shake my head. 'It's okay. I was already feeling pretty rattled. We've just gotta hope that the coastguard find us soon.'

'Or Cariss's daddy.'

I laugh. 'Yeah, with his crack unit of Navy Seals.'

'Or failing that, maybe he'll call the A-Team.' The Flea grins, but then he looks around the beach and starts to frown. 'I wonder where Belle got to.'

Secretly I'm pretty relieved she hasn't turned up. It's nice just hanging with the Flea and not having to worry about being shouted at. 'Maybe she's back at camp.'

The Flea nods. 'I hope so. I hope she's getting some rest. She hasn't been sleeping too well at all.' He turns to me and tilts his hat back off his face. 'So, tell me a bit more about yourself,

Miss Grace. What other writers do you like, apart from the literary legend that is F. Scott Fitzgerald?'

The Flea and I end up talking under the trees for most of the afternoon. By the time the others trudge up from their game, breathless and flushed, I know all about his childhood travelling Europe with his playwright dad and actress mom and he knows all about my summers in South Carolina, huntin' and fishin' with my grandpa. I decided to save him from any tales of parental hell, seeing as it was our first ever proper conversation.

'That was awesome!' Jenna exclaims as they reach us. 'Todd and I rock.'

I look at her and force a smile.

'Todd and you cheat,' Dan mutters. 'Don't you guys know it's against the rules to distract the opposing team by making faces at them?'

'Don't be a sore loser, bro.' Todd puts his arm round Dan's shoulders. His tan is even darker now and his hair almost white blond at the ends, bleached by the sun.

'How you doin', Grace?' Dan says with a grin.

'I'm good, thanks. The Flea has been the perfect companion.'

Jenna raises her eyebrows at me. 'I say we go back to camp and have something to eat. I'm starving.'

There's a hungry chorus of agreement and we all start

heading back. Todd doesn't even look in my direction and I'm glad.

'I need to lie down,' Dan says. 'I'm beat.'

'You're beat*en*,' Cariss retorts.

'Beaten by cheats,' Ron says sulkily.

'Yeah, right. It's very undignified to be a bad loser, you know,' Jenna says with a grin. 'Oh my God!' She stops in her tracks and claps her hands to her mouth.

'What is it?' the Flea asks. Then he grabs my arm and looks at me in horror.

The camp has been trashed. The sticks and branches from the shelter, and all of our belongings, are strewn across the floor like a whirlwind's ripped through. Jenna runs a little ways in, then stops dead.

'My bed!' she gasps.

There, in the middle of her yoga mat, is a dead fish, its insides ripped out and smeared all over the purple fabric, like a piece of roadkill.

Chapter Sixteen

'Where is she?' Jenna screams, looking around wildly.

'Who?' I say, stepping toward her.

'That bitch, Belle. Where is she?'

'Hang on a second,' the Flea says, 'You don't think –'

'Who else could it be?' Jenna yells. 'We've all been down by the sea all afternoon.'

The Flea shakes his head. 'But Belle wouldn't do something like this.'

'Oh, no? After the way she behaved toward me this morning, I wouldn't put anything past her.'

'But this is sick.' Todd looks around the camp. 'Why wreck the whole shelter? What did the rest of us do to deserve this?'

'What did *I* do to deserve this?' Jenna covers her face with her hands.

'Hey, don't cry,' Todd says, putting an arm round her. Jenna buries her face in his chest. Ron comes over and pats her awkwardly on the head.

I look around at the carnage, confused. Sure, Belle seemed pretty strung out this morning, but would she really do this? And if she didn't, who did?

'Where is she?' Cariss hisses at the Flea.

The Flea looks shell-shocked. 'How would I know? I haven't seen her since she went off this morning, but I'm telling you, this wasn't her.'

'She did look pretty crazy, bro,' Dan says, putting his arm round the Flea's shoulders.

'What's going on?'

We all turn round at the sound of Belle's voice.

'Where have you been?' the Flea cries.

Jenna runs past him to stand right in front of her. 'How could you?'

'How could I what? Oh my God!' Belle gasps as she sees the wrecked shelter.

'You think this is funny?' Jenna says, pointing to her yoga mat.

Belle looks at the mat and takes a step back.

'What the hell were you thinking?'

Belle stares at Jenna blankly. 'Me?'

'Yes, you.'

'You think I – you think I did this?'

Jenna tosses her hair back over her shoulder and glares at her. 'We don't just think you did it, we *know* you did it.'

'But I –'

'You're the only person who's been unaccounted for since this morning. We've all been with each other at all times. So who else could it have been?'

Belle's face flushes. 'Do you really think I'd do something like this?'

The Flea steps toward her. 'I don't, Beau-Belle. I know you could never do this.'

Belle gives him a weak smile.

'Well, then I suggest you both take your things and get the hell out of here,' Jenna says.

'What?' The Flea looks at her like she's crazy. 'Where are we supposed to go?'

'I don't know and I don't care.'

'But . . .'

'Can't we sort this out another way?' I say.

Jenna's eyes spark with anger. 'What other way? She's wrecked our camp, Grace, who knows what she might do next.'

'I agree,' Todd says. 'She's out of control. I don't want her anywhere near me while I'm sleeping.'

Jenna grins smugly. 'Thanks, Todd. How about you, Ron?'

'Oh, I'm with you one hundred per cent.' Ron turns and glares at Belle. 'I say you get out of here right away.'

Jenna turns to Cariss. 'Cariss?'

Cariss turns and scowls at Belle. 'If you know what's good for you, you'll go right now.'

'Dan?'

Dan looks at Belle and sighs. 'I put a lot work into that shelter, man. You can't go round knocking shit down just cuz you're in a bad mood.'

'I didn't knock it down!' Belle practically screams.

Finally, Jenna turns to me. 'Grace?'

Everyone else looks at me, including Belle and the Flea. I feel really confused. I want to believe that Belle didn't do it, but I don't see who else it can have been. She was so mad this morning. Unless . . . for a second it crosses my mind that it could have something to do with the strange whispers I've been hearing – and the story Cruz told me about the voodoo queen. But that's just downright crazy. Ghosts and zombies do *not* exist. Some spooky voodoo spirit did not wreck our camp.

I look at Jenna. 'But where are they supposed to go?'

'I don't give a damn – as long as that girl isn't anywhere near me,' Jenna says.

'Or me,' Cariss adds.

The Flea goes marching over to get his bag. 'Don't worry. If this is the way it's gonna be then I don't want to be around you guys either. Come on, Belle, let's get out of here.'

'What are you going to do?' I say.

'Don't waste your concern on them, Grace,' Jenna says curtly. 'They're not worth it.'

I shoot her a look and she shuts up.

Belle and the Flea get their things while the rest of us watch. I feel sick. As the Flea walks past me he stops. 'Don't worry,' he whispers. 'We'll set up camp by the trees where we were sitting earlier. Maybe it's better this way – less friction.'

'But I hate the thought of you guys down there on your own.'

'We'll be cool.' He gives me a quick smile. 'It's hardly as if we're going far.'

I force myself to smile and nod. But as I watch them trudge off along the sand I finally understand what it means to have a heavy heart.

By the time we get the camp straightened out the sun is starting to set. I sit under a tree and start reading the one and only novel I brought with me. It's about a girl called Casey who discovers that the only boy she has ever loved is actually a werewolf with anger-management issues. I thought it might be fun, but it's kind of sucky. All Casey seems to do is complain about the fact that she's so unlucky in love. She's got a really annoying best friend too – called Fifi. Fifi's favourite pastime is baking cupcakes and saying things like, 'Oh my gosh, I can't believe he, like, grows hair on his back and everything. That is, like, so totally gross-out!'

I sigh and put the book down on the sand. Dan's lying next to me with his baseball cap pulled down over his face and his white iPod wires plugged into his ears. I wonder what he'll do if his battery runs out before we get rescued. I shove that thought from my mind and look over at Jenna and Cariss. They're both still rearranging their clothes. Ron is sat between them and Dan, casting sneaky glances at Jenna while pretending to play a game on his cell phone. I'm aware of Todd's outline in the corner of my vision, but I have no intention of looking at him. Instead, I look down toward the sea. I wonder how the Flea and Belle are getting on. And Cruz.

Then Jenna leaps to her feet. 'I know. Let's practise our routines.' She walks over to Todd. 'Could you help me with my salsa, Todd?'

'Sure.'

I watch Todd get to his feet and treat Jenna to one of his dazzling grins. *I don't care*, I want to shout to him. *I don't care that you're trying to teach me a lesson and that other girls want to go out with you. I'm way too engrossed in my riveting novel.*

I pick the book up again and study the blurb. *Would you give up everything for love?* the strapline asks. *No, I would not*, I answer in my head, as Todd and Jenna start dancing around the fire.

Ron chucks his phone on the floor. 'Goddamn game!'

Cariss finally finishes folding her clothes and gets to her feet so gracefully it's as if she's being pulled up on a string. She's wearing a coral bikini top and sarong. She looks like a beautiful tropical princess.

'Dan,' she says, looking down at him.

Dan sighs, and takes the baseball cap from his face. 'What?'

I wonder how he heard her over his iPod. Maybe he didn't have it on at all. Maybe the battery has already died and putting his earphones in is his way of trying to get a bit of alone time.

Cariss puts one hand on her hip and puffs her lips into a pout. It's like she can inflate them at will. 'Can you help me? With my routine?'

Dan looks at Jenna and Todd dancing. Then, with a pained expression, like he's got chronic toothache, he pulls his iPod buds from his ears and drags himself up and over to Cariss.

I realize it's just Ron and me left sitting down and I feel a rush of panic. The last thing I want is to end up dancing with him, and have his Lego-man head gazing forlornly at Jenna over my shoulder.

I look back at my book. Casey has just decided that if she can't be with her angry wolf-boy then life really isn't worth living, not even when Fifi has brought her a basket of freshly baked red-velvet cupcakes.

'I'm going for a walk,' I mutter, putting the book back down on the sand. No one seems to notice or care. Jenna giggles as Todd spins her around. Dan and Cariss have started bickering about which routine to practise first. Ron's eyes are still firmly fixed on Jenna.

I go to the edge of the camp and look down at the boat to see if I can spot Cruz, but it's shrouded in darkness. I start walking across the top of the beach, alongside the forest.

'*This way* . . .'

I spin around at the sound of a voice whispering behind me. It's the same voice I thought I heard before. But it's even clearer this time.

'Who's there?' I say, quietly, staring into the forest. 'Belle? Is that you?'

A breeze blows through the trees, causing them to part in front of me, like a doorway opening. The temperature seems to drop suddenly and my skin prickles with goosebumps.

'*This way*.'

I see a shadow flit through the trees.

'Belle?' I rub my eyes and squint harder into the dark. Why would Belle be running round in the forest at night? It's hardly her favourite place. She has a freakin' meltdown every time anyone mentions going in there. But if it isn't Belle then who is it? My heart starts pounding so hard I can feel the vibrations in the tips of my fingers. It can't be any of the others. Cruz and the Flea wouldn't fool around like that and the other guys are all at the camp.

It's the ghost of the voodoo queen, the voice in my head booms.

I picture a tall black woman carrying a skull on a string, striding toward me. I frown. Why does my inner voice always seem intent on freaking me out? The wind whistles through the trees like a sigh and suddenly I get the strangest urge to go into the forest. I take a step forward. It's like I'm a puppet and someone else is controlling my limbs. Despite the sudden chill, sweat starts forming on my forehead.

'That's right – this way . . .'

I take another step forward. *No!* I yell to myself in my head. *Don't go in there.* I feel for the wooden flower in my pocket and clutch it tight. Warmth seeps back into my body and the feeling of being drawn in begins to fade. I force my trembling legs to turn round and start walking back to the camp. What just happened? I feel an overwhelming urge to get back to the others. But, just as I get to the alcove of trees, I see a sight that stops me dead. Jenna and Todd are standing behind the trees, out of sight of the others. Jenna is gazing up at Todd while he says something to her. Then she raises her hand and starts stroking his hair. 'Don't worry,' I hear her say, 'I'm always here for you.'

It's like I've been pushed from the top of a skyscraper and I'm plummeting downwards, out of control. I blink hard – but they're still there when I open my eyes – and she still has her hand on his hair. And as the reality hits me I feel sick to my stomach. But not because of him. Because of her. Jenna doesn't know that I've decided to end it with Todd – as far as she's concerned we're still an item. So why the hell is she getting so up close and personal with him? I take a step back and my foot lands on a twig, snapping it. They both look up.

'Oh, hi, Grace,' Jenna says, quickly stepping away from Todd. Even in the gloom I can see her face flushing. 'We were just . . .'

I look at Todd and he runs his hand through his hair, the way he always does when he's feeling uncomfortable.

'It's okay,' I say breezily. 'I only came back to get something.'

I stumble through the trees into the camp, and start rooting through my case. I see my phone at the bottom of the case and instinctively grab it – as if I could dial 911 and have some calm-voiced operator tell me how to save my rapidly disintegrating life. I shove my phone in my pocket, and start walking off toward the beach.

'Where are you going?' Jenna reaches out for my hand as I pass her.

I yank my hand away. 'For a walk.'

I stride out of the camp, my thoughts going into overdrive. Jenna likes Todd. Maybe Jenna's *always* liked Todd. She's just never been able to do anything about it before. But now she's single, she wants him for herself. I think of the first night we were here, and how badly she wanted the boys and girls to sleep separately. I think of how pissed she got when Todd wanted me to go with him to collect firewood, and how happy she was when we turned up and Todd joined in the volleyball. And how little she cared that I'd been sick.

I stop walking. I'm right in the centre of the beach by the HELP sign. I think about going back to the camp and having it out with her; telling her and Todd where to go. But then I remember that they can't go anywhere – none of us can. I swallow down the urge to scream. How much longer are we going to be stuck on this dumb island? What if no one ever finds us? As I look around the deserted beach I don't think I've ever felt so alone. But I don't want to be with anyone either. I remember the cove, and how nice it had felt to be somewhere secluded. I half walk, half run toward the edge of the bay, and carefully pick my way across the wet rocks. I feel exactly how I did the night my dad came into my bedroom, his face a weird shade of grey, and told me he was leaving. Like someone has scooped out my insides, heart and all. I stumble through the dark rocky tunnel and into the inlet.

As soon as I get there I feel better. It's so nice to feel the security of the rocky walls ranging up around me. I take a deep breath and gaze into the sky. There's no sign of the Milky Way tonight, but I can see a thin slice of moon glinting out from behind a bank of dark cloud. I shut my eyes and listen to the gentle lapping of the water on the rocks. When I open them again I spot a broad-shouldered figure sitting on the stone jetty.

Cruz. He's facing away from me, gazing down into the water. I'm not sure I even want to see *him* right now, but there's no way I'm going back to the others just yet. I pull myself up straight and start making my way toward him.

As I get close he hears me and turns round. He looks so genuinely pleased to see me it hurts. My body feels as if it's crumpling in on itself and, before I can do anything about it, I start to cry.

'Hey! What's up?' He scrambles to his feet and strides over.

I stand in front of him, my shoulders hunched and quivering. 'I just – I just want to go home.'

'What's happened?' He looks so concerned it makes me cry even harder.

'Everything's gone wrong since we got here. There's something really freaky going on in the forest, everybody's fighting, and now – now I've realized that I don't even like my so-called boyfriend – and I can't even trust my so-called best friend.'

Cruz looks at me. 'The ice queen?'

I nod.

He sighs. 'I think she is double-faced.'

'What?' I look at him, my eyes awash with tears. 'Oh – you mean two-faced?' And then we both start to laugh. And once I start laughing I can't stop. I think I might be borderline hysterical, but I don't care. At least I'm not crying any more.

When I finally stop laughing, Cruz looks at me and his face goes all serious. 'I want to ask you something, but I'm not sure if it is right for me to say it to you.'

I wipe my face on my T-shirt sleeve. 'It's okay, go ahead.'

'Why are you with him? Your boyfriend.'

'I'm not – with him. Not any more.'

'You're not?'

'No.'

'That is okay then.'

'That's okay?'

He nods. 'That is how it should be.'

'Oh. Yes – that is how it should be.' As I say the words it feels as if a light has gone on inside my mind and suddenly I can think straight again. Of course it's how it should be – Todd and I should never have gotten together. We're way too different. I look at Cruz and smile. 'You're right.'

'I am always right.' For a split second I think he's being serious but then he throws back his head and laughs. 'I was right about you, anyway,' he says softly.

I seem to have forgotten how to breathe. 'What do you mean?'

'You aren't like the others. You have – you have fire inside of you.'

'Fire?'

Cruz nods. 'That is a very good thing. Fire is life. It is passion.'

Happiness starts unfurling inside of me like a flower. Is that really how he sees me?

'Do you want to dance?'

I do a double-take. 'What?'

'Do you want to dance? With me?'

'Oh. Okay.'

Cruz holds his hands out to me. I take them. They feel warm and strong.

'This will not last forever, you know,' he whispers.

I step closer to him. It feels so good to hold his hands I wouldn't really mind if this moment did actually last forever. As he looks down at me his dark curls fall softly around his face.

'We will get out of here. You will get home.'

I nod.

He pulls me closer to him and panic starts back-flipping inside of me.

'How are we going to dance? We don't have any music. I don't know if –'

'Shhhh.'

I shut up and look at him.

'We do have music.'

'Where?'

'Listen.'

I hold his hands tighter and listen. The water gurgles against the rocks as it trickles past our feet. In the distance I hear the waves rolling and breaking on the beach. And, mingled in with that, the steady whir of the cicadas from way off in the forest. He's right. We do have music, all around us. I step in closer to him and he places one of his strong arms around my waist. Every cell in my body seems to sigh. I try to hold back a bit, but it's no good – I lean into him and rest my head against his chest. I feel his breath rush through my hair. We start to dance, slowly swaying to the sound of the water. His hand presses into my back, moving me closer to him. Then he starts whispering a Spanish word in my ear. I pull my head back a bit to look at him. 'What does that mean?' I whisper.

'Beautiful,' he whispers back.

I start to laugh. 'I'm not beautiful. I go fishing!' I have no idea why I said this. I can just see the heroines in Mom's Pioneer Romance novels throwing off their bonnets in despair.

Cruz doesn't seem to mind though. He laughs and pulls me back toward him. 'And you are beautiful when you fish.'

'I am?'

'Uh-huh. I love the way you watch the water with such, such – concentration – like this.' He scrunches his eyes and sticks his tongue out slightly – just like I do when I fish. Grandpa always says I remind him of a frog trying to catch a fly.

'And you think that's attractive?'

'Oh yes. Would you do it for me now?'

'What? My fishing face?'

He nods, his eyes twinkling in the starlight.

'Seriously? Well, if you insist.' I pull a real exaggerated fishing face, screwing my eyes up tight and sticking my tongue right out.

Cruz laughs. 'Ah, it is like looking at the Mona Lisa.'

'Yeah, right.'

'Yes, right.'

We both laugh. And then his face goes serious again. He lets go of my hand and strokes the side of my face with the tips of his fingers. I shut my eyes and shiver.

'Thank you,' I whisper.

'What for?'

'For wanting to talk to me.'

'How could I not want to talk to you?'

I keep my eyes closed but I know what's going to happen. And I want it to happen so badly I don't even feel nervous any more. I tilt my face upwards and my lips find his. The kiss is as light as the brush of a butterfly wing and yet it courses through every inch of my body.

I open my eyes and look up at him. He's gazing at me with such intensity it makes me blush, but I can't look away. Then he kisses me again and this time the kiss is so deep and heartfelt I can't tell where my mouth stops and his begins. Finally, we come up for air and I lean into him. He wraps his arms tight around me and rests his head on mine. I feel cocooned by his strength and warmth. And for the first time in what feels like forever, I feel safe.

Chapter Seventeen

'Grace! What the hell are you doing?'

I back out of Cruz's arms and spin round.

A figure is standing on the rocks at the entrance to the inlet. A sudden breeze catches her long hair, causing it to lash out in thin, whip-like strands. Jenna.

Cruz puts his hand on my shoulder. I turn back to him and he raises his eyebrows questioningly. I try, and fail, to smile. 'I'm so sorry, I have to go sort this out,' I whisper. My mouth is suddenly dry and my palms clammy. I have plunged from joy to horror in a single instant.

As I walk over to Jenna, panicked thoughts start chattering in my head like a flock of sparrows. She saw me kissing Cruz. She'll tell the others, and then all hell will break loose. Todd and I are over, but he doesn't *know* that we're over – not officially. So officially I've cheated. But what about what *I* saw happen between Jenna and Todd?

When I get to her I'm expecting her to be angry, but she isn't – she looks genuinely shocked.

'Grace?' she says, her eyes wide.

'What?' I force myself to look at her defiantly.

'What were you doing? Why were you kissing him?' she whispers as she looks over my shoulder at Cruz.

I burn with a mixture of anger and shame. 'What were *you* doing?'

She looks back at me, then immediately looks away. 'What do you mean?'

'When I saw you with Todd. When you were stroking Todd's hair.'

Jenna opens her mouth to speak, but no words come out.

'You like him, don't you?'

'No, I . . .' She pauses for a second. 'Is that what this is all about? You thought that Todd and me . . .' She starts to laugh. 'Oh, no, what a mess!' She takes a hold of my hand. 'Of course I don't like him. He's your boyfriend. I was just comforting him that's all.'

I frown, confused. 'Comforting him?'

'Yes.' She smiles. 'Look, I hope you don't mind, but Todd told me about how you don't want to, you know, sleep with him.'

I hate my stupid face as it starts to flush.

'What you have to understand, Grace, is that guys can be very proud about that sort of thing. For someone like Todd it's a real insult that his girlfriend doesn't want him. And if he knew what you've been up to here, well . . .'

My head starts to spin. I don't know what to believe any more.

'I know you obviously weren't thinking straight – you saw Todd and I together and you jumped to totally the wrong conclusion, but come on, Grace, kissing Cruise-Ship to get revenge? That is so Jerry Springer.'

I look down at the sand, not sure what to think or say.

'But it's okay.' Jenna takes a hold of my arm. 'These things happen. I won't say anything. Let's just get back to camp and get some sleep.'

I look over my shoulder at Cruz. He's standing on the stone jetty staring at us. It's too dark to make out his expression. I feel so torn. I don't want to leave him and yet I feel disgusted with myself. How could I kiss someone while I'm still officially going out with someone else? It makes me no better than my dad.

'Come on,' Jenna says.

I want to call out to Cruz and explain what's happening, but then Jenna will realize he can speak English. All I can do is wave goodbye. Cruz stands, motionless. Feeling sick, I turn and start walking away with Jenna.

'I can't believe you thought I liked Todd,' she says, linking arms with me.

'Yeah well, it's been a long day,' I mutter.

We start making our way across the slippery rocks and into the cave-like tunnel. As there's only room to go single file Jenna has to let go of my arm and she steps ahead of me into the dark.

There's something about not being able to see each other that makes me feel able to lower my guard. 'What's happening, Jenna?'

'With what?' her voice echoes back.

'With us. Ever since we left home it feels like something's changed.'

'Well, something *has* changed – we've been shipwrecked!' She's using the forced, sing-song voice she always uses when she's talking to her mom.

'I don't mean that, I mean between us. You and me. Our friendship.' Then I remember the moment on the boat when we thought we were about to drown and Jenna said she had something to tell me. 'What was it that you needed to talk to me about?'

'What do you mean?'

'On the boat, when the storm hit. You said there was something you needed to tell me. What was it?'

Silence. I keep walking and almost bump into Jenna,

who's standing still in front of me.

'I don't know. I can't remember. I'm sure it was nothing.' Her voice sounds panicky. I can tell she's lying.

I desperately want her to turn round. And when she turns round I want her to be exactly how she used to be. I want her to hug me and tell me that it's just the stress of being shipwrecked that's been making her so uptight. I want her to say that everything's going to be just fine; that we're still best friends, and she doesn't prefer Cariss, or like Todd, and then we can walk back to camp together and pretend like none of this ever happened.

'Come on, let's get back,' she says, without turning round. 'You're right – it's been a very long day.'

As she walks off into the dark I feel our years of friendship slipping like sand from my grasp. I don't know why, but everything is different. And I'm filled with the certain, ominous feeling that nothing will ever be the same again.

Back at what's left of our camp the others are all sitting around the fire staring into the dying flames.

'Where did you go?' Todd says, jumping to his feet as soon as he sees us.

'She was just down by the rocks,' Jenna says quickly.

'Can I speak with you please?' I say to Todd.

He looks at me questioningly.

'Alone.'

Jenna frowns. 'Maybe we should all just go to bed.'

'I need to talk to Todd,' I say, still looking straight at him.

'O-kay,' Todd says hesitantly. Then he walks past me and starts heading toward the beach.

'Grace,' Jenna whispers urgently. But I shake my head at her and go after Todd.

'So. What's up?' Todd says, coming to a standstill by the HELP sign. He doesn't turn round though. I guess he knows what I've got to say isn't going to be good.

'I – I don't think that you and I should go out any more.' My mouth is suddenly so dry I can barely swallow.

He spins round to face me. 'What?'

'I just don't think we have enough in common. I mean, I did to begin with, when you told me about your sister and –'

'What's Ingrid got to do with it?' He stares at me like I'm crazy.

'That night we went for the Infamous Root-Beer Floats? The night you asked me out?'

He nods.

'I thought the fact that we both came from messed-up families meant that we ought to be together. But that can't be your main reason for dating someone. It's nuts.'

Todd frowns. 'I don't come from a messed-up family.'

I sigh and look away. 'No. I don't mean . . . I just mean that you've had things tough too, so . . .'

'So now you're gonna make things tougher?'

'No. Well, I . . .'

He takes a step toward me and I'm amazed to see tears in his eyes. 'I've never told anyone what I told you about Ingrid. I thought I could trust you.'

'You can! I've never told anyone about it either. And I never will. But what I'm trying to say is, just because two people have problems at home it doesn't mean they ought to be together. You have to have other stuff in common too.'

'What other stuff?'

'Like being able to talk to each other.'

Todd shakes his head. 'We are able to talk to each other. What are we doing right now?'

'No, I mean to be able to really talk – and listen.'

'I do listen.' He scowls at me. 'What the hell is wrong with you, Grace?'

Anger prickles beneath my scalp. 'I know, I know, other girls would kill to be in my place. I get the picture. But I'm not other girls. I'm me – and I need to be with someone who understands me.'

I wait for him to start telling me how lucky I am and how great he is, but he doesn't. Instead he hangs his head and scuffs his toe in the sand. 'Did you ever wonder why I asked you out?' he mutters.

I wait till he looks up at me, then I nod.

'It's because you're different to the others.'

I'm shocked. This was not what I was expecting him to say at all. 'What do you mean?'

'You actually care about what I've been through and who I am as a person. Do you know how much that means to someone like me?'

I look at him blankly.

Todd gives a really heavy sigh. 'A lot of times I don't know if girls are just with me cos of the way I look.' Then he frowns and looks away. 'But if you're dumping me then you clearly aren't the person I thought you were.' He takes a deep breath. 'So I'd rather not be with you anyway.'

We look at each other. For a split second I see something like hope in his eyes. Then the moment passes and his eyes harden. I don't know what to say.

Todd shakes his head. 'Great. Well, nice knowing you.'

'Todd!'

'What?'

'Can't we – I mean – do we have to – does it have to be so harsh? Can't we be friends?'

He looks at me and shakes his head. 'No one dumps me and gets to stay my friend. You had your chance, Grace, and you blew it.'

I sigh and look away.

Todd stalks back up to the camp. I feel totally drained, but I know I've done the right thing. I glance down toward the boat. I wonder where Cruz is. Did he stay at the inlet after we left? Should I go look for him and explain why I had to leave?

A piercing shriek rings out from the forest. I guess it's a bird . . . but who knows on this island. It chills me to the core. I turn and hurry after Todd. The thought of roaming off on my own in the darkness is not appealing at all. I'll talk to Cruz tomorrow, when I'm not so wrung out.

When I get to the camp the others are all in bed. Todd is standing by his things, packing his bag.

'It's okay,' I whisper. 'I'll go sleep by the girls.'

He looks at me and nods. And again, just for a moment, I catch a glimpse of the Todd I like.

'I'm sorry,' I whisper, my eyes filling with tears.

He nods again and puts his stuff back down.

I pick up my case and drag it past the dying fire and over next to Jenna. I lie down on the sand. My body feels as heavy as lead.

Jenna opens her eyes and looks at me. 'What happened?' she whispers. Seeing her lying so close to me reminds me of the countless sleepovers we've had in the past, but it just makes what's happened tonight all the more painful.

'I need to get some sleep,' I whisper back. 'Night.'

I roll away on to my side and wait for her to say, 'Don't let the bedbugs bite' like she always does. But she doesn't say a thing. The silence is filled with the shrieks and hisses from the forest. I pull my towel blanket up over my head and try counting my blessings. But this time none come.

The smoke swirls around my face, forcing itself up my nose and into my mouth. I bring my hand up to try and stop myself choking. Then I open the door. The heat beats me back like a physical being. I hunch over, gasping for air. But then I hear the baby crying from along the hall. I have to get to him. I have to save him. I stagger blindly into the heat.

'Burn! Burn! Burn!' The men yell.

Why? Why are they doing this? Why didn't I keep his crib in with me? I can't let him die. But I can't breathe. There's too much smoke. Oh please. Oh no. Why has he gone quiet? Don't die! Please, don't die!

I sit bolt upright, shaking violently. The smoke still swirls all around me, but now it's cold. And damp. I blink hard and the nightmare fades. It's not smoke – it's some kind of mist. I'm in the camp. There's no fire. No baby. I pull up the hood on my sweatshirt and hug my knees to my chest. Why do I keep having this dream? And then I remember what Cruz told me, about Hortense's house burning down, and her baby dying. My skin starts to prickle. Am I dreaming about Hortense? But that doesn't make any sense – I was having the dream about the fire before I even know she existed.

'Jenna?' I hear Cariss say. 'What's going on?'

I look down to my right and can just make out Jenna asleep next to me.

'It's okay,' I whisper to Cariss. 'I guess it's some kind of sea mist.'

I hear Cariss sigh. 'How are the helicopters gonna find us if it's like this?'

But there's a dullness in her voice – like she doesn't really believe the helicopters are going to come any more.

'What's up?' Dan mutters. I hear him fumbling about. 'Hey! What's happened?'

'It's okay,' I say. 'I think it's a sea mist, it'll clear once the sun comes up.'

Jenna stirs next to me.

'Jenna, wake up!' Cariss says loudly. 'The whole island's been taken over by a hideous fog.'

'Oh my God,' I hear Ron call out. 'I can't see a thing!'

'Jenna,' Cariss says again, louder.

'What?' Jenna sighs and sits up. 'Oh, shit!'

'Exactly!' Cariss exclaims. 'I swear, this place is a freakin' nightmare. If I run out of hair serum before we're rescued I think I'll die.'

'Here's hoping,' Dan mutters.

'Don't think that just because you can't see me I'm not giving you a filthy look,' Cariss says.

'Well, don't think that just cuz you can't see me I'm not showing you my ass,' Dan replies. 'Cuz I am. Both cheeks.'

Cariss shrieks. 'Oh my God, you're so gross!'

I lie back down and gaze up into the mist. It's like looking into a veil of cobwebs.

'Hey, Todd, man, wake up,' Ron says. 'Check out the mist.'

Todd groans. 'I only just got to sleep.' I hear him move about. 'Geez!'

Jenna pulls her hair back and looks at me. 'What happened with you guys last night?' she whispers.

I shake my head. 'Not now,' I whisper back.

Jenna frowns.

I shut my eyes. I need more time alone, even if it's just inside my head. I picture my bedroom. I imagine I'm curled under the patchwork quilt on my bed, listening to the sounds of my neighbours floating in through the window. I miss home so much I actually ache. It's so ironic. All the hours I spent lying on my bed feeling mad at my parents and wishing I could escape, yet right now I'd give anything to be back there, listening to rock ballads and writing angst-ridden entries in my journal. Part of me doesn't want the mist to go, so I never have to face Todd or Cruz or Jenna again. But maybe this will be the day we finally get rescued. It's only because we're on the island that things seem such a mess, I remind myself.

'I think it's starting to clear,' Ron says, and he's right because when I open my eyes I can see him now, and behind him I can just make out Todd's outline.

'Thank God for that,' Cariss says.

'Shall we go get some coconuts?' Jenna says, standing up.

'Sure.' I get to my feet too. Anything's better than lying there driving myself crazy.

'You okay, bro?' Ron says to Todd as he gets to his feet.

'I'm fine,' Todd says defiantly.

We wait for Dan to get up, then all head down the beach.

'I think we should try looking for something else to eat,' Dan says. 'Seriously, I think I'm starting to turn into a freakin' coconut.'

'No, you're just naturally hairy,' Cariss snips. It looks like she's going to launch into another full-blown Dan-attack when she pauses suddenly, her eyes wide.

We stop to look at her and I immediately get a sinking feeling.

'What's up now?' Dan says. 'You run out of hair serum? You broke an eyelash?'

Cariss just shakes her head and stares in front of her.

We all turn and follow her gaze.

Cariss slowly points to the HELP sign. The mist is curling off the letters like smoke, but it's still clearly visible.

Instead of spelling HELP, the letters now spell HELL.

Chapter Eighteen

There's a moment where we all stand motionless like we're in a freeze-frame and then we start racing toward the sign. As my feet pound across the sand I try to figure out what's happened. Maybe the wind blew the sticks out of place in the night? But as soon as I get up close I can see that somebody has actually wiped out the letter P, dug out a letter L in its place and refilled it with sticks. There's no way it could have been an accident.

'I hate this place,' Cariss wails.

But Jenna frowns and shakes her head. 'Don't panic. I think we all know who's responsible.'

Cariss stares at her blankly. 'Who?'

Jenna looks over to the cluster of palm trees where the Flea and Belle have set up camp.

'Of course,' says Ron, shaking his head. 'To get revenge for being made to move.'

'Man, that girl is insane,' Todd mutters.

'Come on,' Jenna says. 'Let's go have it out with her.'

'Hey, we don't know it was . . .' I begin, but the others are already making their way across the beach. As I follow them through the mist my body feels wearier with every step. When is this nightmare going to end? Why do so many bad things keep happening? By the time we get to the palm trees all I want to do is bury myself deep into the sand and never come out.

Belle and the Flea are huddled together talking. When they see us Belle groans and pulls her knees closer to her chest. The Flea looks as exhausted as I feel.

'I suppose you think that's funny?' Jenna says, standing in front of Belle with her hands on her hips.

Belle sighs and looks at the ground. 'What now?'

'Doing that to the sign.'

Belle looks genuinely confused. 'Doing what to the sign?'

'Changing HELP to HELL.'

Belle frowns at her. 'What?'

'You heard.'

'I heard, but I don't get what you're trying to say.'

Cariss comes and stands right next to Jenna. 'Don't you think it's bad enough being stuck here without you playing your immature games?'

Belle gets to her feet and glares back at them. 'I don't know what you're talking about.'

The Flea scrambles to his feet and looks over at the sign. He gasps in shock. 'Whoa.'

'Exactly.' Jenna snaps, keeping her eyes on Belle.

'But Belle didn't do that,' the Flea says, looking back at Jenna.

Cariss turns to face him. 'How do you know?'

'I've been with her all night.'

Cariss gives a snarky little laugh. 'Well then, maybe you both did it.'

The Flea takes off his hat. His face is pale and his eyes are ringed with dark shadows. 'That's crazy. Why would we mess up the one thing that could get us rescued?' He gestures at Belle and himself. 'Does it look like we're having the time of our lives here?'

I look at Belle. Her black hair is scraped right back into a ponytail and her face is etched with worry lines. She seems to have aged ten years since we've been here.

Belle runs over to the sign. 'We've gotta change it back,' she cries. 'What if the coastguard come? They won't know we need help.'

We watch as she starts frantically trying to rearrange the sticks.

'I don't think she did it,' Dan says.

I nod. 'The Flea's right. It wouldn't make any sense. We've

all seen how desperate she is to get back home.'

The Flea gives me a grateful smile.

Jenna frowns.

'Well, if she didn't do it, who did?' Cariss asks.

Jenna looks straight at me. 'What about Cruise-Ship?'

'No way!' I say. The others all turn to look at me. I eye-swerve Todd's glare. 'Why would he do it? I'm sure he wants to get away from here just as much as the rest of us.'

'Exactly,' says the Flea. 'Why would any of us do it?'

'But how do you know that?' Jenna says, still looking at me. 'I mean, how well do any of us know him?'

'He has acted pretty strange since we got here,' Ron says.

'We've all acted pretty strange since we've got here,' I say, looking straight at Jenna. She looks away.

'Yeah, what about the way he freaked out when we found the pendant?' Todd says.

I sigh. 'He didn't freak out, he just walked off.'

'That was pretty weird though,' Dan says.

Ron nods. 'It was very weird. And what about the way he treated you, Jen, when you asked him to dance with you?'

Jenna shakes her head theatrically. 'Don't remind me.'

'He's given me the creeps ever since we got on the boat,' Cariss says. 'The moment I discovered he couldn't speak English I got a really bad feeling about him.'

'Are you for real?' Anger fills me, red and hot.

Cariss glares at me. 'What?'

'The guy doesn't speak English so that means there's something creepy about him?' I turn to Jenna. 'And he tells you he doesn't want to dance with you, so he has to be insane?'

Ron gives a sarcastic little laugh. 'Any guy who doesn't want to dance with Jenna must need their head examined.'

Jenna treats Ron to one of her most dazzling smiles. Then she turns to me and shakes her head. 'Grace, I have to tell you I'm getting more than a little pissed with you right now. If I were you I'd be very careful what you say to me.'

I stare at her. I know exactly what she's implying – if I say any more she'll tell everyone she saw me and Cruz kissing last night. But if she wants to play that game she's forgetting the things I know about her – things she would *hate* for everyone to know. And the more I think about it, the more mad I get at what a major hypocrite she's being.

'I'll say what I like,' I tell her. 'You're not the only one who's a little pissed right now.'

'Grace, I'm warning you.'

'No! *I'm* warning *you*!' I yell. My whole body is crackling with rage. 'I don't think you're in any position to judge anyone.'

'I think you should cool it, Grace,' Todd says, going to stand next to Jenna.

Seeing them standing so close reminds me of how I saw them last night and it makes me even angrier. I keep on staring at Jenna, determined not to be the first to look away. Jenna finally looks down. I glance around and see that everyone else is staring at me – even Belle, who's stopped re-building the sign and is looking at me across the beach, open-mouthed. Great. Now I guess they all think *I'm* the crazy one.

'We sure are getting to see everyone's true colours in this place,' Cariss says smugly.

I glare at her. 'Yes. We sure are.' I turn away from them. 'I'm going for a walk,' I mutter and start storming up the beach. If I stay there any longer I know I'm going to say something I'll regret.

'Grace!' I hear the Flea call out after me, but I keep on walking. I take a deep breath to try and calm myself and immediately start to cough. The sickly sweet scent is back again and seems to have wrapped itself around me. Even when I pull the top of my sweater up over my nose, the smell seeps through the fabric and down into my throat. I want to turn and run back to the others but I can't. My limbs feel as if they've been put in iron casts.

'*Don't be afraid*,' I hear the voice whisper, clear as a bell. This time, it's like it's coming from inside my head. '*Come to the forest*,' she says.

My left leg steps forward, then my right. It's the weirdest sensation. My mind wants me to run the opposite way, screaming, but my body won't obey.

'*That's right*,' the voice urges. '*Come to me*.'

My legs keep moving robotically toward the forest. The trees loom above me like giants, their branches huge arms beckoning me closer.

My legs move faster and my heart starts pounding in time. I want to yell at my body to stop but my thoughts are so confused, like my mind can't find the right words any more. I want to go to the forest. I *need* to go. But what about the others?

'*You don't need the others*,' the girl's voice soothes. '*They don't matter any more. They don't understand*.'

I run into the forest. She's right – the others *don't* understand – all they want to do is bitch and fight. I need to find this girl; she knows what I've been going through; she understands.

'*Just keep coming, you'll find me*.' Her voice is as smooth as honey. It has a slight accent that I can't quite place.

I run past the tree with the skull. It's waving back and forth, but there's still no breeze. I don't feel scared. I don't feel anything apart from the desperate need to keep going deeper into the forest. I have to find her. I have to.

I get to the end of the clearing and start scrambling through some bushes. I see a shadow flit by on the other side.

'*Come on – follow me!*'

I fight and claw my way past the tangle of sharp branches – I need to catch up with her, I –

And then I hear something crack over to my left.

'*NO!*' her voice screams, suddenly shrill and harsh.

It's like being jolted from a dream. As I turn round to see what made the noise all of the life rushes back into my body. I look around wildly. It's like being trapped inside a giant web of green. Plants close in on me from every side. Then I hear another twig snap and the sound of someone gasping. My skin crawls with fear.

'Who's there?' I say, my voice trembling. I reach into my shorts pocket for the wooden flower Cruz gave me and start moving quietly through the bushes in the direction of the noise. I stop when I hear the sound of someone breathing heavily. I crouch down and peer through the leaves, and see a sight that nearly makes my heart stop. A man is staggering through the trees on the other side of the bushes. He's literally just a few feet away from me, but it's so dark he looks like a shadow.

'Wait!' I shout, pushing my way through to him. 'Please. You have to help us. We're shipwrecked. We –'

But I'm so desperate to get to him I don't look where I'm going. Something catches my ankle and sends me flying forward. I land flat on my face and pain floods into my leg, raw and hot.

'Please stop!' I cry, trying to free my ankle from a thick, prickly vine. But as I pull the vine off it tears into my skin, causing blood to spring up like drops of red ink. I grit my teeth and pull myself up . . . but the man has gone. I spin around, trying to spot any sign of life, but there's nothing. Until I hear a hissing noise over to my right. I turn and see a snake gliding along a branch toward me.

I try to swallow, but my mouth's too dry. I can hear my blood pounding; every nerve ending in my body is on high alert. I start backing off very slowly. My foot hits something round and hard. My ankle rolls but I manage to steady myself. I look down and see a bottle on the floor. It's made of thick brown glass, slightly misshapen. It's the kind of bottle you might find in an antique store – the kind pirates would store their grog in. Keeping my eyes fixed on the snake, I slowly bend down and pick up the bottle. The snake starts uncoiling itself upwards until it looks just like the symbol on the pendant. I force my shaking legs to straighten, then edge back through the bushes and find myself in the clearing that leads to the beach. Then I turn and run, as fast as I can.

Chapter Nineteen

'So what did he look like?'

'Did he say anything?'

'How old was he?'

I sit on the sand, trying to get my breath back while the others cluster round, firing questions at me.

'What do you think's in the bottle?' the Flea asks.

I shrug. 'I don't know.'

'Shall we open it and see what it is?' Dan says.

'I don't know,' Jenna says. 'I say we go look for him first.'

'Yeah.' Todd brushes the sand from his shorts like he's preparing for battle. 'Come on, before he gets too far away.'

'But the snakes!' Cariss says, folding her arms. 'I'm not setting foot in there.'

I get to my feet and pain rips through my ankle. There's

a ring of pink in the sand from my blood.

The Flea grabs a hold of my arm. 'There's no way you're going back in there either, Grace. You need to get that cut seen to.'

'There's a first-aid kit on the boat,' Belle says. I look at her and to my surprise she actually smiles at me. 'Remember, when I cut my head in the storm?'

I nod. I do remember. I remember watching Cruz bandage her. My heart does some kind of freaky double beat as I think of having to see Cruz again after last night. Then I look at Jenna. She's glaring at me the way her mom glares at her when she hasn't done enough dance practice. She turns to Ron, Dan and Todd.

'Let's go,' she says.

'I'm staying here,' Cariss says, sitting down on the sand as if to prove her point.

'Yeah, you said that already.' Dan looks at her and shakes his head.

Jenna crouches next to Cariss. 'Okay, hun,' she says, squeezing Cariss's hand. 'We won't be long.'

Even after everything she's done I still feel a stab of hurt watching them.

'You take care in there,' Cariss says.

'Oh, I'll be fine with these guys,' Jenna says breezily as she gets back up, holding the bottle.

'I'll take Grace down to the boat to get her ankle seen to,' the Flea says, smiling at me. His smile is like an airborne hug, and it fills me with relief that we're friends.

Belle walks over to us. 'I'll come too.'

Jenna turns away. 'Fine. Come on then, guys, let's go.'

Todd looks at me for a nanosecond, then looks away.

Despite everything, a wave of dread washes over me as I think of them going into the forest. I wonder if I should tell them about the freaky feeling I had of being pulled in before. But there's no way of explaining it without sounding totally nuts. 'Be careful,' I say quietly.

Todd nods. Then they all start walking up the beach.

'So, are you guys going to the boat?' Cariss asks as soon as they've gone.

'Yes, *we* are,' Belle says, making it clear Cariss isn't welcome to join us.

'I guess I'll just wait here then,' Cariss says.

'You do that,' Belle snaps. 'Are you okay to walk, Grace, or do you want to lean on me and Jimmy?'

'I think I'm okay,' I say, but as soon as I put my weight on my foot I wince from the pain. I guess I must have sprained my ankle when I fell.

'Come on, hitch a ride,' the Flea says, offering me his arm. Belle immediately walks around to my other side and offers me hers.

'Don't worry about me,' Cariss calls after us. 'I'll just do some yoga.'

'Great idea,' the Flea yells. Then he drops his voice to a whisper. 'Hope you get stung by the cobra.'

Belle and I start to giggle. Then Belle looks at me and smiles – a genuine, shy smile. 'Listen, Grace, I'm real sorry for what I said to you yesterday. I know you're not like them. I had no right speaking to you that way.'

Just like when the Flea smiled at me, I feel another rush of warm relief. I give her arm a squeeze. 'Thanks.'

We carry on walking slowly toward the boat. 'What you said before was awesome,' the Flea says. 'It was like watching Judge Judy in action. When you said, "No, *I'm* warning *you*," I nearly died!'

Belle laughs again. But I feel a little sick. I can't believe I even considered telling the others about Jenna. No matter how much of a bitch she was being, she didn't deserve that. There's no doubt about it – this place is starting to make us all wacko. Look at what happened to me in the forest.

I feel a sudden, overwhelming urge to see Cruz – he's the only person I can tell about what really happened; the only person who won't think I'm going nuts. I hope.

But by the time we reach the boat a new set of worries is crowding my mind. Is Cruz mad at me for going off with Jenna last night? Does he think I regret kissing him? *Do* I regret kissing him? I'm so confused by everything that's happened I don't know what I think.

Belle shouts something in Spanish. There's no sign of life on the boat. Maybe Cruz is at the inlet. But then Belle calls out again and Cruz slowly emerges from the hold. His chin is shaded in dark stubble and his eyes look hollow with tiredness. I clench my hands together as he stares down at me blankly. Then Belle tells him something in Spanish and he looks back at me, his eyes now wide with concern. He says something to Belle then disappears back into the hold.

'He's going to get the first-aid kit,' she explains.

I nod, unable to speak. Seeing Cruz again has made at least one thing clear – I definitely don't regret kissing him.

In a few seconds Cruz is back and leaping down from the boat. He crouches in front of me and takes my foot in his hands. Leaning on Belle and the Flea, I lift my leg slightly so he can get a better look at my ankle. Cruz opens the first-aid kit and takes out some sterile wipes. Very gently he wipes at the torn skin. I grit my teeth as the antiseptic burns into me. Once he's cleaned the cuts he fetches a dressing from the box and bandages it in place. Then he says something to Belle in Spanish.

'He says no swimming for a couple of days,' she tells me.

I look down at Cruz and nod.

He lightly strokes the sole of my foot with his thumb. It's

such a fleeting thing that no one else would have noticed, but every nerve in my body seems to be throwing a party.

Cruz lets go of my foot and starts packing up the first-aid box. I sit down on the sand to rest my ankle.

Belle begins telling Cruz about the man in the forest.

I watch his face as she recounts my story and again I feel all weird inside as he frowns with concern.

When Belle's finished, Cruz says something to her and she nods.

'He's asking if you'd like to have a lie-down on the boat,' she explains. 'You look as if you could do with some rest.'

'You do look pretty pale, honey,' the Flea says.

I glance at Cruz and he nods at me.

'Okay,' I say. 'But what will you guys do?'

'I say we go get some coconuts, I'm starving,' says the Flea.

Belle nods. 'You'll be okay with him,' she says to me. 'He's a really nice guy.'

I smile. If only she knew. Then Cruz holds out his hand to me. I take it, and hope he can't feel that I'm suddenly trembling. As Belle and the Flea head off, he helps me up the ladder on to the boat.

'Grace, what are you doing?' I hear Cariss yell down the beach to me.

'She's getting some rest,' the Flea calls back.

'Yeah, so butt out,' Belle shouts.

With Cruz right behind me, I hobble over to the entrance to the hold. I'm suddenly hit by a terrifying flashback to the moment in the storm when I thought I was going to die. I take a deep breath and head down the steps into the dark.

The hold is a whole lot tidier than when I last saw it. Cruz has got rid of all the water and built a makeshift bed out of seat cushions and life jackets in one corner. A paraffin lamp is burning in another corner. The flickering orange glow gives the place an almost cosy feel.

As soon as we're both down there I start talking. I have to clear things up right away before I can tell him what's happened. I don't care how awkward or embarrassing it is.

'I'm so sorry about last night,' I say, turning to him. 'Leaving the way I did. But I had to go see Todd. To explain.'

Cruz looks at me blankly. 'Explain what?'

'That I couldn't be his girlfriend.' I look away and hold my breath. I feel a weird mixture of sadness and relief. Sadness that Cruz will probably hate me now, relief that I've been honest with him.

'But I thought you and he were not together.'

I look back at Cruz and his bewildered expression makes me feel sick with shame. 'We're not. Not now.' Cruz steps away from me and sits down on the bed. I go and stand in front of him. 'In my head I'd decided to end it with him before I saw you last night. But I was putting off telling him till we got off the island. I thought it would be easier that way.' My face starts to burn. 'I didn't realize that you and I would end up kissing. I'm not the kind of girl who kisses other guys behind her boyfriend's back. When Jenna saw us I felt terrible – that's why I had to go tell him.' I stop, out of breath from talking so fast.

Cruz looks even more shocked. 'You told him about us kissing?'

I shake my head. 'No. No! I just told him I couldn't be with him any more.'

I sit on the bed, as far away from him as I can, feeling completely deflated.

Cruz shifts a bit closer to me. I look down into my lap.

'And what did he say to that?'

'What?'

'When you told him that you didn't want to be with him any more.'

'He told me he didn't want to be with me any more if I didn't want to be with him any more.'

Cruz starts to laugh.

'What's so funny?'

'It makes me think I was right about him.'

'What do you mean?'

'He is a jackal-ass.'

'A jackal-ass?' I'm so puzzled I forget to be embarrassed

and look at Cruz for a moment. 'Oh a jackass!' I start to laugh. 'Maybe. I just wish . . .'

Cruz looks at me and his eyes are soft and twinkly again. 'You just wish?'

'I just wish everything didn't have to be so complicated.'

Cruz taps the side of his head. 'This is where things become complicated. We make them so, in our heads.'

'But, I'm not making this up.'

He smiles and shakes his head. 'So, what is complicated?'

I clasp my hands together, suddenly feeling about seven years old. My first ever relationship has ended in disaster and now I'm insanely attracted to a guy who seems so worldly and cool there's no way I'd be able to keep up. I'm a flat-chested virgin massively out of my depth. And that sounds like a very bad country and western song. *I* sound like a very bad country and western song. I sigh. 'This. This is complicated.' I'm way too embarrassed to look at him. 'Us.' I say it so quietly I'm not sure he's even heard.

'What is complicated about us?'

'How you make me feel.' I immediately cringe. Why did I have to say that?

'How do I make you feel?' He places one of his hands on mine. Tingles start running up my arms like electrical charges.

'Like I've been electrocuted.' Oh God! My face is now so

red I'm sure it must be lighting up the entire hold. 'Sorry. That sounds stupid. I mean you make me feel alive.'

'But I thought electrocuted was dead?'

'It is.' I frown. 'Well, I guess sometimes you can survive an electric shock, if you're, like, wearing shoes with rubber soles or something. Or if you're holding something wooden. Or you're with someone who knows how to give CPR.' My mouth is like a runaway train – I take a deep breath and try to regain some kind of control. 'When I said electrocuted what I meant was all kind of tingly and buzzy inside. Not, you know, like, foaming at the mouth and hair all standing on end.'

Cruz starts to laugh and laugh. At first I feel mortified, but his laughter is infectious and pretty soon I'm bent over double too. Finally we calm down and Cruz shifts round on the bed so that he's facing me.

'When I first saw you I felt as if I knew you already,' he says.

'That's how I felt too! You were exactly like –' I stop myself just in time. Telling him I had an imaginary boyfriend would tip what's already an excruciating mess into complete and utter catastrophe.

'Exactly like?' Cruz grins – dimple, dimple.

'No one.'

'Someone you used to know?'

'Yes. No. Well, he didn't actually exist.' I shrink back against the wall of the boat.

Cruz looks totally dumbfounded. 'I looked like someone who did not exist? Sorry. My English is not the greatest. I don't understand.'

I sigh. *Sometimes, the only way around a problem is through*, I hear my grandpa saying. It's his favourite expression. And let's face it, I've blown any remote chance I had of seeming sophisticated and experienced, so I may as well just bite the bullet.

'I-used-to-have-an-imaginary-boyfriend-and-he-looked-just-like-you,' I say so fast the words practically blur into one. I close my eyes and wait for Cruz to ask me to please leave the boat.

'Really?'

I keep my eyes closed and nod. I am mortified with a capital M and three exclamation points.

'You know, my mother, she says that sometimes if we imagine a thing hard enough we can actually make it into being.'

I open one eye cautiously and squint at Cruz. He's looking all serious so I don't think he's making fun of me.

'What was he called?' he says.

I shut my eyes again. 'What?'

'Your imaginary boyfriend. What was he called?'

Will this torture never end? 'Ashton,' I mutter. I'm so embarrassed even my eyelashes feel as if they're blushing.

'Hmmm.'

'What?'

'Ashton's okay, I guess. My imaginary girlfriend was called Phoenix.'

'You had an imaginary girlfriend?' I'm so shocked at this revelation my eyes pop back open. Cruz is so handsome I'd imagine him having real-life girlfriends pretty much from the moment he left the womb. Like all the other babies on the maternity ward would stop crying and start cooing whenever he was carried past their cribs.

'Sure. It is a lot easier when you're shy. You always know the right things to say to an imaginary girl.' Cruz looks away and I realize that now he's embarrassed too.

'Did Phoenix look like me?'

'No.'

'Oh.'

'My imagination was not that . . . good.'

'Oh.' I try to decode what he just said. It seems like a good thing, I guess. Cruz looks back at me. 'So, tell me, why is this – us – complicated?'

'I don't know. I've never felt like this before. I don't know how to act.'

He frowns. 'Acting is what they do in movies, right?'

I nod.

'It isn't real.'

I shake my head.

'So, don't act.'

'I didn't mean *act* act. I meant I don't know what to do.'

'What do you want to do?'

I cringe. Why does he have to go and ask me that? Now I'm bound to say something stupid again.

'In your heart. What do you want to do? Don't listen to your head – that is where it gets complicated.'

I've never really tried to listen to my heart before. To be honest, most times there's so much going on in my head I don't think I could cope if my heart wanted to join in the conversation too. But I somehow manage to stop myself from saying this to Cruz and instead I focus on just relaxing my body and imagining what it would like to do. I immediately start to blush again. It would appear that it would like to curl up on the bed with Cruz and fall asleep in his arms.

Cruz shifts even closer to me. 'Do you know what I want to do?'

I shake my head, scared to even breathe.

'I want to hold you.'

'Really?'

'Uh-huh.'

'That's what I want too!'

Cruz starts to smile and I swear I can actually feel my heart dancing a jig inside my ribcage. 'So, you see, it isn't complicated at all.' He shifts forward so that he's sitting right on the edge of the bed. 'Do you want to lie down?' he whispers.

I nod. Then I slide down on to my side, right up against the wall so there's room for him to lie next to me.

He lies down and pulls me close. I nestle my head against his chest. I can hear his heart beating. It's pounding as fast as mine. Then he wraps both of his strong arms around me. His skin smells salty, like the sea.

'Are you okay?' he whispers into my hair.

I nod again.

He pulls me even tighter. 'You are not feeling electrocuted?'

I laugh. 'No.'

'You are not feeling complicated?'

'No,' I whisper. I don't feel complicated at all.

Chapter Twenty

At first we just lie there, listening to the lap of the waves on the shore. But then Cruz starts stroking my hair, and it feels exactly like the night before at the inlet. I know he's going to kiss me. But although I want him to kiss me so bad I feel I might actually burst, I know I have to tell him what happened to me in the forest.

'There's something I have to tell you,' I mutter into Cruz's chest.

'Uh-oh,' he says with a nervous laugh.

'No – nothing like that. It's something that happened when I was in the forest.'

Cruz shifts up on to his elbow and looks down at me. His dark curls fall forward and I fight the urge to reach out and touch them.

'What is it?' He starts stroking his finger up and down my arm and I feel electrocuted all over again.

'Well, it felt like I wasn't in control of my body.'

Cruz frowns. 'What do you mean?'

I sit up, embarrassed. 'It was like something – or someone – was making me go deeper into the forest.' I think about telling him about the whispered voice but decide against it. I don't want him thinking I'm totally out of my tree.

'You felt like you were being made to go in there against your will?' Cruz sits upright and stares at me.

'Yes.' I suddenly feel dangerously close to tears. Actually saying what happened out loud makes it seem even stranger – and scarier. 'I don't know what's happening to me.'

Cruz immediately puts his arm round my shoulders. I lean into him and close my eyes but it's no good – I can feel tears burning behind my eyelids.

'When did you last eat?' he asks gently.

'I don't know. Yesterday. Before I got sick. And that's another thing –' I open my eyes and the tears spill on to my face – 'I keep smelling this horrible sickly smell – and – and . . .'

Cruz holds me tightly as I start to cry.

'There are bound to be strange smells in there,' he says gently. 'It's a rainforest. And maybe it is also your hunger – and the heat? Maybe they caused you to feel these things?'

'Maybe . . .'

Cruz gets off the bed and goes over to a cupboard. He takes something out and comes back over and crouches on the floor in front of me.

'Eat,' he says, holding out some kind of candy bar with foreign writing on the wrapper.

'Do you have any more?' I say, eyeing the candy like it's solid gold. Just being in such close proximity to sugar is making me feel high.

Cruz shakes his head. 'I was saving it for an emergency.'

I push his hand away. 'I can't. It's yours.'

'And I'm giving it to you.' He smiles and starts unpeeling the wrapper. I catch a glimpse of chocolate and my stomach flips.

'Can we share it at least?'

Cruz sighs, then he nods and breaks one tiny piece off and hands me the rest.

'No!' I say with a laugh. 'Properly share it.'

'This *is* properly sharing it. You have some and I have some. We are sharing, no?' He pops his piece into his mouth and I can't wait any longer. I take a bite and it's as if I'm tasting chocolate for the very first time. It melts over my tongue and trickles down my throat. My taste buds start hollering fevered whoops to my brain.

'Wow!'

Cruz grins. 'It is good?'

'It's better than good, it's – it's – divine!'

The sugar hits my blood stream almost immediately and I start grinning like a loon.

'Thank you,' I whisper, before cramming another piece into my mouth.

Cruz starts to laugh and sits back on the bed – so close to me I can feel the heat from his skin.

'You are welcome,' he says, brushing his hair back from his face.

And then our eyes meet – and everything else stops. I even put the chocolate down. Cruz takes my face in his hands.

'Grace,' he whispers, and my heart seems to shoot out through the top of my body like a rocket. 'Please, can I kiss you?'

All I can do is nod and, as our lips meet, I picture my heart looping-the-loop all the way up through the Milky Way. I open my mouth slightly. Our tongues start moving together in a beautiful dance. Whenever I kissed Todd I always felt so self-conscious; I always tried to copy what I'd seen couples doing in the movies, but with Cruz I don't need to worry about what to do at all – my body just seems to know. He wraps one arm around me and gently eases me down on the bed. Then he presses himself against me until it feels as if we're joined together. I put my arm round him and pull him even closer. One of his legs wraps itself around me and my entire body shudders with a sensation so pleasurable it weirdly feels almost like pain. We stop kissing for a moment and Cruz smiles at me.

'Wow,' he whispers, 'I –'

But before he can say any more, a loud crack rings out, followed by a scream.

I sit bolt upright on the bed. 'What was that?'

Cruz sits up next to me. 'It sounded like thunder.'

He gets up and makes his way over to the stairs. I limp along after him, my heart pounding, but this time not in a good way.

When we get above deck I nearly fall back down the steps in shock. The sky is practically as dark as night and the air feels charged with static. I scan the beach for the others. Belle and the Flea are standing on the sand looking toward the forest. There's no sign of Cariss.

Cruz starts shouting at Belle in Spanish. 'I am telling them to come on to the boat. It is safer,' he explains. There is another loud crack and a sudden blinding flash of light. The bolt of lightning is so huge it looks as if the sky has split in two. Rain starts lashing down in sheets.

'Get below deck,' Cruz says to me as he gestures at Belle and the Flea to hurry up. I hop back down the stairs. A minute or two later I hear another crash of thunder and then the sounds of footsteps running across the deck. Belle and the Flea come rushing down the stairs. They're soaked.

'Holy barometers!' the Flea exclaims. 'That's one hell of a storm.'

Belle clutches the crucifix round her neck with trembling hands.

'Where's Cruz?' I ask.

'He's gone after Cariss.' The Flea crashes down on the bed. 'She had a total freak-out the minute the first lightning struck.'

'Where did she go?' I ask.

'Off to shelter in the forest,' the Flea says. 'I guess her fear of lightning trumps her fear of snakes.' He takes off his hat and looks around the hold. 'Well, I have to say I'm loving what Cruz has done with this place. His pioneering life-jacket divan is quite simply ground-breaking. Brand new to QVC – the bed that could also save your life,' he says, putting on a deep, presenter-style drawl. 'Perfect for those tiring shipwrecked moments, when you would just kill for a quick nap.'

I start to laugh, but Belle starts to cry.

'Oh, honey, it wasn't that bad a joke. Was it?' The Flea pats the space on the bed next to him and Belle goes and sits down.

I feel a pang of emptiness as I think of Cruz and I sitting in that exact same spot just minutes earlier. Then I think of Cruz out in the storm, going after Cariss, trying to make sure she's safe despite the fact that she's been nothing but vile to him since he met her. I feel a warm glow of pride.

'What if they don't find anyone?' Belle sobs. 'What if we're stuck here forever?'

'Okay, honey, time to take your chill pill.' The Flea hugs

Belle to him and smiles at me apologetically.

I smile back. He really is a great friend to Belle. I'm not sure I could be quite so patient with her constant crying fits and panic attacks.

Another almighty crack of thunder rings out, causing us all to jump.

'I hope Cruz is okay,' I think out loud.

'I'm sure he will be,' the Flea says. 'A little bit of thunder won't faze a rugged adventurer like him.'

I turn away so he won't see me blushing.

'I think I'm going to go up on deck and see if I can see them,' I say.

'Are you sure that's such a good idea? Four hundred and twenty-seven people get struck by lightning every year, you know – and that's in Colorado State alone. It's a more common cause of death than dog-walking.'

I look at the Flea blankly.

He frowns. 'Or was it dog *bites*? Whatever.'

'I won't stay up there long. I just want to make sure they're not in trouble.' I limp back up the steps to the deck. It's still almost pitch-black outside. I can just make out the jagged silhouette of the volcano looming over the rest of the island. The palm trees on the beach are bent double in the wind and the whole forest is swaying violently from side to side.

'Cruz!' I call out. But my voice is instantly drowned out

by the howling wind. Rain lashes my face and stings my eyes. It's no good, I can't see a thing. But then there's another crash of thunder followed by an explosion of lightning. For a split second the whole island is lit up bright white. Almost instantly it's swallowed by darkness again, but what I saw is etched on my memory like photographic negative: Cariss by the HELP sign, her hair swirling in the wind, as she kicks at the letters in fury.

Chapter Twenty-one

'What do you mean, trashing the sign?' Belle's dark eyes narrow with anger.

I limp across the hold and over to the bed. The Flea jumps up to let me sit down. 'Exactly that. She was kicking the sticks all over the place. I yelled at her to stop and she just ran off.'

'What's she playing at?' Belle jumps to her feet then stands there for a moment, motionless. 'Oh my God, do you think she was the one who changed the P to an L? Do you think she's trying to set me up?'

I shrug my shoulders. I'm just as confused as she is. Why would Cariss want to jeopardize our chances of being rescued just to get Belle in trouble?

'So, where did she run to when you yelled at her?' the Flea asks.

'Up the beach, towards our camp.'

'*Your* camp,' Belle mutters.

'Beau-Belle.' The Flea gives her a warning look.

'Just saying.' Belle sits back down on the bed.

'She must have come back out of the forest without Cruz seeing.' The Flea starts pacing around the hold with his hands behind his back, deep in thought.

I think of Cruz roaming around the forest on a total wild goose chase and I get back to my feet. 'I'm going to go see if I can find him.'

The Flea frowns. 'I'm not sure that's such a good idea. Shouldn't we stay together?'

But before I can say anything footsteps pound across the deck above us. We all stare at the hold steps and watch, speechless, as Cariss makes her way down. She's absolutely drenched.

'What the hell are you up to?' Belle marches over to her.

Then Cruz appears on the steps behind Cariss and I feel giddy with relief.

'Pardon me?' Cariss says, stepping past Belle into the hold.

'Grace saw you, you know,' Belle says.

'Saw me what?'

'Destroying the sign.'

Cariss looks at us like we're both deranged. 'What are you talking about?'

'Just now. She saw you kicking the sticks away.'

Cariss turns to me, her eyes cold with fury. 'What is she trying to say?' she hisses. I'm thrown by how angry she looks, but I'm not going to let her bluff her way out of it.

'There's no point lying, I saw you do it. What were you going to do? Let Belle take the blame again?'

Cariss takes a deep breath and narrows her lips into a thin, straight line. 'I don't know what you're up to, but it's not going to work. I've been sheltering in the forest, and then Cruise-Ship came to get me.' She turns to Belle. 'Go on, ask him.'

Belle turns to Cruz and speaks to him in Spanish. He answers her and Belle's face falls. She turns to me. 'He says he found her in the entrance to the forest. He brought her straight back here. She can't have done it.'

'Thank you!' Cariss exclaims and looks at me defiantly.

I look at Cruz. He gives me an apologetic shrug.

'Cariss! Where are you?'

We all jump at the sound of Jenna yelling frantically from the beach.

'Oh, thank God,' Cariss says. She takes a step toward me and leans in so close the rainwater drips from her face on to mine. 'Jenna was right about you,' she hisses, before pushing past Cruz and going back up the steps to the deck.

I watch her go, stunned. What did she mean? What has Jenna been saying about me?

Belle turns to look at me, clearly flummoxed by this latest

development. 'Are you sure you saw her?'

'Yes.' I look down at my hands. They're shaking. 'I swear I did.'

The Flea puts his arm around my shoulder. 'Maybe it was a trick of the light, honey?'

I nod, numbly, but I'm not convinced.

The Flea gets up and goes over to the steps. 'Shall we go see if the others found anything in the forest?'

Belle nods and follows the Flea up to the deck but Cruz and I hang back.

'You okay?' he whispers as soon as they've gone.

I nod. But I don't feel okay at all.

'I found her in the forest,' he says. 'I don't see how it could have been her that you saw.'

'Who was it then?' We look at each other. Cruz's eyes are full of concern. But this only makes me feel cold with fear. First I hear whispered voices, and notice strange smells, now I'm seeing things that can't have happened. What's wrong with me? Cruz takes my hands in his and a little warmth seeps back into my body.

'It's okay,' he says. 'Come on.'

But as soon as we get on deck my heart sinks. The rain has stopped and the storm clouds are turning from black to purple like ugly bruises. Cariss is on the beach talking to Jenna, Todd, Ron and Dan and pointing over at the boat. They all turn and stare at me. Next to them, the HELP sign shimmers under the evaporating rainwater, completely undamaged.

'It must have been some kind of optical illusion, caused by the lightning,' the Flea says, coming over to give my arm a squeeze.

'Now they're going to be out to get us even more,' Belle mutters.

I feel sick. It's going to look like I made the whole thing up. I think of my grandpa's favourite saying again: *No way round it other than through*, and I take a deep breath. 'Come on then, let's go see if they found anything.'

With the others right behind me, I clamber down the ladder, focusing on my breathing. In and out, in and out.

'Grace, is this true?' Jenna says as soon as I get close. 'Did you really make up a story about Cariss destroying the sign?'

I close my eyes and replay the scene in my head. Cariss kicking wildly at the sticks, her hair being blown all over the place in the wind. My heart starts to pound as an awful realization dawns on me. I open my eyes and look at Cariss. Her hair is tied back tightly. Just as it was when we left her on the beach, and when she came down into the hold. I feel sick.

'I thought I saw her.' My voice comes out all trembly and weak.

'It was right in the middle of the storm,' the Flea says. 'When it was real dark and rainy. It must have been a trick of the light – or the dark – whatever.'

I see Jenna glance at Todd and both of them raise their eyebrows. This makes me unbelievably mad. But how can I say anything? I've made myself look a total jerk.

'Did you guys find anything in there?' the Flea asks hopefully.

Dan shakes his head and sighs. 'Just trees, trees and more darned trees. We were afraid we were gonna get lost so we came back out.'

Jenna looks back at me. 'Don't you think you owe Cariss an apology, Grace?'

I grit my teeth. The last thing I feel like doing is apologizing to Cariss – especially when told to do so by Jenna. But the fact is, I did get it wrong. 'I'm sorry,' I mutter. Cruz steps up right behind me. Jenna frowns and looks away. I am so sick and tired of all this playground bullshit I want to scream.

Dan sighs. 'You know what, I just don't believe Grace would make something like that up. She's not that kind of person. I figure Jimmy's right – it must've been the storm making it look like someone was there.' I want to hug him. But then he turns to Todd. 'What do you say, Todd?'

I glance at Todd. He shakes his head and looks at the ground. 'Grace wouldn't lie,' he mutters.

I feel shocked and grateful in equal measure. Jenna looks livid.

'Thank you,' I say.

'So, what do we do now?' Ron asks.

Everyone looks at Jenna.

'I say we eat.' Dan starts rubbing his stomach. 'I don't know about you guys but I'm starving. What do you say, Cruz? Fancy a spot of fishing, bro?' Dan mimes casting out a line to Cruz. Cruz nods and grins.

Dan looks at Todd and Ron. 'Come on then, let's go get us some brunch.'

Cruz glances at me. I give him a quick nod. He, Dan, Todd and Ron all start heading to the boat.

'Come on, Cariss,' Jenna says, linking arms with her and striding off toward the camp.

Belle goes over to the sign and starts studying the letters.

I go stand next to her. 'I'm so sorry. I don't know how it happened, I was sure I saw her.'

I wait for Belle to get annoyed again, but she keeps staring down at the sign.

Then, after a moment, she speaks quietly. 'I believe you.'

'You do?' Once again I feel flooded with relief.

She nods.

The Flea comes and stands with us. 'Yes, it was obviously the storm. I've heard about people who –'

'No, I mean, I believe she actually saw someone,' Belle interrupts.

We both look at her.

'But, Belle, honey, the sign is fine,' the Flea says. 'Ooh, did I just write a haiku?'

Belle turns to us, her face deadly serious. 'That's just it. It wasn't fine before.'

I frown at her. 'What do you mean?'

'Well, before, I'd started turning the final L back into a P but I didn't get a chance to finish it. But look now – it's perfect.'

The Flea and I look down. The letter P *is* perfect, the sticks are all placed so straight it's like they've been arranged with a slide rule. Which is even weirder, given how strong the wind was during the storm.

'And there's something else.'

I look at Belle. 'What?'

Belle points to the bottom of the letter P. The Flea and I lean over to take a closer look.

There, glinting in between the sticks, is the silver pendant.

Chapter Twenty-two

'Well, that most definitely wasn't there before,' Belle says.

I watch, my stomach churning, as the Flea bends down to pick it up.

'Are you certain it was Cariss you saw by the sign?' Belle says.

I close my eyes and recreate the image in my mind again. I want to tell them that I've realized it was someone else. I want to tell them what I'm beginning to suspect. But how can I do that? They don't know the stories about Hortense. It will just sound crazy.

I shake my head. 'I don't know.'

The Flea hands me the pendant. 'That is the one you found before, right?'

I nod. The pendant feels like a burning coal in my hand.

'Well, I say we show it to Cariss and Jenna,' Belle says.

The Flea frowns. 'Oh, I don't think that's such a good idea.'

'Why not?' Belle glares at him. 'This proves Grace saw someone tampering with the sign.'

'Yes, but they'll probably just say we made it up to cover for Grace. I say we leave it for now, let things calm down a bit.'

Belle sighs and turns to me. 'What do you think, Grace.'

'I think he's right. I don't think it's worth it.' I shove the pendant in my pocket.

Belle sighs again. 'Okay.'

'Are you all right, Grace?You're looking mighty pale again.' The Flea takes a hold of my arm.

I make myself nod.

'Let's go get some water,' he says. 'The containers must be pretty full again after the storm.'

'I'll be right behind you,' I say. 'I've just gotta fetch something from the boat.'

The Flea and Belle head off and I clamber back on to the boat. But instead of going down into the hold I walk over to the far side of the deck and pull the pendant from my pocket. After taking a quick glance back at the beach to make sure no one's watching I fling the pendant with all my might into the sea.

Leave me alone! I yell inside my head.

*

When I get back to the camp Jenna and Cariss are huddled over by the remains of last night's fire, deep in conversation. What had Cariss meant when she said, 'Jenna was right about you'? Clearly it hadn't been complimentary. I wonder if they're talking about me right now.

I go over to my case to get my water bottle. They both stop talking and stare at me.

'Leave it to me,' I hear Jenna whisper. 'So, how's your ankle, Grace?'

I look at her, wary of what kind of trap I might be about to fall into.

'It's okay, still a bit sore.'

Jenna nods. 'Did Cruise-Ship take care of it for you?'

Her face is like a smiling mask that only I can see behind.

'Yes.' I feel my dumb-ass face start flushing so I rummage about in my case, pretending I can't find my bottle.

'It was really touching before,' Jenna continues, 'when Todd said that you would never tell a lie.'

Cariss gives a dry little laugh.

'But then, Todd is an exceptionally loyal person.' Jenna cranks up her smile another notch. 'Anyways,' she continues. 'I've been having a little chat with Cariss and she's said she's prepared to forgive you for what happened before.'

I look at Cariss blankly.

Cariss nods. 'But only because anger and resentment are,

like, toxic emotions,' she says. 'I don't want to go getting any premature frown lines.'

'Right.' I really don't trust myself to say anything else.

'So that's nice, isn't it?' Jenna says sweetly. 'There's been far too much ill feeling in the group recently. When the boys get back I think we should all eat together and try and restore some harmony.'

I can't help raising my eyebrows. *What a great plan!*

'What, all of us?' Cariss says, frowning.

Jenna nods. 'Uh-huh.'

'Even Cruise-Ship?'

Jenna bows her head slightly. 'Yes. I figure it's time for me to do some forgiving too.'

Cariss shakes her head in disbelief. 'Wow, that is so generous of you.'

'Thanks.'

I stare at Jenna, trying to figure out what's going on behind the smiling mask.

'Would you tell the others, Grace?'

I nod, caught off my guard.

Jenna sits back and gives a satisfied sigh. 'Great. Can't wait. It'll be fun.'

The meal is about as fun as a dental appointment for a root canal – when you've just been told you've got two weeks to live. Despite it supposedly being a bonding experience, we still end up in our separate groups, with the Flea, Belle, Cruz and I sitting on one side of the fire and Jenna, Cariss, Ron, and Todd on the other. Dan is sprawled out on his bed.

'What say we play a game?' Jenna says as soon as we've finished eating.

I look across at her. I can't shake the feeling that she's up to something.

'What kind of game, Jen?' Ron says, stoking the fire with a stick. Glowing embers shoot up into the dark, then, one by one, turn black and drift back down again like sinister confetti. It reminds me of when I set fire to my cosmic wish list. What a heap of cow crap that was. When I get out of this place – *if* I get out of this place – I'm going to find Happymeal Johnson and demand answers.

'How about truth or dare?' Jenna says, immediately snapping me back to reality. Truth or dare? With a bunch of people who've been at each other's throats these past few days? It sounds like a recipe for total carnage. But maybe that's exactly what Jenna wants . . .

'Cool,' Ron says. 'How are we going to play it?'

Jenna smiles at him. 'We could spin a bottle.'

I glance at Cruz. He's staring into the fire, his face expressionless. I wish I could pretend I didn't understand what was going on too. It's like he's in his own protective bubble.

'Here you go, honey,' Cariss says, handing Jenna her water bottle.

Jenna shakes her head and goes to fetch the brown glass bottle. 'Let's play it with this. The glass will spin better in the sand.'

Clearly she's given this some thought. I shiver and hug my arms tight to my body.

'Come on, guys,' Jenna calls out, 'form a circle.'

With a whole spectrum of enthusiasm, ranging from Ron wide-eyed with excitement to Belle sighing and huffing like a buffalo, we all shift into a circle. I end up between the Flea and Cruz and dead opposite Jenna.

Jenna places the bottle on the sand in front of her and spins it. We all watch as the brown glass glints in the fire light, before the bottle comes to rest pointing at Ron. Disappointment flickers across Jenna's face.

'Truth or dare?' Cariss says.

'Truth,' Ron says immediately.

'Okay, has anyone got a question for Ron?' Jenna asks.

Belle puts up her hand.

Jenna ignores her and looks at Cariss.

'Do you have a skincare regime?' Cariss asks.

'If you had to date one of the girls here, who would it be?' Belle says, ignoring Cariss.

Ron looks at Jenna, confused.

'I'm afraid it's only one question,' Jenna says to Belle, 'and as Cariss asked first . . .'

'But I put my hand up first,' Belle replies, continuing to look at Ron. 'Who would it be?'

Even in the dark I can see Ron's pale cheeks start to burn.

'You only have to answer Cariss,' Jenna mutters.

'Jenna,' Ron says, looking into the fire.

Todd and Jenna both turn to stare at him.

'What?' Jenna hisses.

Ron stays silent.

Next to him, Todd starts shifting uncomfortably.

'Hah! Knew it!' Belle says triumphantly.

Jenna looks mortified.

Ron glances sideways at Cariss. 'And in answer to your question, I do cleanse and tone, but rarely moisturize.'

Cariss nods sagely. 'I had noticed you have quite an oily T-zone.'

'Forget about his T-zone – the guy just declared his undying love for Jenna,' the Flea says, looking more animated than he has done in ages.

'I didn't declare my undying love,' Ron mutters. 'I just said I, you know, *like* her.' He glances at Jenna hopefully.

The Flea rubs his hands, presumably in glee, and turns to Jenna. 'So, how do you feel about Ron, Jenna?'

'It's not my turn for a question,' Jenna hisses.

Ron continues looking at her hopefully.

'Just spin the bottle, will you,' Jenna snaps.

Ron looks broken-hearted. He gives the bottle a token spin and it lurches a couple of places round – to point at Belle.

Jenna's face immediately lights up. 'Truth or dare?'

'Dare,' Belle mutters.

'Okay, I dare you to take a drink from the bottle,' Jenna says immediately.

'Hang on a minute, why should you be the one to give me the dare?' Belle says.

'Because I was the first person to think of something. Now are you going to take a drink, or are you chicken?'

'Don't do it, Beau-Belle,' the Flea says, placing his hand on her arm. 'You have no idea what it is.'

Belle sits motionless, staring down at the bottle.

Jenna gives a dry little laugh. 'Typical.'

'What's that supposed to mean?' Belle frowns at her.

'I should've known you wouldn't have the guts to accept a simple dare.'

Belle pushes the bottle toward Jenna. 'Why don't you drink it then?'

'It's not my dare.'

'I'll do it, Jen,' Ron offers.

'It's not your dare either,' Jenna snaps.

Belle picks up the bottle.

'Don't,' I say. I glance at Cruz. He's looking as worried as I feel.

Belle pulls out the cork and raises the bottle to her mouth.

'Belle! Stop!' the Flea yells.

Belle sniffs at the bottle and pulls a face. 'Ew, it smells gross.'

'Put the cork back in then,' Jenna says quickly. 'Let's just carry on with the game.'

Belle is about to put the cork back in when Ron grabs the bottle from her. He puts it to his lips and takes a huge swig.

'What the hell are you doing?' Todd yells, knocking the bottle away from Ron's mouth.

'Oh my God! What is it?' Cariss gasps, staring at Ron. A dark-red liquid trickles down his pale chin, like blood.

Ron licks his lips and wipes his chin. 'It doesn't taste that bad.' He looks at Jenna hopefully. He's acting so pathetic I almost feel sorry for him.

Todd shakes his head. 'You don't know what's in this thing, dude. It could be spiked.'

'What does it taste like?' the Flea asks.

Ron shrugs. 'I don't know. Kind of spicy.'

'Cool,' Dan says. 'Maybe I'll try some.'

'Don't be so stupid,' Jenna snaps. 'It could be poisonous for all we know.'

'Oh, but you were prepared to make me drink it,' Belle says.

Jenna shakes her head, smiling sweetly. 'No. I knew you'd

never have the guts to drink it. Now why don't you just spin the bottle?'

So she has set this whole thing up, which means that she'll definitely have something planned for me. Thing is, I'm not sure I even care any more.

Belle takes the bottle and replaces the cork. For a moment I think she might shove it down Jenna's throat, but finally she places it on the sand and spins it furiously.

The bottle spins so fast it goes shooting across the circle. It comes to a stop pointing at the gap between the Flea and me.

'Too close to call, spin again,' Dan says.

Jenna shakes her head. 'No, it's definitely closer to Grace, isn't it, Cariss?'

Cariss nods.

'Truth or dare, Grace?' Jenna asks.

'Truth.' I answer, staring at her across the fire. There's no way she's going to intimidate me.

'I have a question for you,' Jenna says immediately.

I bet you do. My heart starts to pound but I carry on looking right at her. 'Go ahead.'

'Have you kissed anyone other than Todd since we've been on this island?'

'Man, what a waste of a question,' Dan says with a sigh.

I can feel Todd's eyes burning into me, but I stay focused on Jenna.

'Why would you ask that?' Belle says. 'It's obvious she hasn't.'

Jenna smiles sweetly. 'Oh, is it?'

Everyone goes deadly silent and still.

'Why are you doing this?' I say.

'Doing what?'

'You know what.'

Jenna continues to smile at me like I'm a little kid in need of humouring. 'I'm just asking you a question.'

'Go on then, answer her,' Todd says. I look across the fire at him, but a sudden gust of wind causes the flames to leap up in front of his face.

Suddenly Cruz gets to his feet. 'This is bullshit!'

Everyone gasps and stares at him, open-mouthed. '*You* are bullshit!' he says to Jenna. 'You want to say something, then say it. Don't play games with us like we are children.'

Jenna's mouth opens and closes like a fish's.

I feel like punching the air for joy.

'You speak English!' Cariss gasps.

Still Jenna doesn't say a word.

The Flea scrambles to his feet and offers Cruz his hand. 'My name's Jimmy the Flea. Very pleased to meet you.'

Cruz shakes his hand and nods. But he still looks furious.

'Man, I did not see that one coming!' Dan shakes his head, looking totally stunned. 'Why didn't you say something, bro? Why didn't you tell us you speak English?'

'So all that time I've been speaking Spanish to you . . .' Belle stares at Cruz, her eyes wide with shock.

'Okay, I'll say it,' Jenna says suddenly.

We all fall silent and stare at her.

'I saw you and Grace kissing when Grace was still going out with Todd.' She stares at Cruz defiantly.

'Holy moly!' the Flea exclaims, looking down at me, his eyes wide with shock.

But Cruz is totally unfazed. 'You know nothing about nothing,' he says to Jenna, practically spitting the words out.

Todd scrambles to his feet and starts making his way round the circle to me. 'Is this true?'

'Calm down, man,' Dan says.

I get to my feet and look at Todd.

'Did you cheat on me with him?' he asks again.

'I'm sorry,' I say. 'It was only one kiss and it wasn't like I planned it or anything. As soon as it happened I ended it with you.'

'But I thought you were the one who ended it?' Jenna looks at Todd, puzzled.

Todd ignores her and comes charging toward me. Cruz steps in front of me to block his way.

'Get out of my way!' Todd yells.

'Todd, be careful!' Jenna cries.

'I'm not afraid of him,' Todd says, shoving Cruz in the chest.

'I said get out of my way. I need to talk to Grace.'

There's a sudden blur of movement, and Cruz has Todd in an arm-lock.

'Oh my God!' Cariss gasps. Even Jenna looks terrified.

'I do not need to listen to your crap any more, and neither does she,' Cruz says to Todd. 'You understand?'

Todd nods, his face flushed with anger.

Cruz lets him go, then he picks up the bottle. 'I say this party is over. Maybe in the morning we can be like adults and try to figure a way out of this place.'

'That sounds like a plan,' Dan says.

'Count me in,' the Flea says.

'And me,' Belle adds, smiling at Cruz.

Cruz says something to her in Spanish and she laughs. Then he looks at me. 'Do you – er – would you like to stay on the boat tonight?'

I nod, unable to speak. Everything has happened so fast it's taking my brain a little while to catch up. I take a deep breath, then start heading over to the trees to fetch my things. When I walk past Jenna our eyes briefly meet. It's like looking into the cold eyes of a stranger.

Chapter Twenty-three

When Jenna was twelve she found out that her dad, who'd left when she was just a baby, had moved back to California. I was staying over at her house at the time, and we were playing our favourite game – reading Jenna's mom's emails while she was at one of her whack-job night classes. When we saw an email from a random guy in her inbox we assumed it was from a new boyfriend and pounced on it.

But when Jenna clicked it open it just read:

I'm sorry – I can't. I have Taylor to think of.

That was it – no sign-off or anything. So Jenna scrolled down to the original email. I remember feeling sick as I read her mom's mail and did the math. The random guy was actually Jenna's dad. Her mom's email had been practically begging him to come see Jenna – which made his curt response all the more heart-breaking.

I wanted to slam the laptop shut and hug Jenna and tell her how sorry I was. But she kept on scrolling up and down – re-reading her mom's email and her dad's reply. I thought she might have cried – I felt close to tears – but she just sat there, her back ballet-straight, her face expressionless. And then she said, 'I guess Taylor must be his new wife then.'

I think I just nodded, unsure what to say. Then, finally, Jenna snapped the laptop shut and said, 'Come on, let's go watch TV.'

And that was that, until about two weeks later, when she came into school, bubbling with excitement. 'I've found my dad's address,' she told me. 'He's living in Santa Monica and I'm going to go visit him. Once he sees me he won't be able to say he doesn't want to know me, right?'

I nodded, but I remember having a really bad feeling about it even then.

The following weekend, we told our moms we were going to hang on the beach for the day and we caught the bus to Santa Monica.

All the way there, Jenna talked excitedly about how her life was going to change once she and her dad were in touch, and how great it would be to be able to escape her mom and go spend weekends with her dad. And how she wondered if they looked alike and what things they would have in common. And then we got to his house.

The moment I saw a swing-set in the backyard my heart sank. Jenna didn't notice it – she'd been too busy brushing her hair and putting on lipgloss. Then taking off the lipgloss because her dad 'might be one of those men who didn't approve of their daughters wearing make-up'.

'Maybe turning up out of the blue like this isn't such a good idea,' I said to her. 'Maybe you should phone him first.'

But, before Jenna could answer, the front door burst open and a little girl of about five came running out. 'You can't catch me!' she yelled, running behind the station wagon that was parked on the driveway.

Jenna and I looked at each other in shock. It was like we'd just seen a ghost. The ghost of Jenna, aged five.

'Oh, yes I can,' a man's voice boomed and Jenna's dad appeared in the doorway. I recognized him immediately from the photo of him Jenna kept hidden in her school locker. Jenna obviously recognized him too because she started shaking like a leaf beside me. We watched, motionless, as he ran around behind the car and scooped the girl up into his arms. Her long blonde hair cascaded down behind her as she tipped her head back and giggled.

'Come on, Taylor, if we don't hurry they'll run out of ice

cream.' A woman appeared smiling in the doorway, holding her purse and some car keys.

'Ice cream! Ice cream!' Taylor squealed.

'I scream, you scream, we all scream for ice cream,' Jenna's dad said, laughing, before bundling Taylor into the back of the car. Then he stopped to kiss the woman and she gave him the car-keys and got into the passenger side. He was just about to get into the driver's seat when he saw us standing there on the sidewalk. My heart nearly stopped beating.

'You girls all right?' he called out.

I looked at Jenna. She just stood there, not saying a word.

'Yes, sir, we're just – just on our way to see a friend,' I stammered.

Jenna's dad smiled and got into the car. We watched as it purred off out of the driveway and down the road.

'He didn't even know who I was,' Jenna whispered.

'Come on, let's go home,' I said, pulling on her arm. But it was like she'd suddenly grown roots. I couldn't shift her at all.

'I want to see inside,' she whispered, nodding at the house.

My heart sank. 'We can't. They've gone out. How can –'

'Come on.' She grabbed my arm and started pulling me around to the backyard.

I'd hoped that when she couldn't see any way in Jenna would realize what a crazy idea it was and agree to go home. But unfortunately a small window next to the back door had been left slightly ajar. Jenna made a beeline for it and, within what was probably just seconds but felt like hours, she'd wriggled through the window and unlocked the back door, and we were standing inside a huge kitchen.

The first thing I noticed – once I'd checked for any security systems we were about to trigger – was how totally different it was to Jenna's mom's house. Jenna's mom's kitchen was snowy white from top to bottom. The kind of kitchen that is so squeaky clean it makes you feel like you should be hosed down with bleach before being allowed to enter. But this was the kind of kitchen you'd expect to see in a farmhouse – with warm red cabinets, a rust-coloured stone floor and a huge oak sideboard. In the centre of the kitchen saucepans of all shapes and sizes hung from the ceiling above a huge stove. It smelt of fresh baked bread and all I could think as I gazed around was that it looked so lived-in and so full of fun. From the jokey apron hanging on the door, to the kid's pictures stuck higgledy-piggledy all over the fridge. I looked at Jenna. She was staring around the room, wide-eyed, drinking everything in. Then she went over and picked up a framed photo from the windowsill. It was of her dad and Taylor. 'She looks just like me,' she whispered.

I put my arm around her shoulders. 'I really think we should go.'

'No!' Jenna shook off my arm and glared at me. 'Not yet.'

'But what if they come back?'

'You keep watch out front. I need to use the bathroom.'

Before I could argue with her she'd raced from the kitchen and I could hear her footsteps pounding up the stairs. I hurried through to a room at the front of the house, which turned out to be the television room, crammed with multi-coloured cushions and throws. I crouched on a beanbag by the window and watched the road outside, my heart pounding.

I heard a toilet flush and then the sound of doors opening and closing upstairs. Then I heard the soft thud of Jenna's footsteps directly above me. I was about to call out to her to hurry up, when I heard a horrible wailing sound, followed by a smash.

'Jenna!' I raced upstairs. I could hear banging and tearing noises coming from behind a closed door on the landing. The door had one of those 'This Bedroom Belongs to' signs hanging on it, with 'Taylor' written underneath in bright-blue letters. I flung the door open and gasped. The room was trashed. Toys and games were strewn all over the floor. Jenna was standing by a wardrobe pulling out handfuls of clothes and ripping at them like she was possessed. Then she went over to the bed and picked up a teddy bear from the pillow.

'What are you doing?'

Jenna turned to me. Her face was bright red and shiny with tears. 'Come on, let's go,' she said, marching past me to the door, still clutching the teddy bear.

'But . . .'

I ran after her, down into the kitchen and out through the back door.

'Why are you taking her bear?'

Jenna turned and stared at me and she looked so crazed I actually felt scared of her. 'Well, she's taken my dad.'

As I make my way down the beach with Cruz and Belle and the Flea I can't stop thinking about this. Jenna swore me to secrecy about what happened – I wasn't even allowed to talk about it with her, let alone anyone else. But it was there all the same; a terrible secret woven into our DNA, bonding us together like we were sisters. I'd seen a part of Jenna no one else had ever seen, but I didn't judge her for it, because I knew how much she was hurting. But now, I keep coming back to one thing – maybe I should have made her talk about it. Maybe if she'd dealt with it properly she wouldn't be so hard-hearted now.

I sigh. Cruz takes a hold of my hand and it's like he's pulling me back to reality. My new reality, in which Jenna and I are no longer friends.

'What happened back there was awesome!' the Flea says, grinning at Cruz. 'Did you guys really kiss? Sorry, none of my business. But did you?'

I nod.

'Sweet!' The Flea winks at me and grins and I feel so grateful for his what-you-see-is-what-you-get, uncomplicated friendship.

'How long have you known Cruz can speak English?' Belle asks.

'Just a couple days.'

'Wowsers!' the Flea exclaims and Belle laughs in disbelief.

I feel shocked too, but for a different reason. Has it really only been a couple of days? It's starting to feel as if we've been on the island for years.

We say good night to Belle and the Flea and carry on to the boat. I wonder what Cruz is thinking. There's so much I need to say to him but I want to wait until we're properly alone. We climb up the ladder and make our way across the deck and into the hold. As soon as we get down there I turn to face him. But the minute our eyes meet it's like all of the words I had lined up in neat little sentences in my head keel over in a dead faint. All I want is to be folded up in those strong arms again. I swallow hard and manage to whisper the only words left standing.

'Thank you.'

He sighs. 'I could not just sit there. I had to do something.'

I nod and smile.

He smiles back, but his eyes look sad. 'I do not like having conflict. But sometimes it is the only way.'

I look down at the floor. 'It felt good – having someone look out for me like that.' I immediately look back up at him. 'Even though I could've taken care of myself.'

He smiles again, and this time it's a proper, happy smile, with both of his dimples sparking into life. 'I know you can take care of yourself. But I told you. Now I have saved your life I am responsible for your well-being forever.'

I suddenly feel very, very tired. 'So, are you responsible for my well-being right now?'

He nods. 'Of course.'

I stand there in front of him for a second, as if plucking up the courage to dive off a cliff. 'Well, if you were to give me a hug it would make my being very well indeed.'

He laughs. 'Is that so?'

I nod.

He steps forward and wraps his strong arms right around me. 'Like this?'

I nod and lean my head against his chest.

'Yes. Exactly like this.'

'And how about this?' Cruz strokes my hair and starts planting gentle kisses on my face.

My head becomes filled with heart-shaped balloons. I can't even nod. All I can do is lift my face to his and hope that he can read my mind.

Cruz makes a trail of kisses from the top of my forehead to

the tip of my nose and down on to my mouth. Then he guides me over to the bed and pulls the blanket back. He gestures at his T-shirt.

'Is it okay if I . . .?' He mimes taking it off.

I nod and watch as he lifts his T-shirt over his head. My eyes drink in the muscular ridges of his abdomen. My fingers itch to trace the thin line of hair forming a path from his navel to the waistband on his shorts. Cruz looks at me. Without thinking I lift my own T-shirt up and off. But I don't feel self-conscious at all. He takes my hand and pulls me close. The warmth of his bare skin against mine feels incredible. We sink down on to the bed and he pulls the blanket over us.

'Hello,' he whispers to me in the dark.

'Hi,' I whisper back.

I feel one of his big hands pressing into the small of my back and my body seems to turn to water, flowing to his touch. This time, when our mouths find each other, it's like we're trying to literally consume each other. He rolls on top of me and I wrap my legs and arms around him as our tongues entwine. His breath quickens and I feel him trembling – both of us trembling.

'Grace,' he half whispers, half moans.

I hold him even tighter. I never want this feeling to end.

He pulls his head back slightly and looks down at me. 'Grace,' he says again, before gathering me into a hug.

'Now, you must sleep,' he whispers in my ear.

My entire body sighs. I don't want to sleep. I want to keep on kissing him forever. But the rhythm of his hand stroking my hair and the rolling of the waves outside blend to form the world's most potent lullaby.

Chapter Twenty-four

I wake the next morning, alone in the bed. I'd been so fast asleep that for a brief, wonderful moment I have no idea where I am or what has happened. But then the hollow ache of hunger starts spreading from my stomach to the very tips of my fingers and toes. And I remember everything.

Hearing the sound of movement from across the hold, I ease myself on to my elbow and see Cruz sitting cross-legged on the floor with his back to me. He's so still I think he might be meditating. I decide to keep quiet just in case, and lie back and watch him instead. And as I do the total randomness of the situation hits me like a freight train. Less than a week ago, Cruz and I were going about our lives, thousands of miles apart, not even aware that each other existed. Now he feels like one of my closest friends in the world. I roll on to my back and frown up at the ceiling. Why do we meet the people we do? Does God, or whoever, sit in some kind of heavenly air traffic control tower, directing the radar blips of our lives so that we connect with the people we're supposed to? Or is it all just completely random?

'What are you thinking?' A soft voice stirs me from my thoughts.

'Oh! Hi.' I roll back on to my side, smiling. Cruz has turned round and is now sitting cross-legged on the floor facing me. He's holding a small, leather-bound book.

'Sorry,' he says with a grin. 'You looked so serious. What were you thinking about?'

I pull the blanket up over my shoulder. 'I was just wondering why we meet certain people. You know, is it fate or is it just totally random?' I plump up my cushion pillow. 'It's a bit dumb really. Are you okay? Couldn't you sleep?'

'It's not dumb.' Cruz gets to his feet and puts the book in his pocket. Just the very act of him standing triggers some kind of carnival inside of my ribcage, with my heart thumping like a giant bass drum.

'I think about that a lot too,' he says. 'I think that everyone we meet, we meet for a reason. Even the jerk people.'

I frown. 'Really? Why do we need to meet the jerk people?'

Cruz comes over and crouches down beside the bed. His face is just inches from mine. My big old drum of a heart pounds double-time. 'To teach us something, maybe.'

'Like what?'

'Well, maybe what we will and will not put up with.'

'Hmm.' I'm pretty sure he's talking about Jenna and Todd so I change the subject. 'I guess I met you so that you would save my life.'

Cruz shakes his head. 'No, *I* met *you* so that I would save your life, but you met me so that you would give me a hug right now.'

I start to laugh. 'You're kidding? So my whole lifetime on this planet has been building up to this very moment?'

'Yes.'

'Wow. I'd better make it an awesome hug then.'

'Exactly.' Cruz is about to get on the bed when we hear the sound of yelling from the beach.

I look at Cruz and sigh. 'What now?'

He holds out his hand to me. 'Let's go see.'

We both put our T-shirts back on and head up on deck. The sun is only just edging over the horizon but it's already sauna-hot. I see Todd and Ron by the palm trees. Todd is yelling at the Flea and waving his arms about like a crazy person.

'Come on,' Cruz says. I follow him across the deck, relieved that my ankle isn't feeling nearly as sore as yesterday.

We climb down on to the beach and start making our way over to them. 'What's going on?' I call out as soon as we get close.

'Why don't you ask your friend here?' Todd says, pointing to the Flea.

The Flea is standing by his makeshift bed in his boxers and T-shirt looking dazed and confused. 'He's saying Belle's done something to Jenna.'

'Where is she?' Todd says.

The Flea's face is ashen. 'I told you, I don't know. I only just woke up.'

Todd scowls. 'Yeah, right. You've been with her all night. You must have known what she had planned.'

'What's happened to Jenna?' I ask.

'What do you care?' Todd snaps.

Ron just stares at me blankly.

Cruz goes over to Todd. 'What is going on?'

Todd ignores him and keeps looking at the Flea. 'Don't mess around, Jimmy. The girl clearly needs psychiatric help and you covering for her isn't helping any.'

He takes a step toward the Flea.

Cruz immediately steps in the way. 'All right. Take it easy. Why don't you say to us what you think she has done?'

'Why don't *you* back off, dude?' Todd yells, then he walks around Cruz and prods the Flea with his finger. 'Where the hell is she?'

I notice the Flea clenching his fists. 'Back off, Todd,' he says quietly.

Todd starts to laugh. 'Or what, you'll bore me to death with quotes from the Discovery Channel?'

My whole body goes red-hot with anger. How dare he talk to the Flea like that? I'm about to yell at him when something incredible happens – the Flea shoves Todd in the chest and sends him staggering backward.

'What the . . .' Todd splutters as he scrambles to keep his balance.

'Oh, why don't you just shut up, you boring, vacuous, pampered little mommy's boy,' the Flea says, his voice as calm as a newsreader's.

Cruz looks at me and raises his eyebrows. I stifle a grin. Go the Flea!

Todd, however, looks apoplectic. 'What did you just call me?'

The Flea purses his lips and looks upward, like he's trying to recall his list. 'Er, let me see, there was boring, vacuous, I think I also said pampered –'

Todd takes a step toward him. 'You –'

But the Flea puts his hand up to stop him. 'I've had to put up with shit from guys like you my entire life,' he cuts in. 'But you know what, we're not in school now, and just because we happen to be shipwrecked on a desert island it does not give you the excuse to go all *Lord of the Flies* on me. I mean, hello, that is so 1950s!'

Todd turns to look at Ron, his eyes wide with disbelief.

'Did you hear what he just said to me, bro? Did you hear what he called me?'

Ron just stares at Todd.

Todd's face seems to have journeyed through the entire spectrum of red and is now venturing into purple. 'Aren't you gonna say something? Aren't you gonna stick up for me?'

'S'bad,' Ron says, before looking off into space.

I stare at Ron. What's wrong with him? It's like he's still asleep.

Cruz goes and stands right next to the Flea. I move to his other side and grab hold of his hand. I can feel it trembling and give it a squeeze.

Todd glares at us. 'Great! Okay, you wanna know what your good buddy Belle's done this time, why don't you come with me?'

I look at the Flea. He nods and we all follow Todd up to the camp.

When we get there Jenna is pacing up and down. Her hair is all over the place and her cheeks are flecked with mascara. Whatever's happened must've been bad if it's stopped her doing her morning beauty routine. Cariss is standing arrow-straight, with a towel wrapped tightly around her shoulders and Dan's leaning against a tree.

As soon as Jenna sees us she goes nuts. 'Where is she?' she yells at the Flea.

The Flea sighs. 'What's she supposed to have done this time?'

'Like you don't know,' Jenna hisses. 'Do you have any idea how dangerous it is pulling a stunt like that? I have could have had a heart attack waking up with that thing dangling in my face.'

'Waking up with what thing dangling in your face?' the Flea says blankly. Jenna stomps over to the edge of the camp and picks something up, then marches back over to us.

'This thing!' She brandishes a straw doll at the Flea. The doll has long blonde hair, just like Jenna's, and someone has painted a face on it, with red trails of blood coming from the eyes like tears. Its entire body has been pierced with long pins.

I look at Cruz and he looks at me, his eyes wide with alarm. One word echoes around my mind, like the call of a ghost.

Voodoo.

Chapter Twenty-five

The Flea looks at the doll. Then he looks at Jenna.

'And when exactly is Belle supposed to have made Voodoo Barbie here?'

Jenna's eyes flash. 'I don't know. Last night, I guess.'

'Right.' The Flea sighs. 'So she just popped along to the local branch of Hobby Lobby to get the materials, did she?'

'Well, I don't know *how* she made it,' Jenna says, her voice high-pitched with frustration. 'All I know is she made it.'

The Flea shakes his head. 'How? How exactly do you know this?'

Jenna's eyes glint with indignation. 'Think of what she's already done! She trashed my bed. Then she physically assaulted me when I told her to quit being a baby. And she was real pissed with me last night.'

The Flea gives a tight little laugh. 'Well, if being pissed with you last night is a motive then I guess that makes at least half of us suspects.'

Jenna's face flushes and she glances at me.

'If she's so innocent then where the hell is she?' Cariss asks.

The Flea frowns. 'I don't know. Maybe she went for a swim?'

'I don't see her,' Dan says, staring down to the sea.

The Flea starts looking worried. 'Well, maybe she's getting coconuts.'

'We already checked,' Todd says. 'And at the inlet. There's no sign of her anywhere.'

I glance up toward the forest. I don't think for one second that Belle made the spooky doll, but why has she disappeared?

The Flea is clearly having similar thoughts. 'We've gotta go look for her,' he says.

'Are you kidding?' Jenna snaps.

The Flea stares at her. 'Something might have happened to her.'

'Good riddance,' Cariss hisses. 'To be honest with you, I don't care if I never see that girl again.'

The Flea marches over to her. 'You,' he says, calmly and concisely, 'are one of the ugliest people I have ever met.'

Cariss staggers back like she's been stabbed.

'Amen, brother,' Dan mutters.

'There's no need to get so personal,' Jenna says sharply.

'Jimmy, your friend Belle is clearly deranged, and you're either in denial or you're covering for her.'

'Oh, come *on*, Jenna,' I say.

Jenna continues staring at the Flea. 'I have nothing to say to you, Grace. You've made your choices, now you have to live with them.'

I stare at her. 'What's that supposed to mean?'

'It means, if you want to hang out with psycho-girl then you have to deal with the consequences.'

'Belle is not a psycho!' the Flea yells before I can say anything.

'She's been acting nuts ever since we got to the airport,' Jenna says. 'The way she was crying like a baby saying goodbye to her mom. And crying nearly every second since we got here. I swear to God, I –'

'Her mom's got cancer,' the Flea says quietly.

'What?' I stare at him, open-mouthed.

The Flea nods grimly. 'She found out right before we left. She didn't want to come at all, but her mom made her. She didn't want her to miss this opportunity.' He gives a sarcastic little laugh. 'Some opportunity!'

I feel a rush of sorrow for Belle – and guilt for the times I've felt mad at her for being moody. 'That's terrible . . .'

The Flea nods, then he turns back to Jenna. 'So, you see, she's got slightly more important things on her mind right now than trying to freak you out.'

Jenna pouts and scuffs her foot in the sand, clearly unsure of what to do or say next.

Dan shakes his head. 'That's too bad.'

'What kind of cancer is it?' I say to the Flea. 'Is it terminal?'

The Flea shrugs. 'It's breast cancer, and they don't know. Her mom had literally just found out a couple of days before we left. That's why Belle's so upset – she's freaking out about what the stress of us going missing will be doing to her mom.' He looks around at all of us. 'Come on, we have to go look for her. There's no way she'd run off without telling me. She's terrified of leaving the beach and missing any rescue helicopters.'

'I guess the only place left to check is the forest,' Dan says.

The Flea gives him a tense smile. 'Cool, let's go then.'

Jenna, Cariss and Todd stay motionless. Ron is now lying down in his bed and appears to have actually fallen asleep.

'I'm staying here,' Jenna finally says, looking down at the sand.

'Me too,' says Cariss, pulling her towel right over her head.

I look at Todd. He goes to sit down next to Ron. Great.

Cruz shakes his head in disgust.

The Flea gives a sarcastic laugh. 'Well, thanks, guys.'

'Somebody has to stay on the beach,' Jenna says feebly.

I shake my head and turn away.

*

I'm starting to think of the forest as a living thing. I don't just mean the plants and birds and animals – it's like the forest itself is a huge living creature, with a mind of its own. As we make our way through the first of the trees, it seems to be in a pensive mood, like it's watching and waiting for something. The squawks of the parrots aren't nearly as loud as normal and the sun filtering through the web of branches overhead is casting an eerie green glow. I sniff the air nervously, afraid that the sickly scent will be back, but all I can smell is hot, damp earth.

'Do you really think she would have come in here by herself?' I say, trying hard not to sound scared.

Cruz takes hold of my hand.

'I don't know,' the Flea says. 'I mean, I guess she could have gotten so stressed she decided to go look for help, but I don't understand why she wouldn't have told me.' He sighs. 'If only I'd woken up. I could've stopped her. Or gone with her at least.'

'It's not your fault,' I say.

'Yeah, don't blame yourself, bro,' Dan says, placing one of his huge hands on the Flea's shoulder.

As we trudge further into the forest I can't help smiling at the sight of broad-shouldered Dan and the whip-thin Flea walking together in front of us. There's something really heart-warming about their unlikely budding friendship – especially in the middle of so much conflict. But then I hear a faint, familiar whisper and I'm filled with an instant dread.

'You okay?' Cruz squeezes my hand, obviously sensing my sudden tension.

I force myself to nod. Maybe it was just a breeze through the –

'*Follow the signs . . .*' I stop dead at the sound of her voice. It's so gentle and soothing, yet there's an ominous undercurrent that chills me to the bone.

'What is it?' Cruz asks.

'Did you – did you hear anything just then?' I whisper to him.

'What did you say?' the Flea calls to us over his shoulder.

'Nothing.' I call back. I look up at Cruz. He's shaking his head.

'Why? Did you?' he asks.

'*Say no*,' the voice whispers. '*You mustn't tell them about me.*' She sounds slightly panicked now, almost like she's pleading with me.

'No,' I say.

Cruz grips my hand tighter.

I can't tell him. He'll think I'm going crazy. Maybe I *am* going crazy.

We carry on walking. I focus on my breathing to try and stay calm.

After about five minutes I hear her voice again. '*Look to the left.*'

I automatically do what she says. Cruz follows my gaze.

'Hey,' he says.

We all stop.

I look at him. 'What is it?'

He's pointing at a huge cluster of purple-leaved plants in between two trees.

I frown, confused. 'What?'

'*Go closer*,' the voice whispers. I walk over to the plants and the others follow me.

'Looks like some kind of tropical fern,' the Flea says.

'That shit's not poisonous, is it?' Dan says.

Cruz shakes his head. 'No, that's not it.' He points to the middle of the cluster, where some of the fern leaves have been squashed flat against the floor. 'Somebody has been walking through here, see?'

'Holy footprints!' the Flea exclaims. 'You're right.'

We make our way through the purple ferns. My head is in turmoil. What if we're being led into a trap? But how can I tell the others I'm hearing voices – or *one* voice at least?

'Oh my God,' the Flea exclaims. 'A footpath.'

Sure enough, hidden behind the ferns, there's a narrow dirt path, cutting like a secret tunnel through the wilderness. Cruz takes a couple of steps forward, then pauses again. He points to a cracked twig in the middle of the path. 'Someone may have stepped on it,' he explains.

'Man, his CSI routine's good!' Dan exclaims with a chuckle.

'*Come down the path*.' The whisper coils around me like smoke.

I jump and Dan frowns. 'What's up, Grace? You okay?'

'Yeah, I . . .'

'*If you want to see your friend again, come down the path*.' The voice is still a whisper, but this time it's a lot more insistent. Her accent is really strong, European maybe.

'Do you think Belle would have come along here though?' the Flea asks. 'I mean, if she'd found the path wouldn't she have come back and told us about it?'

'Not necessarily,' I say, my stomach churning. 'Maybe she was so excited to find it she kept going.' I'm well aware how lame this sounds, but if the voice I keep hearing is for real, and Belle has come down here, then we have to do what it says.

'Okay, let's head on for a bit then,' the Flea says.

I'm aware of Cruz looking at me, but I can't meet his gaze, I can't let him know that something is up.

'*Good*,' the voice whispers in my ear. '*Keep going. Your friend's waiting for you. Keep looking for the signs*.'

What signs? Who are you? I yell back inside my head, but there's no reply. I'm eaten up with fear. I want to believe that the voice is just a figment of my imagination – even though that will make me a certifiable nut – but it feels so separate from me, so real. And if it is real, how do I know it's telling the truth?

After a while, the path starts to twist and turn and the trees and vines on either side get thicker and taller. It reminds me of the fairy tale, Sleeping Beauty, where the vines grow so high while the princess sleeps, they swallow up the entire castle. I'm about to take a sip from my water bottle when I hear the voice again.

'*Look right, Grace.*'

It's not just the fact that she knows my name, but the way she says it like she's known me for years, that totally freaks me out.

Clenching my fists, I glance right and see a flash of bright colour amongst the green. There, caught on the end of a branch, is a tiny piece of pink fabric.

My heart leaps. 'Hey, take a look at this,' I call out to the others, temporarily forgetting my fear.

They stop and gather round. Cruz carefully removes the fabric.

The Flea gasps and claps his hand to his mouth. 'It's the exact same colour as the top Belle was wearing last night!'

We all stare at each other while we process this piece of information. All I can think is, the voice must be for real.

'Come on,' the Flea says, marching on along the path with real purpose now. 'Beau-Belle!' he calls out. 'Can you hear us, honey?'

There's a loud squawk from somewhere way above us and

the sound of beating wings. I shiver. Belle wouldn't come this far into the forest on her own, I just know it. But if not, who did she come with? I wait, half-expecting the whispering woman to answer me.

'Belle!' the Flea calls out again. 'It's me, Jimmy.'

The Flea and Dan stop dead in their tracks. We've reached a fork in the path.

'Which way?' the Flea says, looking back at Cruz and me with panic in his eyes.

Cruz shrugs.

'*Go right*,' the voice whispers, and it feels so close I have to look over my shoulder to make sure no one's there.

'I say we go left,' Dan says. 'That way's deeper into the island. If we go right we might end up going back the way we came.'

'*No!*' the voice says. It has a harder edge now and it makes me shudder.

'I don't know – maybe we should try right,' I say.

'Why?' Cruz asks, staring at me real intently.

'I don't know – I just have a – a feeling, that's all.'

'Hmm, not so sure we should be basing our decisions on feelings right now, Gracie,' the Flea says with a tired smile. 'Dan's right, we don't want to end up going back on ourselves.'

'*Make them go right!*' the voice hisses. All around us the plants start swaying and bending as if they're getting mad too.

'Damn, I hope there isn't another storm coming,' Dan says, looking upward.

'I really think we should go right,' I say again. My heart is hammering in my chest. I don't know what to do. Again, I wonder if I should tell them that I've been hearing a voice. Should I tell them what it's saying to me? But if I do that, they'll all start quizzing me, and we'll lose time. We need to keep moving to find Belle.

Cruz puts his arm round my shoulders. 'How about we go left first and if we don't find anything, we come back and go right?'

'Sweet,' Dan says.

'Good plan,' says the Flea.

I nod. As long as we end up going right, surely that will be enough.

We start heading along the left pathway. The wind whips up even stronger, until it begins to sound like someone, or something, is howling. It's just the wind, I tell myself. I grip on to Cruz's hand, feeling sick with dread. I'm sure we've made a huge mistake coming this way – that *I've* made a huge mistake allowing the others to come this way.

But we carry on and, after a couple of minutes, the Flea, who'd been bounding on ahead of us, comes to an abrupt standstill. 'Look!' he cries back at us.

We all stop behind him and peer into the gloom. In front

of us the pathway suddenly widens into a clearing. And there, in the middle of the clearing, I can just make out the glowing remains of a fire.

Chapter Twenty-six

As we reach the clearing the boys turn to look at each other, their mouths open in disbelief. I'm also way too shocked to say a word. The clearing is formed by a circle of skyscraper-tall trees. Their top branches have woven together to create a roof high above us that not even the finest ray of sunlight can penetrate. But the darkness isn't the freaky part. The freaky part is the fact that there are miniature crosses made from sticks hanging from almost all of the lower branches. There must be hundreds of them. Then I notice something else – around the edge of the clearing, on the floor, someone has arranged a ring of stones, with weird symbols painted on them in red and black.

'Belle?' the Flea whispers.

'Hey, CSI? What kind of spooky shit is this?' Dan says to Cruz.

Cruz shrugs his shoulders.

The Flea bends down and picks up one of the stones. 'What do you think these are for?'

'They are runes, I think,' Cruz says.

'What are runes?' Dan asks.

'Symbols from an ancient alphabet,' the Flea says. 'Some people believe they have magical properties.'

'They could be for protection,' Cruz says.

I frown. 'What do you mean?'

Cruz points to the ring of stones. 'Placed in a circle in this way, it could be they are meant as a protective barrier.'

'Protective barrier against what?' Dan asks.

No one answers.

High above us the wind rushes through the tops of the trees with a high-pitched whistle. I feel an overwhelming sense of foreboding.

'Somebody must be staying here,' the Flea whispers, nodding toward the smoking remains of the fire.

'It's the freakiest campsite I ever saw,' Dan whispers back.

'Look.' The Flea points to a tree next to him.

I lean closer and see a piece of paper skewered on the end of one of the branches.

'There's writing on it.' The Flea carefully removes the paper from the branch.

We all hunch over to take a closer look. There are two lines of handwriting scrawled across it. My heart sinks when I see that it isn't English.

'I wonder what it says,' the Flea murmurs.

'Home, sweet home?' Dan grins, but I can tell from his eyes that he's scared too.

'It is in Spanish – from the Lord's Prayer,' Cruz says, studying the writing.

'It is?' Dan frowns.

'And lead us not into temptation, but deliver us from evil,' Cruz reads.

'Whoa . . .' Dan shakes his head.

There's another gust of wind, stronger this time, causing the stick crosses to sway wildly, clunking against each other like wind chimes.

The Flea turns to me. 'Do you think it could belong to the man you saw yesterday?'

I nod slowly. 'I guess.'

'You don't think . . .'

We all look at the Flea, waiting for him to finish.

'What?' Dan says.

The Flea looks around nervously. 'You don't think that whoever it is has Belle?'

'But how would they have gotten her off the beach without you hearing?' I say.

'Yeah, man, there's no way that chick would be taken

anywhere she didn't want to go without putting up one hell of a fight,' Dan says.

Cruz walks further into the clearing. 'Look.' He points over to the far edge.

We gather round him and I see that he's pointing to something tucked beneath one of the bushes. Cruz bends down and pulls out an old canvas rucksack. We all look at each other, then Cruz slowly unzips it. The bag is full of clothes. A man's clothes. One by one, Cruz pulls out tattered, dirty T-shirts and pairs of shorts. Then, finally, he takes out a notebook. It's so old and worn the cover is falling off. Cruz opens it and flicks through and I see page after page of tiny scrawled handwriting.

'Is it in Spanish?' the Flea asks.

Cruz nods. 'It's a journal.'

'Dear Diary, I'm stuck on this screwed-up island with no one but parrots and snakes for company,' Dan says in a jokey voice. 'Good job I got my cross-making to help pass the time!'

I almost laugh, but stop as soon as I see Cruz frowning as he reads.

'Is everything okay?' the Flea asks.

Cruz nods and slams the notebook shut. 'Sure. Okay, we need to keep going. We need to find Belle.'

I really don't like the sudden urgency in his voice.

Clearly neither does the Flea. 'What is it?' he asks. 'What did you –'

'Shhh.' Cruz holds up his hand and the Flea falls silent.

'What is it?' Dan whispers.

We all listen. And then I hear it – the sound of someone or something moving, right on the other side of the clearing.

We all tiptoe over to a gap in the trees. I'm sandwiched between Cruz and Dan, with the Flea right behind me. As we peer into the gloom I have to try real hard to stop myself from screaming.

There, standing right behind the trees, is a man. His hair is matted and long. His thin face is streaked with mud, and his clothes are dirty and torn. But it's his eyes that are the most freakish thing about him – they are the palest blue I've ever seen – almost white against all the dirt and the hair. I wonder if he's the man I saw yesterday – I *think* so, but it's impossible to know for sure. If only I'd gotten a better look at him.

He points a shaking finger at us. His nails are long and twisted, like talons.

'Espiritu!' he cries, his voice brittle and wavering. 'Espiritu!'

'What's he saying?' Dan hisses at Cruz.

Cruz puts his hands up like he's surrendering.

'Does he mean, spirit?' the Flea asks.

Cruz nods and starts talking quietly in Spanish to the man, his voice low and reassuring.

'Is he warning us?' I say. 'Does he think he's seen a spirit?'

Cruz nods. 'He thinks *we* are spirits.'

'What the hell?' Dan exclaims, looking at the man. 'We ain't no spirits. We're real live flesh and blood, look.' He takes a step forward and the man lets out a piercing scream, before turning and fleeing down the path.

'Damn!' Dan exclaims.

'Come on.' Cruz starts running after the man. We all follow him. We've only gone a few yards when the man trips and falls over. As we gather round him he looks up at us, his face ashen with terror. He isn't as old as I'd first thought, just really dirty – and really scared.

'Espiritu!' he cries out over and over again. Then he starts reciting something in Spanish.

'What's he saying now?' the Flea asks Cruz.

'The Lord's Prayer,' Cruz says. 'He's trying to protect himself from us.'

'But why?' Dan says. He crouches down to talk to the man. 'Dude, we're just a bunch of kids from America, we ain't gonna hurt you.'

The man shrinks so far down into the ground it's like he's willing it swallow him up.

'Ask him if he's seen Belle,' the Flea says to Cruz.

Cruz starts talking to the man, again in a real calm voice, but the man just keeps on chanting to himself, over and over.

'What are we going to do?' the Flea asks, his voice trembling with despair. 'If that *was* a piece of Belle's top back there he might have seen her. She might have come right through here.'

Cruz frowns. Then he fumbles in his pocket for something. He takes out the small leather-bound book I saw him reading when I woke up this morning. He holds it out to the man. The man takes one look at it and falls silent. Then he reaches out a trembling hand and takes it from him.

'What did you give him?' the Flea asks.

'A Bible,' Cruz whispers.

The man hugs the book to his chest and starts to cry. Then he starts saying another word over and over.

'He's thanking me,' Cruz explains. Then, gently placing a hand on the man's arm, he asks him something.

The man starts to nod vigorously.

'What did you say to him?' Dan asks.

Cruz turns to us and smiles. 'I asked him if he'd seen Belle.'

Chapter Twenty-seven

'Where is she? Where did she go?' the Flea cries at the man, causing him to look totally freaked out again.

'Go easy,' Cruz says, 'If he gets scared he will not tell us anything.'

Cruz asks the man another question, and he gestures further into the forest.

'He says she went that way,' Cruz translates.

The man says something else and Cruz's face falls.

'What? What is it?' the Flea cries.

'He is saying, "they took her".'

'Who took her?' The Flea grabs the man's shoulder. 'What did you see?'

The man clutches the Bible to his chest and starts chanting.

'Oh God!' The Flea looks around in despair. 'What do we do now?'

Dan gets to his feet. 'I say we go get the others. We don't know what we could be dealing with here. We need everyone with us.'

The Flea starts pacing back and forth. 'But if we go back we're going to lose time, and he isn't going to want to go with us, is he?'

Cruz frowns. 'We cannot leave him. He will run away.'

Then I have an idea. 'How about I go back and get the others and you guys stay here with him?'

Cruz immediately shakes his head. 'It isn't safe for you to go off alone.'

'I'll come with you,' Dan says.

I shake my head, even though the thought of going back through the forest alone scares the hell out of me. 'No, you guys need to stick together. What if whoever's got Belle comes back?' I force a smile at Cruz. 'I'll be fine. I have a brown belt in jujitsu. All I have to do is follow the path, it's not like I can get lost or anything.'

Cruz frowns. 'I don't want you going off on your own in this place – it is too dangerous. None of us should be alone in here.'

'Okay, I'll go with Grace,' the Flea says. He looks at Cruz and Dan. 'It makes more sense for you guys to stay here,' he nods at the man, who is now leafing through the Bible, 'in case you need to restrain him or something. The only brown belt I've got is from Gucci and made of leather. But any sight of Belle and you better holler.'

Dan nods. 'We will, bro.'

'And you shout if you need us,' Cruz says.

I nod. We look at each other and for a split second I time-travel back to last night on the boat, falling asleep in Cruz's arms. What I would give to be back there right now and for none of this to have happened. I give Cruz a weak smile, then the Flea and I turn and start heading down the pathway.

We make the journey back in silence, but I bet the Flea's head is as noisy as mine with panicked thoughts. When we finally get back to the clearing leading to the beach, I link arms with him.

'Don't worry, once we've got the others with us I'm sure we'll find her.'

The Flea frowns. 'You think?'

I nod. 'Of course.'

But he looks away, and I can tell from the way he keeps blinking that he's close to tears. 'She's my best friend, Grace. She's the only person apart from my parents who's always accepted me for who I am. I know she can be hot-headed but she has a heart of gold. I don't know what I'd do if . . .'

I squeeze his arm tighter. 'She's going to be fine. You'll see.'

I spot a patch of blue sky at the entrance to the beach. 'Come on, we're nearly there.'

I let go of his arm and we start running. We burst out of the forest and head straight for the camp. But when we get to the alcove of trees we stop dead.

'What's going on?' The Flea looks at me, his eyes wide with alarm.

I shrug my shoulders, too shocked to say a word.

The camp has gone. Everything has gone – apart from Dan's things, and my suitcase standing bolt upright on the sand next to the charred remains of the fire. But I'd left my suitcase on the boat . . .

I run out of the camp and look down toward the sea. I clap my hand to my mouth in shock. Jenna and Cariss are standing by the edge of the water, watching as Todd and Ron push the boat out into the sea.

'No!' I yell at the top of my voice. I turn back to the Flea. 'Go get Dan and Cruz.'

The Flea still looks stunned. 'But . . .'

'Go!' I scream at him.

The Flea starts backing off toward the forest.

'Quick!' I yell. Then I start running down to the sea as fast as I can. I have to stop them. They can't leave us here.

'Stop!' I yell as I get to the HELP sign, and this time Todd hears me because he stops pushing and turns round.

'What are you doing?' I cry.

Jenna says something to Todd, then she comes running up to meet me.

'What's going on?' I gasp, almost hysterical with panic.

Jenna looks down at the sign. 'We've had enough waiting around. We're going to find help.'

'But what about Belle?' I clutch my side and gasp for breath.

Jenna looks at me, her gaze ice-cold. 'What about her? I'm sorry about her mom and all, but that really doesn't excuse the way she's behaved since we got here.'

I grab a hold of Jenna's arm. 'You don't understand. Belle's been taken. We've found this crazy guy in the forest. He says he's seen her; that someone has got her. We need your help.'

Jenna's icy mask slips and she looks genuinely shocked. 'Really?'

I feel a massive wave of relief – hopefully now I'll be able to get through to her. 'Yes. You guys have to help us. God knows who's got her.'

Jenna looks down toward the boat.

Todd and Ron are standing there in the shallow water, watching us.

'Come on, Jen,' Todd shouts.

Jenna turns back to me. 'I'm sorry, we can't,' she whispers.

I stare at her in disbelief. 'What?'

'We can't. We have to go.'

'But –'

'There's something wrong with Ron, he's acting real strange. We have to get him to a doctor.'

'What do you mean, strange?'

Jenna glances down at Ron, then back at me. 'It's like he's in some weird kind of a trance. I'm worried it's . . .'

'What?'

'Whatever he drank from that bottle last night.'

The panic inside of me reaches a crescendo. 'But the engine on the boat's broken, you're just going to drift.'

Jenna nods. 'I know, but at least there's a chance someone will find us.'

'But what about the rest of us?' I fight the urge to fall to my knees and start out and out begging.

'We'll send someone to get you as soon as we find help.' She smiles at me and for once it doesn't seem fake; it seems apologetic.

'Come on, Jenna,' Cariss calls from the boat. 'We have to go.'

Jenna suddenly takes a hold of my hand. 'Come with us, Grace.'

'What?'

'Now. Come with us.'

'But what about the others?'

'I told you, we'll send help for the others.'

'But we can't just leave them here. Didn't you hear what I said? Belle could be in danger.'

'But so could Ron!' Jenna's gaze hardens. 'I'm sorry, Grace, but Ron is my friend. That girl has been nothing but a bitch to me since we got here. Why should I feel any loyalty to her after the things she's done?'

'But she didn't do them!' It takes every fibre in my body not to grip her by the shoulders and shake her. 'And even if she did . . .'

Jenna looks at me. 'Even if she did, what?'

I take a deep breath. 'It's no worse than what you did to Taylor.'

Jenna gasps.

I reach out to grab a hold of her arm, but she's backing away like I'm trying to burn her. 'I'm sorry, I didn't mean to –'

'You . . .' Jenna's eyes are wide with shock . . . 'you promised me. You said you'd never mention it.'

'I know, but don't you think you're being a – hypocrite?'

Jenna stops dead. 'A what?'

'A hypocrite.' My hands are shaking and my mouth is dry. Talking about what happened after all these years of silence feels like opening some kind of Pandora's box. I don't know what might come flying out, but I'm desperate. I have to get Jenna to see sense.

Jenna blinks hard and bites her bottom lip. For a moment, I

think she's going to cry. I step toward her, tears welling in my eyes, but as I reach out to her again, the icy mask returns. She looks at me and shakes her head, then turns and starts running toward the water.

I stand there for a second, paralysed with disappointment. How could she freeze me out like that? How could she not understand what I was trying to say? Panic jolts my body back into action and I start racing after her. I catch up with her just as she reaches the boat, which is now fully in the water. 'Please!' I yell. 'You can't leave us here.'

The others start climbing the ladder on to the deck.

'Quick, Jenna, get on board,' Cariss calls over her shoulder as she climbs.

'You can't go,' I yell up at them. 'You've gotta help us.'

'I told her we'd send help as soon as we get picked up,' Jenna says to Cariss, as she starts to climb the ladder.

Despair weighs down on me like a coat made of lead.

I grab on to Jenna's leg and start pulling at her.

'Get off!' she shrieks.

'Todd, please!' I yell, looking up at him on the deck.

'I'm sorry,' he says. 'We can't just stay here. Ron needs help.'

I look at Ron standing motionless on the deck, staring out into space.

'But what about Belle . . .?' My voice fades along with my hope.

A huge wave rolls in and sucks the boat back out with it. I run after it and the water rushes up to my waist.

Jenna goes to stand right by Todd.

'Bye, Grace,' she says, as if she's just popping out to fetch some groceries.

I want to throw my head back and wail. Another huge wave rolls in, crashing in front of me and catching me full in the face. I stagger backward, choking and rubbing the salt water from my eyes. When I manage to open them again the boat is pulling away rapidly. I stand there watching, helpless, until it is just a dot on the ocean.

Chapter Twenty-eight

I run faster and faster through the forest, pain eating into my ankle with every step. *All I want is to see Cruz and the Flea and Dan*, I silently plead to whoever might be listening. I'll dedicate my life to charity, I'll never bitch about my parents again, I'll deliver all of my homework assignments on time. Just please, please let Belle and the others be okay and let us find a way out of here.

And then I hear a noise behind me. A rasping, breathless noise. I spin around.

'Who's there?' I call into the gloom. I can't see anyone. I feel for the wooden flower in my pocket and carry on, thinking of Cruz, and reassuring myself that it won't be long till I see him. But I hear the rasping sound again. Louder this time. For a split second I wonder if Jenna and the others had a change of heart. What if they've come back to help us? I look back over my shoulder.

'Who's there?' I shout again, my voice trembling slightly. 'Jenna? Todd? Is that you?'

There's a sudden flutter of birds' wings way up high in the treetops above me, like something's startled them into flight. I get a sick feeling in the pit of my stomach and turn and start running again. It's just the wind, I tell myself. Don't let it freak you out. But it feels as if the pathway's never going to end; like I've been doomed to run down this tunnel of green forever. My hair is sticking to the sweat on my face and my heart is pounding. *Please let me get to them soon. Please let them be okay*. And then I see a figure racing down the pathway toward me. Cruz! I launch myself at him and into his arms. He grips me tight like a vice and starts saying something in Spanish over and over in my ear. Then he leans back slightly to study my face.

'Are you okay?'

I nod. 'Yes, but the others –' I break off, willing myself not to cry.

Cruz frowns. 'Jimmy – he told us that they were trying to take the boat. Is that true?'

I nod. 'They've taken it.'

'What?' Cruz looks furious. 'But the engine is not working. They have no idea what they're doing.'

'I know, but they wouldn't listen.'

Cruz looks down the pathway as if he's seriously thinking about chasing after them.

'It's too late – they've gone,' I say quietly.

Cruz sighs, then he puts his arm round my shoulder and hugs me to him. 'Come on,' he says, leading me back down the path.

In the clearing, Dan and the Flea are huddled in conversation by the man. As soon as they see us Dan races over. 'Did you get them to stay?' he asks. 'Please tell me you got them to stay.'

I shake my head, unable to look at him – or anyone. 'No, they've gone.'

'But what about us?' Dan takes off his cap and shakes his head in disbelief.

'What about *Belle*?' the Flea says.

'I told them about Belle, but they were too worried about Ron.'

Dan frowns. 'What's up with Ron?'

'He's acting real spaced-out. Jenna's worried it might have been whatever he drank from that bottle.'

Dan nods. 'He was pretty weird when we got up this morning.'

Cruz starts pacing around the clearing. The man watches him nervously through his matted hair.

'They said they'd send help as soon as they get picked up.' But doubt and guilt have wormed their way into my mind.

Was there more I could have done? Could I have stopped them going if I'd tried harder?

'They are so stupid!' Cruz snaps.

The man jumps to his feet and starts muttering. Cruz says something soothing to him in Spanish and it seems to pacify him.

'Did you tell them about him,' the Flea says, gesturing at the man, 'and what he said about Belle being taken?'

I nod.

'I don't know how those guys can live with themselves,' Dan says, putting his cap back on and pulling it down tight.

Then, suddenly, the man lets out a piercing shriek and points a trembling finger toward the entrance of the clearing. As I turn to follow his gaze I hear the same rasping sound I'd heard on my way back through the forest.

A figure is standing in the gap between the trees. It's wearing a tattered, hooded robe, the colour of sand, and is so old and stooped it's hard to tell if it's a man or a woman. But then it raises its head and I see that it's a woman. Her long grey hair hangs in cornrow braids and her face is so dark and wrinkled it looks as if it's been mummified.

She stares at the man through lifeless eyes, her breath rasping around the clearing like a stormy wind.

The man looks about in terror, then his eyes meet mine.

He starts saying something to me in Spanish, and although I

can't understand, I can tell from the way he's talking that he's pleading with me. Then he says a word I *do* understand, over and over again, and it makes the hairs on the back of my neck stand on end.

'Hortense! Hortense! Hortense!'

Chapter Twenty-nine

The man grabs a cross from one of the trees and holds it out in front of him, his hand trembling. Then he starts backing out of the clearing.

Cruz and I look at each other, and I know from the fear in his eyes that he's thinking the same as me – Hortense *does* exist and she's standing right in front of us.

The woman takes a step into the clearing, her withered arms raised toward us, her crooked fingers quivering. The temperature immediately plummets and goosebumps erupt on my skin.

'Okay, what kind of messed-up old folks' resort *is* this?' Dan says.

'Come on, let's get out of here.' Cruz starts ushering us out of the clearing. As I hurry past him he grabs hold of my hand

and I feel a welcome rush of warmth.

The path on the other side is much wider and less tunnel-like than the one we came down. But this makes it real hard to keep track of the man, who's able to weave in and out of the trees.

The Flea leads the way as we race after him, followed by Dan, then me and Cruz.

'Do you think that was her?' I whisper to Cruz as we run. 'Do you think that was Hortense?'

'I don't know,' he whispers back. 'But I think maybe, yes.'

I glance over my shoulder. There's no sign of the woman following us. But I guess if she is an evil spirit like in the story she'll be able to spring up anywhere.

Up ahead of us the man suddenly breaks away from the path, charging straight into a cluster of bushes. He screams something, then his voice tapers off into silence. The Flea and Dan charge into the bushes after him, then stop suddenly, pulling each other back and yelling in fright.

Dan turns to us and shakes his head. The Flea stands statue-still, looking pale and shell-shocked.

I limp up to them and peer over the Flea's shoulder. 'Oh my God!'

We are standing right at the edge of a huge canyon. On the other side of the bushes is a sheer drop of at least a couple hundred feet.

'Where did he go?' I ask, knowing the answer but not wanting to believe it.

The Flea swallows, then nods downwards.

Holding on to Cruz's arm I lean forward and there, far below us, I see the man's body splayed out on the dusty red ground.

I turn away with my hand to my mouth, fighting the urge to vomit.

Cruz bows his head and makes a quick sign of the cross, then he puts his arm around my shoulders and holds me tight.

Dan starts pacing back and forth. 'I guess he didn't know what was on the other side of the bushes. I guess he was just trying to hide from that – that thing.'

Cruz shakes his head. 'He knew.'

The Flea's eyes widen in horror. 'What do you mean? Why would he go running through there like that if he knew what was on the other side?'

'He knew he was going to die.' Cruz's voice is barely more than a whisper. 'When he was shouting, right before he went – he was asking God's forgiveness for killing himself.'

'Man!' Dan takes off his baseball cap and wipes his brow. His eyes are shiny with tears.

'What *was* that thing?' the Flea says, looking back the way we came. 'Why would he choose to die rather than face it?'

We all follow his gaze back into the forest as if expecting

Hortense, or whatever it was, to come rasping through the trees at any moment.

'Belle!' the Flea yells, making us all jump. 'Can you hear us, honey?'

There's a chorus of screeches and squawks and the forest falls silent again.

'*Don't be scared.*'

My skin crawls at the soft, sinister purr of her voice. I look at the others. They're still staring at each other, shell-shocked.

'*Follow the sound of the drums.*'

What drums? I look around in panic. Why can no one else hear her?

Then Cruz frowns. 'What's that sound?' he asks.

My heart leaps. Can he hear her now too? 'What sound?' I ask cautiously.

'Some kind of drumming,' he says.

My stomach lurches.

Dan and the Flea start to nod, and then I hear it too – a very faint drumming sound, like a distant heartbeat.

The Flea glances around wildly. 'Where's it coming from?'

'I think it's someplace over there,' Dan says, pointing deeper into the forest.

We start walking back along the footpath. No one says a word. I try to process what just happened. Somebody died. Right in front of me. And although I didn't know the man, and although he was pretty darn scary, it doesn't make it any easier to take. The others must be feeling the same, they're all looking completely devastated.

After we've been walking for a couple of minutes, the Flea puts up his hand. 'I think we're getting closer.'

We stop and listen. The drumming is definitely getting louder.

The Flea looks at us, distraught. 'What the hell is going on here? Where are we? What's happened to Belle?'

Dan slings his arm round the Flea's shoulder. 'Hey, take it easy, bro. It could be some kind of party.'

The Flea raises his eyebrows. 'Right. Well, given the state of the islanders we've encountered so far, you'll forgive me if I'm not in too much of a hurry for an invite.'

'Come on,' Cruz says. 'We have to check it out.'

As we head deeper into the forest the drumming gets louder and louder. Every few seconds I glance back over my shoulder, expecting to see the robed woman lurching after us, but as suddenly as she appeared, she seems to have vanished – swallowed up by the forest's web of green.

We reach a point where the footpath curves sharply to the right. We follow it round and find ourselves at the entrance to a huge clearing. Ahead of us, at the far end of the clearing, is a sheer wall of flame-red rock.

'Wow!' Dan tilts his head back to take it all in.

I do the same. The craggy rock seems to stretch up forever.

'The volcano!' the Flea gasps.

I feel Cruz's fingers linking with mine. I grip his hand tightly. The drumming seems to be coming from right inside the volcano, but how can that be? Then I spot a cave mouth carved into the base of the rock, partially hidden by a curtain of vines. As I point to it I notice that my hand is trembling.

'Look,' I whisper.

'Belle!' the Flea calls out. 'Can you hear me?'

'Shhh!' I grab his arm. 'We don't know who's in there.'

The drumming stops.

There's a moment's silence and then the echoing sound of footsteps running away. We stand there for a second, frozen to the spot, until the sound fades to nothing and all that's left is the distant squawk of a bird.

'Come on,' I say, tiptoeing forward. My heart has taken over where the drumming left off, pounding like crazy inside my ribcage. Cruz grips my hand tighter. The Flea and Dan come right up close on my other side, so we're moving together as one unit. When we reach the volcano we press our backs against the rocky wall and start edging our way toward the entrance. As I psych myself up for whatever might be waiting inside I'm hit by such an aching need for my parents it nearly floors me. What if I never see them again? I take a deep breath. I *will* see them again. I have to see them again.

When we reach the entrance we all exchange weak smiles. Cruz squeezes my hand tightly. I take another step to my right and peer inside. At first I see nothing but darkness, but then my eyes adjust and I make out a flickering light from quite a long way in. I nod to the others and we all file inside.

Up ahead of us, all around the edge of the cave, are what look like hundreds of candles, glowing like animal eyes in the dark. It looks kind of pretty – until we get closer – and I see that each candle has been placed inside a human skull.

We look at each other, open-mouthed with horror.

'What *is* this?' the Flea whispers.

I look up at Cruz. The candlelight is making shadows dance on his face, but I can see that his eyes are wide with fear. 'Come on,' he whispers. 'We have to keep looking for Belle.'

We walk past the first of the skull lanterns. Above us, wherever the crags in the cave wall form a natural cubbyhole, someone has placed a religious figurine. I move a little closer to a statuette of the Virgin Mary and immediately step back again. Just like the doll Jenna found hanging over her bed, the Virgin Mary has red trails coming from her eyes like tears of blood. I glance at a few of the other statuettes and see that they all do. I want to turn and run out of there as fast as I can, yelling for help at the top of my lungs. But there's nowhere to go and there's no one to help us.

Cruz nudges me and points to the floor in the center of the

cave. I take a sharp breath. Someone has drawn a huge snake in the dirt – above the letter H.

'Hey,' the Flea gasps, 'it's the same as the symbol on the pendant.' He goes a little further into the cave. Then he stops dead in his tracks and turns back to us, shaking his head. 'Oh my God!'

I hurry over to him. 'What is it?'

'Beau-Belle,' the Flea whispers, turning to face the very back of the cave. His whole body is shaking violently.

I try to swallow but my mouth's too dry. What's gotten him so upset? Summoning every last drop of courage, I turn and follow his gaze to the far end of the cave. What I see makes my legs buckle with shock.

Belle has been laid out on some kind of wooden altar.

We all run over to her. Her eyes are shut and her face is waxen.

'Oh, no! Oh, Belle!' The Flea reaches her first and grabs her body to him. Her arm hangs down by her side, totally lifeless.

I turn to Cruz, my eyes filling with tears. 'We're too late.'

Dan comes and stands beside me as Cruz bends down and presses his fingers to the side of Belle's neck. 'I can feel a pulse,' he says.

The Flea looks at him. 'But I can't feel her breathing.'

'It's very faint,' Cruz says. 'Come on, let's get her outside.'

But before we can move a sudden breeze rushes in, filling the cave with a terrible sighing sound. The candles inside the skulls start flickering like crazy.

'Quick!' the Flea says.

Another gust of wind rushes in, more powerful this time, and one by one the candles are snuffed out and we're plunged into darkness.

'Okay, everyone hold on to Belle and don't let go,' Cruz says.

I reach out and take hold of Belle's cold, limp hand. I hear Dan, Cruz and the Flea moving about in the dark and then feel Belle's body being lifted.

'Let's go,' Cruz says.

We start stumbling back in the direction we came, but the darkness is so dense it's impossible to see a thing and we end up crashing into the wall.

'Hold on,' Dan says.

I hear a clicking sound and see a small flicker of light.

'Your lighter!' the Flea exclaims.

'Yes, sir.' Dan holds up the lighter and we're just able to make out the way to the entrance before another gust of wind blows it out.

After what feels like forever, we stagger back into the clearing and lay Belle on the ground. All around us the trees bend and sway, the moaning wind making it sound as if they're in pain. The Flea kneels down next to Belle and gently places her head on his lap.

Belle frowns.

'Beau-Belle! Can you hear me? Squeeze my hand if you can hear me.' The Flea looks up at us excitedly. 'She squeezed it!'

High above us the sky darkens. I look up, expecting to see a storm brewing, but the sky is filled with huge clouds of birds, all fleeing the forest like they've sensed something terrible's coming.

Belle moves her head from side to side and moans. 'Jimmy?' she whispers.

The Flea bends down over her. 'Yes, honey, it's me. Everything's okay. You're safe now.'

Belle slowly opens her eyes and squints up at us. 'What happened? Where are we?'

'We're by the volcano,' the Flea says, hugging her to him.

'But how . . .?' Belle closes her eyes.

'Somebody brought you here,' the Flea says softly. 'Do you remember who it was?'

Belle keeps her eyes shut and shakes her head.

'I say we get out of here before they come back.' Dan looks toward the cave.

Cruz nods. 'Are you okay with that, Belle? We can carry you.'

Belle nods. 'I don't remember anything,' she whispers. Then she opens her eyes and looks at me. She looks so frightened. I crouch down next to her and take her hands in mine. They're still icy cold. I try to rub a little warmth back into them.

'It's okay. You're back with us now.'

Belle gives me a weak smile and tries to shift into a more upright position.

'What's the last thing you do remember, honey?' the Flea asks.

Belle frowns. 'I remember eating fish – and playing that dumb game of Truth or Dare. I remember everyone fighting. And then going to bed, and saying a prayer for my . . .' She looks down suddenly. 'Oh, no!'

The Flea looks at me, alarmed. 'What is it?'

Belle stares up at him, panic-stricken. 'My mom's necklace. It's gone!'

Chapter Thirty

I creep back into the cave, with Cruz right behind me.

'What makes you so sure it is in here?' he whispers.

'I'm not.' I turn to him. 'But I had to do something. It's Belle's one link to her mom. We've gotta at least try and find it.'

I take hold of Cruz's hand and he strokes my palm with his thumb. Then he pulls me to him and his lips press on to mine. The kiss only lasts a second but it fills me with strength. 'Let's go,' I whisper.

We creep further through the gloom with me flicking Dan's lighter on and off to guide the way.

'Shall we look over by the altar thing?' I whisper. 'Maybe it fell off when they put her there.'

Cruz nods, then he bends down and picks up one of the skulls.

'What are you doing?' I hiss.

'Getting a candle, to help us search.'

'Oh.' I watch as he carefully removes the candle from the base of the skull. 'Is it – does it feel real?'

Cruz holds the candle out for me to light. 'Yes, it's real, look.'

'No, not the candle – the skull, does it feel real?'

Cruz nods and it feels as if the blood in my veins has frozen solid. Who did the skull belong to? I look down at the letter H drawn in the dirt on the floor. 'Hortense is here, isn't she?'

I want him to say no and tell me I'm being dumb, but Cruz just nods. My stomach starts to churn.

'You know when I was reading the man's diary before?' Cruz whispers.

'Uh-huh.'

'He wrote that he'd come here to see if the legend was true, to see if Hortense really did exist.'

I look up at him. 'And?'

'And it looks like he found her. In the very last entry he says that she was hunting him like a wild animal.'

My teeth start chattering as I think back to the horrific woman who'd come staggering after us in the forest, and how the man had fled from her to his death – exactly like hunted prey.

'Come on, we must hurry.' Cruz takes my hand and leads me to the altar. We shine the candle over it but it's completely bare. Cruz looks at me and shrugs. 'Nothing.'

'What about underneath?' I crouch down and start feeling around cautiously in the dirt. I jump as my fingertips brush against something solid. It feels curved, like a cup maybe, but it's too wide. I feel it some more. It feels like a plate, or a bowl. A sudden breeze rushes past the back of my neck, bringing with it the sickly incense scent.

'*I've waited so long for you to come to me.*'

The whisper makes my skin turn icy cold, and I feel like my heart has stopped. But I try to disguise my fright, and peer over my shoulder into the gloom. *Are you Hortense?* I ask silently.

'*Yes.*' The whisper rushes past me – *through* me – chilling me to the core. '*You have the girl,*' she whispers gently, '*now I need you to come to the back of the cave. Alone.*'

No! I yell back in my head.

The smell intensifies. '*Do not be afraid. I have done so much for you. Now it is your turn to help me.*'

I look around blindly. What is she talking about? She hasn't done a thing for me – apart from freak me out ever since I got here.

'*Yes, I have. I took revenge upon the friend who betrayed you.*'

'What?' I'm so shocked I say it out loud.

Cruz places a hand on my back. 'You okay?'

'Yes. Sorry. I thought I heard something.'

'*The friend with the long pale hair,*' she whispers in my ear.

'*Every time she hurt you I hurt her back. Now you must help me. Come to the back of the cave.*'

I want to yell no. I want to yell at Cruz to help me. I want to get up. But I can't do anything. My body feels weighted to the ground.

'What did you think you heard?' Cruz asks.

'*Tell him to leave.*' Her voice is louder now, deep and rich, like a cello.

The sickly smell swirls around me like a thick fog. My mouth is opening. I can't stop it. Why can't I stop it? I mustn't tell him to leave, I –

'Cruz, you have to go. You have to get out of here,' I hear myself saying.

'What?' His voice sounds echoey and far away.

'You have to –' I go to put the bowl down and my fingers brush against something hard and pointy.

My thoughts are blending together in a thick soup of random words. I can't remember why, but I know I have to pick this thing up.

'*Leave it!*' her voice roars in my ear, angry and fierce.

My fingers clamp round it tightly. The pointed edges cut into my skin. It feels like a cross. And then I remember. It's Belle's mom's crucifix. Belle! I have to get it back to her.

'*No!*' the voice hisses.

'Grace, are you okay?'

I feel Cruz's hands on my arms. He's pulling me up. I grip the crucifix tighter. I can hear someone gasping for breath. 'Who's there?' I cry, and then I realize that it's me.

'Come on.' Cruz's voice is in my ear. His arms are round me, holding me tight. My whole body starts tingling as the life rushes back into my limbs. It hurts so bad. Clutching the necklace and the bowl, I let Cruz guide me back through the cave.

'*Don't leave me. I need you. It is destiny!*' Hortense cries as we leave.

And her voice fades to nothing.

Find anything?' the Flea calls as we come staggering out of the cave.

I blink at the sudden brightness of the light.

'Are you okay?' Cruz says, gripping my shoulders and staring into my eyes.

I nod and take a few deep breaths.

'Grace, are you all right?' Belle asks. She's sitting right up now and not looking quite so pale.

I nod again, then open my tightly clenched fist and see her crucifix. 'I got it. I got the necklace.' Then I look at my other hand and what I see make my legs turn to jello. 'Oh, God! How . . .?'

'What is it, Gracie?' the Flea calls.

I drop down to my knees and put the bowl on the ground in

front of me. 'I don't understand. How did it get here?'

Cruz crouches down next to me, and puts his hand on my back. 'What's wrong?'

'How did what get here?' Dan asks, coming over.

I can't tear my eyes from the bowl. 'It's – it's . . .'

'It's what?' Cruz says gently, looking at the bowl.

'It's mine.'

'What do you mean, it's yours?' Dan stares at me, bewildered.

I pick up the bowl with trembling hands. The bottom is coated with a thick, black dust, but I can see the inscription running around the rim.

Vivre éternellement dans l'obscurité de la lune.

I think back to the night before we left for the trip, sitting by my bedroom window, setting fire to my cosmic wish list, and saying those exact same words as I watched the glowing embers drifting off into the dark sky. I shiver and Cruz pulls me closer to him.

'How can this be yours?' he says.

'My dad got it for me when he went on holiday – Oh, God!' I look at Cruz, terrified, as I remember. 'When he went to New Orleans.'

Dan shakes his head and starts to chuckle. 'Honey, I think they would've made more than one of them. I don't think this is your actual bowl.'

The Flea nods. 'Exactly. Although it is quite unusual looking.'

I look back at Cruz. He's staring at the bowl. 'What's that beneath the writing?'

I wipe the dust away and see the engravings I'd dismissed as some kind of hieroglyphs before – tiny snake symbols above the letter H.

Chapter Thirty-one

Apart from the odd moan from Belle as she's carried by Dan and Cruz, we start the journey back to the beach in total silence. I guess we're all too stunned to speak. When I'd finally managed to compose myself I told the others I was just being stupid about the bowl and that it was the shock of seeing something so familiar that made me freak out. I'm so confused I can barely think straight, but one thing I do know for sure is that I don't want to scare them even more. There's only one person I can tell.

I glance over at Cruz. His face and arms are glistening with sweat as he carries Belle. He looks at me and nods and I feel the tiniest ray of hope. Maybe he'll be able to figure out what's been happening here, once I tell him everything. I start going over the facts in my head, like I'm preparing a presentation.

Dan's right – the bowl can't be the actual one my dad gave me – but it is identical. And it does have Hortense's symbol on it; the same symbol as the one on the pendant and on the floor in the cave. All this time Hortense's voice has been leading me to it. Belle was like the bait to reel me in. But why? And why would she have done all of those horrible things to Jenna for me? Why does she need *me*?

When we get near to the clearing where we found the man, the Flea takes hold of Belle's hand. 'This next bit gets a bit spooky, honey, but it's okay.'

Belle looks at him, alarmed.

But when we enter the clearing it's like the man never existed. The whole place has been stripped of every single cross and stone and piece of paper. Even the remains of the fire have vanished.

The Flea looks at us in panic. 'But . . .'

'What is it?' Belle says. 'What's happened?'

Cruz smiles down at her. 'Nothing. Everything is cool.' He looks at the Flea and shakes his head, as if to say, don't frighten her.

The Flea gets the message and forces a grin. 'I was just kidding, hun.'

'Weird thing to kid about,' Belle mutters, but she clutches her mom's necklace to her chest and closes her eyes.

As we carry on down the pathway Dan looks at the Flea.

'We're gonna have to tell Belle about the others.'

The Flea nods.

'What about the others?' Belle murmurs without opening her eyes.

'They've gone to get help,' the Flea says. 'In the boat.'

Belle looks at us in panic. 'In the boat? But none of them knows how to sail.'

I nod. 'I know. But they're hoping that if they drift far enough they'll come across another boat.'

'But what about us?' Belle cries. 'How could they leave us? Why didn't you stop them?'

'Grace tried to, hun,' the Flea says, squeezing her hand.

Belle looks at me, her eyes wide with fear.

'I'm sorry,' I whisper, my eyes starting to burn.

'It's okay. I'm sorry for shouting.' Belle closes her eyes again and sighs. 'I'm just so tired.'

We finally get back to the purple ferns and the Flea and I hold them apart so Dan and Cruz can carry Belle through. When I see the light filtering through the trees leading to the beach I want to cry with relief.

Quickening our pace, we stumble out of the forest and collapse down on to the sand.

'Thank you, thank you, thank you!' the Flea exclaims, lying on his back and gazing upwards. The sky is pale blue with smudges of rose-pink cloud. It feels weird emerging into something so pretty after everything we've just been through. Kind of unreal somehow.

I roll on to my side and look down at the dark-blue ocean. I imagine the boat adrift in the middle of it and it makes me shiver. Belle curls up on her side, clutching her mom's necklace. I go fetch a towel from my case and place it over her. She looks up at me and smiles. 'Thanks, Grace,' she whispers. She still looks real tired. I wonder what happened to her while she was with Hortense.

Dan looks around what's left of our camp. 'So, what do we do now?'

'How about Grace and I go and get some fish?' Cruz says. 'And you guys make a fire.'

Dan nods. 'Okay.'

'Why don't you bring the bowl – to put the fish in?' Cruz says, looking at me pointedly.

I nod. He knows I have more to tell him.

The Flea glances back at the forest. 'I say we move further down the beach, away from – you know . . .'

We all nod.

'And tonight we take turns keeping guard,' Dan says. 'I ain't having no psycho old lady attacking me in my sleep.'

My excitement at making it out of the forest starts fading

fast. We might have made it back to the beach, but we're still stuck on the island – without the boat and with God knows who.

As if reading my mind, Cruz takes hold of my hand. 'Come on, let's go.' He turns to the others. 'Yell if you need us.'

'Oh, don't you worry about that!' the Flea says, starting to gather some sticks for the fire. 'I'll holler so loud they'll hear me on Pluto.'

As soon as we're out of earshot of the others I turn to Cruz. 'I have to tell you something.'

Cruz nods. 'I have to tell you something too.'

I look at him, scared. 'What is it?'

'No, you go first.'

Swallowing my embarrassment, I tell him all about my bowl and the cosmic wish list and how I recited the inscription as I set light to the paper. Thankfully we reach the pitch-dark tunnel to the inlet just as I get to the bit about the dreams I've been having and the whispered voice I've been hearing, and how she told me she was Hortense, and what she told me in the cave.

When we emerge into the light on the other side I wait for Cruz to shake his head and look at me like I'm nuts, but he doesn't. He just leads me over to the rocks, and gestures at me to sit down.

'You should have told me about hearing her voice,' he says softly.

I flush. 'I wanted to, but I didn't want you thinking I was crazy.'

He takes a hold of my hand and squeezes it tightly. 'I would never think that.'

His gaze is so genuine and so concerned I'm flooded with regret. If only I'd had the courage to tell him sooner. 'Thank you,' I whisper.

He leans over to kiss me and I'm almost overcome with gratitude and relief. How would I ever have gotten through the past few days without Cruz?

'So, what do you think about the bowl?' I ask nervously.

Cruz takes it from me and reads the words around the rim. '*Vivre éternellement dans l'obscurité de la lune*.'

'What do you think it means?' I say.

'Well, "*vivre éternellement*" it means "live forever", and I am pretty certain "*l'obscurité*" is "the dark".' Cruz replies.

I think of Belle's lullaby about the moon goddess Luna. 'And "*lune*" could be moon,' I suggest.

Cruz nods. 'Yes. That's right. So, "Live forever in the dark of the moon".'

'But what does it mean?'

Cruz shrugs.

I take a deep breath, knowing that once I've spoken my deepest fear out loud it will probably make it seem all the more real. 'Do you think that the bowl – or bowls – once belonged to Hortense? When she was in New Orleans? I remember my dad saying it was an antique when he gave it to me – I wish I'd paid more attention now. To be honest I was pretty annoyed he hadn't gotten me something a little more exciting, you know?'

Cruz gives a wry laugh. 'I bet you do not think that now!' Then he sighs. 'This is going to sound a little bit crazy . . .'

I shake my head. 'Trust me, nothing you say could sound any crazier than the thoughts I've been having.'

'Well, suppose Hortense put a spell of some kind on the bowls when she was in New Orleans.'

'Okay.'

'And she left one behind – the one your father ended up buying. Then, when you did the cosmic star thing, you somehow released the spell.' He takes a hold of my hand and stares at me intently. 'You said that you feel as if she's been leading you to her? As if she wants something from you?'

I nod.

'Maybe what you did with your bowl started that. That would explain why you've been dreaming about her too.'

I look at him and gasp. 'Oh my God, the first time I had the dream was right after I used the bowl. I thought it was because I'd set fire to my wish list. But it wasn't – it was her. And that means . . .' I look away. I can't bring myself to say it. If using the bowl started a chain of events to bring me to Hortense then it means that I'm responsible for everything that's happened since. I'm responsible for us getting shipwrecked.

'It's not your fault,' Cruz says quickly. 'You are not the one who cast the spell, if that's what this is. You are not to blame for what has happened. She is.'

I make myself smile and nod but Cruz must sense my unease because he hugs me to him.

'But it doesn't matter,' he murmurs into my hair, 'because maybe it is all going to be okay anyway.'

I frown. 'What do you mean?'

'Well, when you refused to obey her in the cave –' I nod – 'Maybe that broke the spell.'

I look up at him hopefully. 'You think?'

He nods. 'We made it out of there, didn't we? She didn't come after us.'

'Yes.' I start to smile. 'She wouldn't have let us go, would she? I mean, if she could've stopped us.'

'That is what I'm saying.'

I sigh and look down at the clear turquoise water streaming by us. 'But we're still stuck on this dumb island. How do we know she won't try something else?'

'We don't. But . . .'

'But what?'

Cruz starts to grin.

'What is it? Why are you smiling?'

He takes my hands in his. 'I didn't want to say anything in front of the others, just in case it is, you know, a false alarm.'

'Just in case *what's* a false alarm?'

'I think I know a way to get us out of this place.'

'What? How?'

Cruz kisses me on the nose, then gets to his feet. My heart is thumping so hard I can feel the blood pulsing in my ears. Is he serious? Has he really found a way out of here? I scramble up as Cruz pulls the man's tattered journal from his pocket. He opens the journal at the very end. On the inside of the back cover is a hand-drawn map. Three words are written at the top in wonky capitals.

I read them out loud. 'Île de Sang.'

'Look.' Cruz points to a narrow cove on the map where the man has drawn an arrow and written something in tiny print.

'What is it? What does it say?'

'It says "boat". I think maybe it is where he hid his boat. When he first came to the island.'

'You're kidding? But how do we find it? How do we know where we are?'

Cruz grins at me, his brown eyes twinkling. 'Aha, so you might be a champion at fishing and a brown belt in jujitsu but you cannot read a map.'

'Yes, I can.' I grab the book from him and study it.

'Look. Here is the volcano,' Cruz points to a red peak in the centre of the map.

I look at him and raise my eyebrows. 'I did figure that one out.'

'And here is our beach.' He points to a large bay at the bottom of the island.

I frown at him. 'But how do you know it isn't one of the bays on the other side?'

Cruz smiles and points to a compass symbol in the corner. 'Because the sun – it rises behind the volcano, so our beach has to be on the west coast.'

I look at the bay. It's right next to the narrower inlet with the arrow pointing to it. 'But that means . . .'

Cruz smiles. 'I know.'

I look around. 'The boat's someplace here?' I whisper, hardly daring to say it.

'Uh-huh.'

'But where?' I turn a full three-sixty degrees, trying to spot a possible hiding place, but the inlet has no trees or plants and no tucked away corners – everything is visible.

'The only place I can think of is back there.' Cruz nods toward the tunnel leading to the beach.

'But we've been through so many times and never seen a thing.'

'I know. But it is so dark in there. And we weren't looking for a boat before. Come on.' He grabs my hand and we scramble back across the rocks toward the tunnel.

'We have to feel the walls inside,' Cruz says. 'He might have found some kind of – what is the right word? A space? Like a hiding place? You take the left side and I take the right.'

We start fumbling our way along the tunnel. The walls are cold and slippery and coated in thick strands of seaweed. I start having serious doubts about Cruz's theory. How could the man have hidden a boat in here? How would we not have stumbled into it before? I'm about to tell Cruz not to get his hopes up when he lets out a cry.

'What is it?'

'Come here.'

We're at the mid-point of the tunnel where it's so dark I can't even see an inch in front of my face. Cruz grabs my hand and guides it over to the right. I feel the cold solid wall, then the slimy curtain of seaweed gives way to open space. I pull my arm back in shock.

'Put your hand through,' Cruz says, gently easing my arm forward again.

I reach through the seaweed – the tunnel wall has completely disappeared.

'Now reach down,' Cruz says, guiding my hand downwards.

I feel something smooth. I start groping at it wildly. It goes on and on. It's big enough to be a boat, but I can't let myself believe until I'm totally certain. I reach upwards and feel some fabric bound around a pole.

'The sail,' I whisper.

I feel Cruz nodding behind me.

I turn around and sink into his arms. 'We've found a boat!'

'We have.'

And now I start to cry, great big, heaving sobs. All I can think of is how Jenna and I had stood right in this very spot – the night she caught me kissing Cruz – the night everything started going wrong. If only one of us had slipped, and brushed against the boat. How differently would things have turned out?

Cruz hugs me tighter, his warmth and his strength wrapped around me like a blanket.

'I told you I would get you out of here,' he whispers in my ear. 'I told you I would keep you safe.' His lips start brushing my face, kissing away my tears. I tilt my head so that my mouth can find his and we kiss until all of my sadness is transformed into twenty-four carat joy. It's like Cruz is some kind of freaky love alchemist. 'I mean it,' he whispers, cupping my face in his hands.

'I know,' I whisper back. 'You are responsible for me now you've saved my life.'

'Not just that,' he says, pulling me closer.

'What then?'

He falls silent for a moment. And in that moment a word echoes back at me – filling my mind, my body and, for all I know, the whole darn tunnel.

'I think I love you,' Cruz murmurs.

I stare at him in shock. It's as if he's opened the top of my head and plucked out exactly what I wanted to say to him.

'Grace! Cruz!' Dan's voice reverberates down the tunnel, making us jump apart. 'You guys need any help catching some fish?'

'It's okay,' Cruz calls back. But I can feel him still looking at me in the dark.

I stand there, paralysed, his words ringing in my ears. *I love you, I love you, I love you*.

'Are you coming back already?' Dan's voice gets a little louder as he starts heading toward us. 'You catch anything?'

'We did,' Cruz says. 'But not a fish.'

'Say what?' I hear Dan scrambling closer through the dark and I take a deep breath of the cool damp air and try and re-enter the earth's orbit.

'Do you have your lighter?' Cruz calls out to Dan.

'Sure.'

I hear a click and see a tiny, wavering light up ahead. 'This way,' I call out to him. Then I take hold of Cruz's hand and squeeze it three times – *I. Love. You.* – like I'm talking to him in Morse code. I don't know if he gets what I'm trying to say, but he squeezes my hand back and kisses the top of my head.

After a few seconds Dan reaches us.

'Turn on your lighter,' Cruz says.

Dan clicks the lighter and I pull back the seaweed. Cruz was right. There's a huge alcove in the tunnel wall, and tucked inside it is a boat.

'You are kiddin' me!' Dan exclaims.

I crouch down and start to laugh and laugh. It's like my brain can't cope with the sudden bombardment of awesomeness – it's become too wired up for doom.

Dan leans forward with the light. The boat is packed with storage boxes. Cruz pulls one out and opens it. It's crammed full of canned food and bottles of water.

'Oh man, are you guys seeing what I'm seeing or am I just having some kind of freaky starvation-induced hallucination?' Dan whispers, picking up a can of hot dogs.

'It looks pretty real to me,' I whisper back.

Dan checks the can with his lighter. 'They're still in date!' He starts to whoop and jump around and Cruz says something very happy-sounding in Spanish. I just carry on laughing like a loon.

'So, all this time,' Dan says, his voice helium-squeaky with excitement. 'All this time we've been living off frickin' coconuts, there's been a mini Walmart right under our noses!'

'Is everything okay?' the Flea calls down the tunnel. 'I heard a load of shouting. 'What are you guys doing?'

'Wait there,' I yell.

Cruz hands Dan and me a box each and we start making our way back along the tunnel.

'Did you get some fish already?' the Flea shouts.

Dan chuckles. 'No, sir, but we got you some hot dogs.'

'Er, not funny, Dan,' the Flea calls back. 'Joking about food with a starving man is kind of like joking about the ozone layer with Al Gore. Very poor taste.'

Dan laughs even harder. 'Jimmy, man, you crack me up.'

The Flea gives a sarcastic cough, but I just know he'll be grinning from ear to ear.

As soon as we reach the bend in the tunnel leading to the beach I see the Flea's thin silhouette against the setting sun.

'What's going on? What do you guys have?' the Flea says as we reach him.

'What do we have?' Dan says, his eyes wide. 'We've got *food*, bro! Real life, canned food!' He plonks his box down on the sand and opens the lid.

'Holy groceries!' the Flea exclaims. 'Where did you find this?' He looks at me. 'Grace, please tell me I haven't fallen asleep on the beach and this isn't just some cruel dream.'

'You aren't dreaming,' I say with a smile so wide I think my face might actually split in two.

'And that isn't the best of it,' Dan says.

'It's not?' the Flea says, dreamily studying a can of peaches.

'Nuh-huh.' Dan shakes his head. 'They also found a boat.'

The Flea puts the peaches down. 'Okay, now I know you're shitting me.'

I shake my head. 'He's not. We did. Hidden in the tunnel. The food was stored inside it.'

The Flea stands frozen for a moment, then he flings his wiry arms around me and hugs me tight. 'So does that mean . . .?' He drops his voice to a whisper. 'Are we able to get out of this place?'

Cruz nods. 'It is just a small sailing boat, but it looks in quite good shape.'

The Flea looks stunned. 'But how did you find it?'

I grin at him. I can't *stop* grinning at him. 'There's a map in the man's journal. The boat was his.'

Dan sighs. 'Well, I'll be . . .'

I turn to Cruz. 'I wonder why he didn't use it to escape.'

Cruz sighs. 'Who knows? I think that whatever happened to him here – it made him lose his mind.'

Dan nods. 'Yeah, I don't think that poor sucker even knew what a boat was any more.'

We all fall silent for a moment. Then Cruz puts his hand on my shoulder. 'How about we eat and rest up tonight, then leave at first light, when we can look out for rocks?' he says.

'Aye, aye, captain!' The Flea gives Cruz a theatrical salute, then he grabs Dan's arm. 'Come on, let's go tell Beau-Belle. She is not gonna believe this!'

As I watch them striding off up the beach, I can't stop shaking my head.

'What is wrong?' Cruz asks softly.

'Nothing's wrong!' I turn to him and smile. 'I'm so happy right now, I actually want to jump for joy.'

Cruz raises one eyebrow in that impossibly cute way of his. 'So, why don't you?'

I raise my eyebrows back at him. 'Well, maybe I just will!' And with that I start leaping up and down like a demented kangaroo.

Cruz grabs hold of my hands and joins me. And we jump and jump until my head is spinning and my jaw is aching from laughter. Then, finally, we crash down on to the sand. Cruz pulls my body into his until our hips are moulded together. I run my fingers through his tumbling curls and sigh.

He looks at me and smiles – a shy, questioning smile. I trace my finger along the chiselled line of his cheekbone. There's so much I want to say to him. So much I want to share with him, confide in him, laugh about with him. So much I want to do with him. But right now all that can wait. Right now I just want to say one thing. I brush back his hair so I can whisper in his ear.

'I think I love you too.'

Epilogue

Hortense stands at the edge of the forest, looking down at the beach. Their fire is almost out now, its embers glinting like rubies in the dark, and they are asleep. She had come so close today. If she'd reached out in the cave she would have been able to touch the girl's snowy-white skin. But something had gone wrong; something she hadn't considered when she cast the spell all those years ago. The girl has fallen in love; she could feel it radiating from her like a force field.

She feels for the pendant around her neck and traces her finger over the snake. '*You cannot escape me*,' she whispers. Halfway down the beach she senses the girl stirring and moaning in her sleep. Nothing is more powerful than what now connects them. That girl is her only way back; her only chance of being reunited with her baby. The young man is an inconvenience, no more. Once he is out of the picture all will be as planned.

She looks up at the waning moon and smiles. Not long to go now. Not long at all. Then she pulls up her hood and melts back into the forest.

They're not off the island yet . . .
DON'T MISS THE
DRAMATIC SECOND BOOK IN
THE SHIPWRECKED SAGA
COMING SOON

Acknowledgements

A massive thank you as always to my wonderful editor, Ali Dougal, for your eagle eye and expert guidance. Thank you also to my US family – I hope Grace makes a worthy fictional addition to the Delaney clan! Huge thanks and love to Sara Starbuck – my fellow pirate of the pen, true friend and chief cheerleader. I am forever indebted to you. Thank you, thank you, thank you to all of the readers who have taken the time to send me such lovely emails – your feedback means the world to me. And thank you to Rob Tinsley – the real-life Cruz – for letting me shamelessly steal your life from Facebook, and teaching me the proper way to drink from a coconut.